SEARCH NO FURTHER

AJ CAMPBELL

SEARCH NO FURTHER

by AJ Campbell

JOIN MY READERS CLUB

As a member of The AJ Campbell Readers Club, you'll be the first to know about my upcoming book launch promotions, get sneak previews of my book covers and receive free periodic downloads of my work. Upon joining, all new members will receive a copy of *Choices* – a FREE short story, exclusive to club members. See the back of the book for details on how to join. I look forward to welcoming you personally.

For Mr C.

ONE

'Don't be fooled, my dear child.' Nonna's voice rings with contempt. 'Some would love nothing more than to see me take my last breath.' She nibbles at a sliver of king prawn from the seafood crudo, one of the many sharing slabs on offer today.

Amused, I turn to my grandma. 'Nonna! What's that supposed to mean?'

She has one eyebrow pulled up. 'I know…'

A horde of screaming children interrupts her reply as Mr Polka Dot and his assistant finally show up: the entertainment duo I've arranged for the next hour and Nonna has paid for. The party for the princess is in full swing at De Rosa's restaurant – a cosy slice of Italian life smack bang in the middle of London's East End. You are lucky to bag a table unless you book well in advance. The usual crustless sandwiches, cocktail sausages, and bowls of crisps you'd expect at a kid's birthday party are nowhere in sight. No! Today, as every day, it's all about the food at my nonna's restaurant. Cara De Rosa wouldn't have it any other way.

Sparing no expense, she's been planning this party for months with the dogged determination that each attendee will never forget the spread on offer. 'Great-granddaughters are only eight once,' she repeated when I suggested Lola and her friends would be content with pizza and ice cream. Heightened by the festive cheer of mini rolls exquisitely crafted to resemble reindeer, and Christmas trees formed from folded cucumber shavings and topped with a star cut from a sliced carrot, all held together with a cocktail stick, the spread is mouth-watering.

The usual strategic layout of rustic tables has been changed into three long rows. The birthday girl and her guests occupy the middle row, over which float twenty pink and purple balloons – one for each child to take home with their opulent party bags. More extravagance Nonna ordered without my knowledge. Above these balloons, in the centre of the table, hovers a number-eight-shaped helium balloon bigger than the party girl herself. Two rows of tables for the adults flank an over-excited Lola and her guests – Nonna's friends, and the selected few who were lucky enough to gain entry because of their association with their child.

Wine flows freely, as the adult guests pick at plates of antipasto. 'We're trialling a new menu,' Nonna proudly informed everyone upon their arrival, her theatrical, radiant voice resonating throughout the restaurant. I love her voice; most people do. It's tinted with a lush Italian accent that sounds like it could, at any moment, break out

2

into an operatic aria. 'Be honest and tell me your thoughts,' she said, the smile on her face affirming her confidence that every guest will adore the latest concoctions. We are opening a new branch of De Rosa's a few miles away in trendy Islington, and she is keen to go a bit more upmarket to suit the local clientele. I say *we*, but I should really say *they*, as it's my older sister, Milana, who works on that side of the business with Nonna. I'm a waitress. I should add "general dogsbody" to this, as I'm the one who always seems to end up with the tasks no one else has time for. But not for much longer. I have plans. I just need to buckle down to execute them. January will soon be here.

The new menu is a sophisticated display of colourful Italian indulgence Nonna and Milana have been working on for months, along with Papa, who runs the kitchen. I've been sampling everything on offer today. I can't help myself. I pick up my third skewer – an artistic arrangement of tortellini and cubes of white cheddar encased in slices of salami, secured either end with a plump olive. I take a bite, staring at one of the many contemporary canvases for sale, produced by local artists and displayed on the original brick walls. An ardent supporter of the local community, Nonna sells the paintings and gives the artists all the proceeds. "These people earn so little from their beautiful work," she has always told me.

The produce we sell in the deli that is attached to the side of the restaurant, Nonna sources locally as well. This time of the year, she packages various non-perishable delights and presents them in attractive Christmas hampers, which she decorates herself. It's a task she starts towards the end of September, when she returns from her annual two-week vacation in Italy. The mounds of goodies take over all of the four spare bedrooms in her and Rik's house.

'He's late,' Nonna says, irritated, nodding over at Mr Polka Dot.

'Only five minutes,' I say. 'Not an issue.'

She is a striking woman, my nonna. If I look as good as her when I'm her age, I'll have zero complaints. We held her sixty-fifth birthday party here last year. No expense was spared at that celebration either. I haven't inherited her looks. Not to my eye, at least. She is light-skinned for an Italian, possessing more of a yellow undertone to her complexion. In contrast, I've inherited a darker olive one from my mamma, Bettina, who also works in the restaurant. Nonna tells me that when she was my age, she had an abundance of dark, curly hair like me, but she dyes hers an ash blonde and it's styled in a long bob. We both have dark, brown eyes, but the only similarity I can see to Nonna is the large beauty spot that protrudes equidistant between our left nostril and our heart-shaped lips. When I was at school, I hated my beauty spot. I wanted to have it removed. I even investigated surgical procedures. Then, on my first day of sixth form, I met Matt in our English Lit class. He told me my beauty spot was what had attracted him to me in the first place, and I stopped investigating.

Matt.

I touch the sore on my left hand. It feels particularly painful today.

'At least the adults can eat in peace.' Nonna waves to

one of the waitresses. The flushed-faced girl, an agency temp we hire from a local company for occasions like today, rushes over. 'Time to serve the next course, please,' Nonna says, tapping the face of her fitness watch. A piece of jewellery out of keeping with her usual attire, but she has a heart condition and likes to keep track of her rhythms.

'Kitchen said another five minutes,' the young waitress says, rubbing the palms of her hands together. She is dressed in De Rosa's standard uniform – jeans and a black T-shirt with De Rosa's fancy red logo embossed on the front.

'Not ready! Why ever not?' Not waiting for an answer, Nonna snatches the white napkin from her lap and slaps it on the Scandinavian snowflake design tablecloth. She stands and pats her partner, Rik, a slim man of Malaysian descent, on the shoulder. 'I'll be back in a minute, my love. I must organise this circus in the kitchen. Make sure you give everything a try. I want your honest opinion.' She pecks him on the cheek.

Rik grins. They have been together for two years or so, and he is used to her fiery nature by now.

I wish the family had all got used to him.

Rik and I exchange looks of mutual amusement. You have to know Nonna to appreciate that an over-generous softer side exists to the acerbic wit and razor-sharpness she will display to people who hack her off. At fifty-six, Rik is ten years her junior, which surprised me when she first told me. His well-lined face that suggests he has many stories to tell if one would care to listen, makes him appear

5

around the same age as her. Distinguished-looking, he is sharply dressed in a gunmetal grey suit. The suit is expensive. You can tell from the high-quality fabric and perfect cut. Nonna bought it for him for his birthday last month, along with an Audi TT to replace the aged Golf he used to drive, much to the repugnance of Papa and his brother Franco.

'She wasn't feeling good earlier,' Rik says. 'I keep telling her. She's meant to be relaxing and letting the others run the rest of this show.'

'She said she will once the food is here.'

'Pity Zach couldn't be here today,' he says.

I shrug. 'The stag party was booked last year; before we even met. He's the best man; he couldn't exactly drop out. I've been meaning to ask you. Do you have a stag party planned? Nonna said she hasn't got time for a hen party with the wedding so close.' I elbow him and laugh. 'Thanks for giving us plenty of notice, by the way.'

'You know Cara. When she gets that bee in her bonnet.'

We exchange knowing smiles. Yes, I know Nonna well. She is my best friend. 'Don't tell her, but I've been organising a few of her friends for a small get together.'

'When're you going to fit that in? Cara said this place is booked solid until you close on the twenty-third.'

'It's going to be a post-wedding hen party. When you get back from your honeymoon in the New Year.' I slide my handbag off the back of the wooden chair and dig out my hand cream. The cracks have started to open. God, I hate this time of year.

Mr Polka Dot's assistant, an enthusiastic young magician, mingles with the adults while Mr Polka Dot continues performing his show for the kids. Lola turns to wave, sharing her excitement with me. I smile at her. She looks cute, I must admit, sitting amid her friends, clothed to leave no doubt in any partygoers' minds whose birthday we are here to celebrate. The ostentatious bow attached to the back of her eye-wateringly expensive satin dress is almost as big as the number-eight-shaped helium balloon. There's no party prize for guessing who financed that. I watch my daughter with humble adoration. She's the type of child who dances through life like an enchanting fairy, sprinkling her magic onto every situation. I'm so blessed to have her.

I turn to a hand tapping my shoulder. 'Sienna, come with me. I want to show you something.' Nonna grabs my forearm, allowing me no choice but to obey her order. Glancing over my shoulder, I search for Lola, but she is too preoccupied to notice me leaving. Along with the rest of the party guests, she is engrossed in the magic wand a zealous Mr Polka Dot is tapping against his patent top hat.

Nonna leads me towards the back of the noisy restaurant and into the large kitchen, an overheated sauna of a room, bustling with chefs in the final preparations of a meal for the adults waiting to be fed. Their musical Italian accents sing a song of happiness as they chop and cut, slice and stir. Culinary delights sizzle in pans on the giant burner ovens bordering the back wall, filling the air with the savoury aroma of basil and roasted garlic. Large square plates of sliced spinach torta and hand-painted bowls of citrusy salads line the stainless steel prep stations, along with baskets of seeded flatbread.

Nonna is a woman of considerable panache, favouring flowing dresses and matching head scarfs worn in different styles depending on her mood. Today her dress is silver. It shimmers like fish skin, and the skirt sashays around her legs as she flows around the kitchen, instructing people to hurry along. 'How long, Don? People are waiting.' My red-faced papa is busy arranging creamy ricotta on the top of a giant bed of roasted pumpkin. He tosses an empty baking tray towards a pile of washing-up by the sink. It whangs against the stacked dirty pots. 'Soon, Mamma, soon, relax,' Papa replies, dabbing his forehead in the crook of his arm. Picking up a plastic container, he sprinkles the cheese with pomegranate and pumpkin seeds, while ordering his staff to get a bloody move on.

I walk over to use the hand-washing sink. As I'm dabbing my hands dry on a paper towel, Cara diverts me to a worktop at the back of the kitchen. 'Voila. This is what I wanted to show you.' Her sweeping hand, jangling the collection of silver bangles circling her wrist, presents a cake. I gasp. I can't help myself. This isn't the unicorn one Lola saw in Tesco and told us she wanted. This is more like an offering for a Hollywood star than a birthday cake for an eight-year-old schoolgirl from East London. Three stacked tiers, approaching a metre high, are topped with a pair of fondant ballerina shoes so delicately crafted they look real. The intricate ribbons of the shoes entwine and trail to the bottom tier. 'You think she'll like it?' Nonna asks. Her eyes sparkle in answer to her question, as does her new diamond ring. I want to ask her what happened to the cake Lola chose and tell her there was no need for such extravagance. But lost for words, I pull a face to express I love it, and so will her granddaughter.

'I saw a picture of this one in a magazine and knew Lola would prefer it, so I popped into Katie's Cakes. You know Katie? She often pops in here for a morning coffee. She has set up a new business making cakes from home. I showed her a picture and gave her a deposit. It's always good to help out new businesses.' She spins around and shouts at Papa. 'We need to get moving, Don. People are waiting for food.' Poor Papa is sweating in the heat of the kitchen despite the back door being ajar.

'Nearly there, Mamma. Chill. Go sip wine. Five. I need five more minutes.' Papa darts from one work surface to another like a busy ant. He strides over to the back door and pushes it fully open before returning to his team and hurrying them to bring the banquet together.

A waft of cigarette smoke sends Nonna into a fit of uncontrollable coughing. She storms towards the door clutching her chest. A set of fairy lights illuminates the courtyard garden. 'Milana De Rosa, you disappoint me,' she shouts at her granddaughter sitting alone outside. 'I never thought I'd see the day.'

I'm as surprised as Nonna to see my sister smoking. Unlike me, Milana has never been one to light up alone. More the sort to accept a cigarette from a group of friends during a Friday night out if everyone else is having one. She runs a hand through her mane of long, lustrous hair. The kind that could be used in an advert for the best ever conditioner. Lucky for her, she was blessed with straight hair; as opposed to my wild curls, which not even said conditioner could tame. She turns to face us. 'Sorry, Nonna.' Milana bends towards an ashtray in the centre of the table, her slight frame shivering in the winter chill.

'You allow this, Don?' Cara throws her arms up to her son.

'She's nearly thirty years old, Mamma.' Papa shrugs, raising the palms of his hands to the ceiling. 'What do you expect me to do?'

Nonna turns to me, still coughing as though she has something stuck in her chest desperate to escape. 'I purchased this outside seating furniture for the staff, not for my grandchildren's sneaky cigarette breaks. Why do you kids smoke, anyway? It's so *eighties.*' She shakes her pursed fingers, shaped like a pinecone, towards Papa. 'You need to have some control over your kids.' She clutches her chest. 'I'm so tired of it all.'

'Are you OK?' I ask.

Her tone suggests she is not, that she would share her worries if she wasn't hosting an afternoon to be remembered. 'The party will be over before any food has been served. I'll join you in a minute.' She dismisses me from the kitchen. 'I can't relax until this lot have got their act together.'

As I leave, I hear her chivvy up Papa and his team of chefs. I pop into the ladies and wash my hands before returning to the table. Rik smiles and holds up a bottle of Soave. 'This is a new one Cara has asked me to try. The wholesalers have it coming up on offer. Fancy a glass?'

'Sure.' We discuss the conveyor belt of button-popping food starting to arrive as Cara returns to the table. She stops short of her chair and stares around the room.

'You OK, love?' Rik asks, his brow wrinkled with concern.

She doesn't acknowledge him. Her eyes have shrunk to the size of raisins in the deathlike whiteness of her startled face. Something isn't right. Her confused gaze fixes ahead, as though she is witnessing a tragic scene unfolding.

'Nonna?' I say, terrified.

She turns and stares at me, her eyes piercing into me. 'You have to help me! Sienna, you…'

'Cara?' Rik pushes his chair back.

Nonna staggers like a drunk and tumbles forward. She grasps her chest with both hands. Her legs are shaking uncontrollably. She looks at me in desperation, trying to speak, but words don't make it past her lips. Rik jumps up. He tries to catch her, but misses as she shrinks into a ball of hopelessness, slumping to the floor with a thunk.

TWO

The noise level plummets across the restaurant as Rik drops to kneel beside his fiancée. He rolls her onto her back. 'Cara, Cara,' he says, vigorously rubbing her collarbone.

The skin around her lips is turning blue. 'We need to get an ambulance,' I say.

'Call one, now,' he says.

I remain motionless, shocked into stillness.

'Sienna, ambulance. Now!'

'I'm on it,' says a man springing into action to the left of me, who I've never seen before today.

Mamma appears. 'What's happened?' She pulls a band from her wrist and ties her frizzy hair into a stubby pony-tail before crouching at Nonna's feet.

'She collapsed, Bettina,' Rik says, checking Nonna's airways and pulse. He removes his jacket and tosses it towards his chair, beads of sweat bubbling on his forehead.

Milana instructs Mr Polka Dot to take the kids to the

deli next door. 'Don't let them see this.' She points towards an archway at the side of the restaurant. 'Carry on entertaining them in there.' Racing over to us, she demands people to stand back. She orders Mamma, 'Get Papa from the kitchen, quick. And help with the kids.' She grabs her hair and tucks it under the collar of her shirt as she kneels at Nonna's side.

Rik shuffles on his knees beside me, opposite Milana, with Nonna's body slumped between us. He takes charge, surprisingly calm in the chaos developing. Interlocking his fingers, he starts compressions.

'Someone get down to the pub and get the defibrillator!' Milana shouts.

The mother of one of Lola's school friends pushes her husband. 'Go. Be quick. I'll sort the code and call you.' The startled man collides with an onlooker as he tears towards the exit, calling he will be back as quickly as he can.

The children file out of the restaurant like a line of soldiers. Some dare to sneak a glimpse as they march through the archway to the deli. They're not stupid. They are aware something is up. I try to spot Lola, but can't see her.

'You OK to take over?' Rik says to me. I'd rather Milana did. We are both trained first aiders, but she'll do a better job.

'We need to work together,' Rik says to the two of us. He gives two rescue breaths. 'This is not a job for one person.'

'I'll take over.' Milana hitches up her shirt sleeves and

places her hands, one on top of the other, in the middle of Nonna's chest and starts pumping.

Rik shouts to the human wall of gaping spectators mumbling amongst themselves, aghast at the events developing. 'Everyone, please stand back. Give us some space.'

'Stand back,' Milana repeats.

'Ambulance is on its way,' a voice calls out.

'What's happened?' asks Papa appearing from the kitchen. 'Is she going to be alright?' With his arm, he wipes away drops of sweat that are dribbling down his face.

'I think it's another heart attack,' Rik says, astonishingly confident. How can he keep so calm?

'What can I do?' Papa asks.

'Nothing. It's all under control,' Rik replies.

My lips tremble. 'Nonna! Nonna!'

Milana barks at me. 'Concentrate, Sen. This is no time for emotions. Concentrate.'

'Push harder,' Rik tells her. 'Stop at thirty; you know the drill.' He looks at me. 'Check for breath when Milana stops.'

I do as I'm told and rush around to Nonna's head. When Milana reaches thirty, I lower my ear to Nonna's mouth. There's nothing.

'Take over when I've given some breath,' Rik instructs me. His calmness is waning. Shock pains his expression as he taps Nonna's face and tells her to wake the hell up.

After Rik gives her life-essential breaths, I move around to her side and start pumping, repeating the cycle. 'Nonna! Nonna! Wake up,' I say. Rik instructs me to pump harder. 'We need that defibrillator. What's happened to it?' he asks the woman who sent her husband to the pub.

'He's coming,' she replies.

At thirty, I stop. Rik rechecks her breath and shakes his head. 'Are you OK to carry on?' he asks.

'Can you?' I say, more than ready to hand over the CPR reins to stronger forces. He commences compressions. A guest shoves a mobile phone in my face. 'A lady from 999 wants to talk to you.' Milana grabs the phone and briefly answers questions from the emergency services, informing them we are administering CPR. Rik continues to pump, but signs of life are not forthcoming. I mutter Nonna's name, begging her to wake up.

There's a flurry of activity as an ambulance arrives. A middle-aged paramedic runs in, carrying a defibrillator and medical bag. His blue eyes are sunk in circles of darkness, suggesting he's been on shift way longer than he'd like. 'That was quick,' the guy who made the initial call observes.

'We were on the way to a nearby job and got diverted. Sometimes, luck is on our side.' The paramedic dumps his bags amongst the commotion and plucks two rubber gloves out of his trouser pocket. He snaps them on and asks Rik to continue whilst he gets set up. 'Give us the order of events. What happened?' he says.

Assessing the scene, the paramedic efficiently switches on his machine. Another paramedic appears with a medical bag. The two of them talk between themselves, as one attaches the defibrillator and the second takes over from Rik. Their conversation is so calm it's as if they are dealing with something as simple as a sprained ankle, not a stopped heart threatening the life of the woman before them. I want to scream at them to hurry up. Do something, quick. A second ambulance pulls up outside, and another two paramedics run in. One is on the phone. The other converses with the initial two.

Whilst all this is happening, Rik relays the day's events, with Milana butting in here and there. The rotating light from the ambulances parked on the pavement outside casts an eerie sense of foreboding onto the situation. I stare at Nonna, silently begging her to stay with us. She can't leave me. Not now. I need her.

'I can't believe this is happening again,' Rik says. He has been here before. He was with her when she had her first heart attack. They didn't know each other at the time. They were sitting at a table next to each other in a restaurant somewhere in London. Rik performed CPR on her and saved her life. Shortly after, he moved in with her – much to the disdain of the family. But that's a tale for another time. 'She's been getting herself so worked up recently,' Rik says.

Papa chips in, addressing Rik. 'It's all the stress. It's not good for her. This needs to stop. You need to put an end to it.'

'Not now. This is not the time,' Rik barks at him. He unbuttons his shirt cuffs and rolls up his sleeves. He wipes his brow and reaches for his jacket. Digging into the pocket, he says, 'I keep telling her to slow down, but she won't listen. When she woke up this morning, she said she didn't feel well. I suggested she stay in bed, but, as always, she said she had too much to do.' Fumbling around in his wallet, he produces a folded-up piece of paper the size of a business card and recites the list of Cara's prescribed medication. Daily pills to lower blood pressure and cholesterol, to help with chest pain, to avert clotting, and to prevent strokes and heart attacks – not that the latter appears to have done any good.

'When you say she didn't feel well this morning, can you expand on that, please?' the paramedic says.

'She said she felt sick and had a headache. She thought she might be coming down with a bug. She's been feeling tired lately. But then, this is a hectic time of the year for her. She's been getting up later and wanting to go to bed earlier. We were invited to dinner at our friends' house on Friday evening, but she cancelled. That's not at all in Cara's nature.'

Milana pipes up. 'She never cancels anything.'

'Never,' I say for what it's worth. 'But she has a lot going on.'

It all happens so quickly. Before we know it, Nonna jolts awake. Confused and distressed, her eyes dart around the people encircling her failing body as if she is looking for someone. 'Nonna.' My voice is a whisper. I'm surprised she hears.

Her eyes, wide with horror, fix on mine, and she mouths, 'You have to help me.'

THREE

Once Nonna is safely in the ambulance, Rik climbs in. When he is seated, I wave at him, holding a pretend phone to my ear. 'Call me. I'll come up to the hospital later,' I shout out as the doors slam shut. As the ambulance pulls into the road and heads for the hospital, I stand beside Milana, shivering in the cold. 'I can't believe what's happened,' I say, transfixed on the small crowd gathered in the street. People are loitering outside the shops opposite, gawking. Before storming back inside the restaurant, Milana shouts at them, asking if they haven't got anything better to do.

I follow her inside where the atmosphere is subdued. The smell of leftover food lingers, and the guests have dwindled to a few stragglers; most people grabbed their kids and left at the first opportunity. Mamma started to disperse them before the medics arrived. She dumped a box containing twenty party bags and told them to help themselves, advising they best collect their child and leave by the deli entrance. The remaining few are sipping cups of sweet tea or taking swigs of whiskey Mamma has generously sloshed into large tumblers. Something she wouldn't have dared do on Nonna's watch. 'Have this.' She raises a glass towards me. 'I think you need it. What a shock.'

I wave the glass away. 'I'm going to drive to the hospital later.' Wanting to get out of here as soon as possible, I help the other waitresses ferry plates of leftovers and untouched food into the kitchen. Lola is amusing herself with her bestie, opening gifts piled high on a table in the corner.

I'm collecting the balloons when Uncle Franco and Aunty Jenni arrive, the shock on their faces asking what the hell has happened. Jenni removes her coat, straightening her floaty tunic over her fancy leggings which have silver studs running up the sides. 'Whatever's gone on?' she asks.

'Shame to see you couldn't even make it on time for your great-niece's birthday,' Mamma butts in as Franco and Jenni stare around the restaurant. Milana grabs a glass, half-fills it with whiskey, and hands it to Franco who gives Lola a wink.

'I thought we were coming to a party,' Franco says, ignoring Mamma's harsh words, as most people do. Because Bettina De Rosa has little good to say about anyone or anything lately. I'm not being mean when I say this. I'm simply stating the truth. I don't know what's got into her. Papa blames the hormones. I'm not so sure. Franco stares over at Lola and lowers his voice. 'Is someone going to tell us what has happened?'

'Drink?' Milana asks Jenni, holding up a bottle of the leftover Soave.

'Just a water.' Jenni's eyes dart sideways to her husband. 'Looks like I'll be driving.'

Milana opens a bottle of Evian and plonks it on the bar. She nods at Jenni. The bar is adorned with twinkle lights. Nonna bought these in the January sales this year to complement her boxes of De Rosa's Christmas décor. Papa pours the Evian into a glass and hands it to Jenni. 'We think Cara's had another heart attack,' he says.

It's incomprehensible to think of someone as super-fit and healthy as Nonna with heart issues. She's an inspiration for women of all ages, the epitome of later-life health. Every morning, early, she power-walks her neighbour's golden retriever, Benny, around the park. And, before breakfast, she practices yoga in her insulated garden room. A daily regime she says I should take up. 'It would do you a world of good,' she says. If only I had her enthusiasm. And every Wednesday evening, she and Rik attend Latin American dance classes. So, it's hard to believe she had a heart attack two years ago, a bad one. They found a ninety per cent narrowing in one of the coronary arteries, which resulted in surgery to have three stents fitted.

Milana gives a rundown of the afternoon's events which ignites an argument of fire when Franco questions why the hell didn't Papa accompany their mamma in the ambulance.

'Rik insisted he went,' Papa says.

Franco thrusts his hands out in front of him. 'Then why

didn't you insist some more? She needs her real family with her.' He locks his jaw, seething through tightened teeth. 'Not him.'

'I'm telling you. The man wouldn't back down,' Papa says.

'You're always so bloody weak,' Franco says to his brother.

Here we go. I should be used to this. Franco and Papa wrangle in Italian, using their hands as well as their voices. Nonna is forever telling them to quit their bickering. Neither realise their ongoing battles will never find a winner. They have inherited their mamma's fire. Pity they use it as a weapon against each other rather than as fuel to search for a truce. I watch their identical bushy brows rise and fall in time with their hands, their dark eyes flaming to join in the fight. If it weren't for Franco's professionally trimmed beard and shoulder-length hair, they could be mistaken for twins. Except Franco is two years older than Papa. Nonna often tells stories of their younger days when they modelled designer clothing for a big-name Italian brand. It's not hard to see why.

Their squabbles have always amused me. It's like watching a comedy show, although today is no laughing affair.

Jenni tries to pacify an agitated Franco. 'Come on. Calm down. Why don't I drive you to the hospital?'

Franco flaps his hand in Jenni's face, silencing his wife. 'You should've gone!' he says to Papa, switching back to English. 'Mamma needs us.'

They switch to speaking Italian again, going at it like a couple of wolves, verbally tearing at each other's throats. The tension between them vibrates in the air. I balance a plate of party food on my forearm, pick up another in each hand and make for the kitchen. I've heard enough. I want to get to the hospital. 'Five minutes, and we'll get going,' I whisper to Lola as I pass.

When I reach the kitchen, the atmosphere is grave compared to earlier. Even the tinsel looping around the overhead saucepan rack seems to have lost its sparkle. All the kitchen staff adore Nonna. She's a diamond-tough one to please but, along with her wicked sense of humour, that's why they all respect her. I put the plates on the counter, where a couple of sombre chefs are boxing torta and packing leftovers into recyclable containers. 'Sienna, you must take some of this home,' Jared says.

Jared is my favourite chef. A product of the Prisoner Apprenticeship Pathway from Brixton prison, he is another one of Nonna's give-back-to-society projects. Nonna is friends with the prison governor. They often lunch together. She invited Nonna to visit the onsite restaurant, the prison's training project established to reduce reoffending rates by giving prisoners the chance to gain academic qualifications in the catering industry. 'Prisoners entering the programme are nearly fifty per cent less likely to reoffend,' Nonna told us all when she arrived back after her lunch that day. 'Wouldn't it be great to help one of these troubled men?'

'Why give us the bother?' Papa said, aggrieved she hadn't discussed it with him first. 'I'm the one who's going to have to work with him. What did he even end up in prison for, anyway?'

'A drug-related offence. Nothing that'll affect us here.'

Jared was at the end of a three-year custodial sentence. A lenient result, but the judge had seen him as a victim of exploitation rather than a hardened criminal – and he had fully cooperated with the police. The day Nonna first met him, a year ago, she decided then and there she would be offering him a position in De Rosa's, despite the subsequent objection from the family. Not that I was party to that contention. I was ill at the time, going through one of my bad patches that has periodically struck me down for the last five years on the day December starts.

I twist the imaginary band of gold on the third finger of my left hand.

Oh, Matt.

'There's enough food here to feed you and little Lola for a week,' Jared adds. 'Take what you can.'

'Sure.' Any help I can get, I won't refuse. I fear deeply for what the coming days are going to deal out.

When I leave to collect more plates, I bump into Franco, entering the kitchen. 'I was coming to find you.' He reaches out and draws me into his arms. 'Are you OK, la mia bella nipote?' He has always called me this – *my beautiful niece* – when he knows I'm upset, ever since I can remember. 'I'm sorry we were late, and I wasn't here to help you. I got caught up. Don't you worry. Nonna is going to be fine. She's a strong woman.' He squeezes me tight. 'If you need anything, you know where I am.'

Jenni is knelt, chatting to Lola. They are attaching paper

outfits – sparkling bomber jackets and leather trousers and little black dresses – to mini cardboard figures. Lola seems oblivious to the drama that has played out before her. She stops dressing the cardboard imitation of Taylor Swift and frowns at Jenni. 'I don't understand.'

'Your birthday present from Franco and me is a party for you and your friends. I need to OK it with your mum, but next Saturday, you can come to the salon after it closes at six o'clock for a pampered princess party. I'll style your hair and paint your nails, and I'll order some of those glitter tattoos you love.'

Lola's little mouth breaks open a wide smile. She nudges her bestie sitting beside her. 'Can Tiffany come?'

'As long as it's OK with your mum.' Lola and Jenni both look at me questioningly.

I nod my agreement, telling Lola to start packing her presents into the plastic containers I brought along for the purpose.

'Franco suggested it,' Jenni says when Lola is out of earshot. 'He thought it would make up for the disaster today.'

'That was kind of him,' I say. This is Franco all over. Despite being a bit of a rogue, he is a loveable character. Except when he is arguing with his brother.

'Poor darling, she has missed her party,' says Jenni, slipping an arm around my shoulder. 'Are you OK, sweetie?' She's attractive, Jenni, stunning. Spider eyelashes framing stormy-blue eyes, delicate lips, wispy layers cut in a pixie wedge: it all suits her elfin face.

I agree Jenni can be annoying at times, with her faint cockney accent and ability to talk for Britain. And, according to my mamma, for most of the northern hemisphere too. "Words tumble out of that woman's mouth as if they're late for an interview," she says whenever she has to spend time with Jenni, which is as little as she can get away with. The pair of them agree on little. Jenni and Franco are both hairdressers and own a salon at the other end of the road, where Nonna visits every Saturday afternoon for her weekly wash and blow-dry. I say own, but that's not entirely accurate. Nonna has a sixty per cent stake in Hair by De Rosa. According to Nonna, the friction between Jenni and Mamma started the day Jenni permed Mamma's hair, after which she was over-enthusiastic with the scissors, leaving Mamma looking like, in Mamma's enraged words, a pathetic poodle.

'Franco is always telling her, "Slow down, Mamma. You'll end up in an early grave." Especially with her heart problems. But there's no telling a woman like Cara De Rosa, is there?' I shake my head at her indisputable statement. 'If you need me to help with Lola after work at all this week, shout. I'm busy at the salon every day until six, and we're meant to be having our work Christmas party here on Thursday. Who knows if that will happen now, though? Anyway, just drop me a text if you need me, and I'll see what I can do.'

'Would you mind Lola while I pop up to the hospital? I might not be able to see Nonna, but at least I can give Rik some support.'

'Sure. I'll stay here with her until you get back.' She digs her hands into her slim hips, shaking her head at Franco and Papa who have started another argument. 'Never a dull moment with this lot, eh?' she says, giving me a tight-lipped smile. 'Too many conflicting agendas. There's going to be a murder here one day.'

FOUR

It's eerily quiet, devoid of any human activity, as I run along the hospital corridor. The fluorescent lighting has been dimmed, the shiny red floor like a river of dark blood. When I arrive at Nonna's ward, I buzz my arrival at the intercom and wait for someone to let me in. I squirt a liberal helping of gel into my palms and rub it in, wincing at the pain it causes my cracked hands. I really must get some of that cream my friend Maddie recommended. It's written down somewhere on the back of a cigarette packet. I can't afford for the sores to get any worse, not with the restaurant so busy. I won't be able to work. I stand waiting for a while, reading the notices on the door, even though I'm the last person who needs educating about hand-washing and infection control.

My OCD started five years ago. Well, that's what Mamma and Milana call it. Nonna has a more accurate assessment of my obsession. Guilt. Every time she catches me at the sink, she gently reminds me guilt cannot be washed away. These days, the daily pill I pop keeps it under control. I spurt another dollop of gel onto my sticky fingers.

Fed up with waiting, I slip in behind a doctor carrying a takeaway coffee and a bar of chocolate, oblivious to my presence. Next to the visitors' waiting room, I back up against the wall to allow a group of medics dressed in theatre blues and surgical scrub caps to push a bed and equipment along the corridor. Not wanting to stare, my gaze falls into the small room to see Rik sitting on the sofa at the far end. His knees support his elbows, and he is tapping a leaflet against the edge of the table and staring at the floor in a trance of helplessness.

When I step into the room, he glances up from his bent position. 'What's the latest?' I ask.

'She's out of it. I popped for a coffee,' he says as if defending himself. He tosses the leaflet about cardiac rehabilitation onto the table. 'She's not in a good way.' He looks ill himself, his light brown skin grey with worry. 'They believe she's had another heart attack, but they can't say for sure until her bloods come back. Ninety-nine per cent she has, though.'

I sit beside him, staring at a sad-looking Christmas tree in the corner reflecting the ambience of the place. 'We're lucky she got a bed so quickly,' I say.

'There's nothing lucky about any of this.'

'She's in the best place,' I say, because fewer words suit such a situation. I should know. I've trudged this path before. Nothing anyone can say can mitigate the agonising distress.

'I don't understand how she could've deteriorated in only a few days. I thought she had a bug.' He bangs the palm of his hand on his temple. 'I can't believe it has come to this. It's worse than her first heart attack. Different, somehow.'

I listen to him relay the events of the past week. Guilt creeps through me for not realising Nonna has been feeling so poorly. But then that's Nonna for you. Never one to bow under pressure, however tricky or complicated the circumstances, she was back at work the week following surgery after her last heart attack as if she'd popped into hospital for the removal of a wart. She doesn't talk about that time. "Put the past behind you, and the future is brighter," she always tells me.

I wish I could put the past behind me.

I squeeze Rik's forearm. 'I'm going to see her. You finish your coffee,' I say, softly.

I walk along the centre of the ward, thinking about how hard this must be for him. Franco and Papa have disliked Rik since the day he arrived in Nonna's life; despite the fact he saved her when she suffered her first heart attack. The dislike has mushroomed since Nonna announced their news last Monday. She had called a family meeting, insisting everyone attend. Monday is the only night the restaurant is closed. Nonna calls it family night, and she has always had an open house policy for anyone to drop in at any time for leftovers from the restaurant or whatever she has thrown together beforehand. It's a tradition carried on from when my Nonno Nico was alive. It used to be a fun evening when he was still around. Milana and I would take turns choosing what to play from the treasure chest of games he stored in his leather footstool. Milana lost interest as the teenage years arrived, but I have never grown tired of those nights and still take Lola most weeks. Over the years, Nonno Nico taught me to master the game of backgammon and guided me from a mediocre to a strong contender for even the most experienced player.

Last Monday, Lola was setting up the backgammon board for the two of us, like I've taught her, when Nonna's announcement astonished everyone but me. Franco and Papa were bickering over the accompaniments for this year's Christmas dinner. Mamma was lolling in the corner of the sofa, nursing a whiskey and talking to Jenni, who was flicking through a magazine she had fished out of her bag when Mamma fixed herself a third drink. Milana was on her phone, flicking through Instagram. I knew what was coming. Nonna had already shared her news with me. 'Listen up, everyone,' Nonna said, taking Rik's hand and beaming at him. I've noticed the special smile she reserves for him. It reaches her eyes and makes them perform a little jig. 'We've something important to announce.' She peered around the room then back to Rik. There it was again – that little dance in her eyes. Rik looked uncomfortable. I knew why. Everyone was thinking about the consequences for themselves of what they anticipated was coming, especially Franco, who, when pushed too far, has a temper as hot as Papa's spicy penne arrabbiata. The grin on Nonna's face grew even wider, if that were possible. She threw out her left hand. The rock on her third finger sparkled like her voice. 'Rik and I are officially engaged, and we are getting married on January the third before we head to Bermuda.'

At first, mumbles and gasps echoed around the room like the lyrics from a bad song. 'Don't worry. It'll only be a small affair,' she added. 'Just the family and a few friends.'

I stifled a giggle. Affairs of this nature are never small where Cara De Rosa is concerned. I raised my clapping hands, encouraging everyone to do the same.

'I've organised it all. We've booked the town hall and a table for twenty in that lovely French restaurant we went to for my sixtieth. Remember it?' She leaned into Rik's shoulder. 'I don't expect any of you to do anything other than put on your fancy clothes, turn up, and wish us well.'

Was I the only one to clock the brief glare she directed Franco and Papa's way?

When I arrive at Nonna's bed, she is asleep. She looks in a bad way. Her pallid complexion matches the white sheets, her face gaunt and crumpled like a piece of paper ready for the bin. I remove my coat and wash my hands in the small sink, watching the attending nurse hold a thermometer in front of Nonna's forehead. The nurse records her findings and straightens the bedsheets. I scrape a plastic chair along the floor until I can't get any closer to Nonna. 'What's happening?' I ask the nurse.

She opens the Santa-shaped metal claw holding her hair in place at the back of her head, and tucks in some stray strands. 'Are you family?'

'Granddaughter.'

She rambles on but adds nothing to the information I gained from Rik.

As soon as the nurse leaves, Nonna's eyes open. She blinks rapidly. 'They're talking rubbish,' she says. Her breathing is laboured. 'I know my body.' She drags her hand to her chest. 'It's not my heart.'

I take her hand. 'They're doing tests, Nonna.'

'What tests?'

'Blood tests. Remember last time? Blood test will confirm if you've had a heart attack or not.'

'I heard.' She moans, massaging her chest. 'But they're wasting their time.'

'What do you mean?'

She stops blinking and narrows her eyes, staring intently at me. 'They want me dead.'

FIVE

I flinch. 'What're you talking about? Who wants you dead?'

Nonna's hand clutches her hospital gown. She looks like she has aged twenty years. 'I'm dying. Help me.' She retches. 'Killing me.'

'Don't be silly.' This is so unlike her. She's clearly confused. I reach for a sick bowl in time to catch the vomit shooting out of her mouth. She carries on, heaving and retching.

The nurse returns. She encourages Nonna to let it all out until she has nothing left. 'That's it, my love,' she says, wiping Nonna's mouth. She reassures her before taking the bowl away. Nonna's eyelids droop, and she softly mewls like a baby.

'Nonna. Tell me what you mean,' I say, trying to placate her. I gently shake her shoulder, but I'm unable to fight the sleep she needs to mend her broken body. Her eyes close tightly.

Rik appears and pulls a chair up to the other side of the

bed. He clasps his hands together, his knuckles as white as the face of the woman lying between us, who he can't take his eyes off. We sit in silence for a while, trying to deal with the shock. How did it come to this?

Trying to fill the silence, his voice cracks as if his vocal cords have been ripped apart. Like my heart has at seeing Nonna lying here in this state. 'She loves you the most, you know. You and Lola. She's so proud of you. The way you've coped as a single parent all these years.'

His words are no surprise. I've known since I could understand family dynamics, I'm Nonna's favourite grandchild. Milana blames our mamma. On her thirteenth birthday, Milana told me she recalled when I was born. Why she chose that day to tell me this, I couldn't say. I was ten at the time, but looking back, her words reflected the chip on her shoulder. 'Mamma wouldn't leave the house because she couldn't stop crying. Papa took me to a childminder every day. Mamma never once took me to school. Papa did.' The pattern continued. Mamma returned to work soon after I was born, and Nonna raised me, along with a local nursery. I can't remember a single time Mamma ever doing the school run either. When I started school, Nonna used to take both of us.

Rik looks so sad sitting there, his usual sleek appearance creased with worry. He needs to freshen up. When she wakes, Nonna will frown at his crumpled shirt stained with marks from the afternoon's unfortunate events.

If she wakes up, that is.

The thought that she won't recover terrifies me.

Nonna is my rock.

"You are the daughter I never had," she has always told me.

And she is the mamma I never had. Nonna has always been there for me. She was the one who caught me when the surgeon, who tried with his team for more than twelve hours to save Matt's life, released those devastating words, "He didn't make it." And she was the one who helped me the most through the year following Matt's death. The year of the assault course. Mountains to climb, hurdles to overcome, as all the firsts came at me like deadly rockets: the first Christmas, birthdays and anniversary without him.

It was Nonna who delicately picked up the fragile pieces of my broken life and carefully assembled them back into something like normality. In the early days, when I couldn't get out of bed in the mornings, she would arrive and take over, chatting to Lola as she got her ready for the day. And, after dropping Lola at nursery, she would come back and wash the dishes, run the hoover around, before dragging me up. Nonna had to pick Lola up from nursery, too, until she finally managed to get me to talk to a friend of hers, a retired therapist, who made me realise something. History was repeating itself. I was turning into my mamma. And I didn't want that for my daughter. So, for the sake of Lola, and with the help of my daily pill, I slowly rebuilt a sense of normality.

I can't lose Nonna.

'You should go home and rest,' I say to Rik.

He rubs the palms of his hands together. 'I want to be here when she wakes up.'

'You need to pace yourself. I can stay for a bit. Jenni

won't mind having Lola a while longer. Franco and Papa will be here soon.' I restrain the words he knows are teetering on the tip of my tongue – *and it's probably best you're not here when they arrive.*

I take Nonna's hand and repeat her name, willing her to open her eyes. I want her to explain herself, tell me more about the disturbing thoughts in her head, but there is no response. She looks so pale, so deathly grey. If it weren't for the rise and fall of her chest, you might think she was already in heaven. We sit in silence until I can take no more. 'Would you like some water?' I ask Rik. He nods.

I walk over to the freestanding water cooler by the nurses' station. Filling two plastic cups, I return to Nonna's bed to see a young woman in a white coat as I approach. At first, I think she is a physio until I notice the stethoscope around her neck. Are doctors getting younger, or am I getting older? With her flawless skin and plaits, she looks like she could be my au pair, not someone responsible for saving people's lives. She is preparing Nonna's arm to take some more bloods. I stand at the end of the bed, waiting for her to finish. Her reindeer earrings waggle as she speaks. Lola would love them. 'It'll only take a few minutes, and I'll…'

A croak from Nonna stops the doctor mid-sentence. 'Be quick, be quick.'

As shocked as I am to hear her voice, Rik asks her if she is OK, but Nonna doesn't reply. Rik reassures her, asks her questions, but there's no response. Only after the doctor has left us does Nonna half-open her eyes. She stares at

Rik. Her voice is a murmur amongst guttural moans. 'Gianni. You must stop Gianni Bellini.'

'Ssh, ssh,' says Rik. 'You mustn't worry yourself. I'll take care of everything.'

She doesn't respond. My eyes dart from her to him. I say his name, but he doesn't seem to hear. 'Rik,' I repeat, louder. Only then does he allow his eyes to meet mine. 'Who is Gianni Bellini?' I ask.

He turns away, staring at Nonna. I prompt him to answer me. His reply is vague. 'You heard wrong. She means Jovani Bachini.'

'Who's he?'

He blinks rapidly. His jiggling leg vibrates the bed, flickering the strand of tinsel attached to the metal bed frame. 'A man who had some business dealings with her. Nothing for you to worry about.'

'Why has he got to be stopped? What's he trying to do?'

'Forget it. It's all sorted.'

Nonna has always taught me: "Watch out for people who give vague answers and can't stop fidgeting. They are liars."

Who is Jovani Bachini?

SIX

With Lola tucked up in bed, I tidy her room, scooping up items of clothing from the floor.

Did I change my clothes ten times a day when I was her age? Afterwards, I straighten the rest of the place. It doesn't take long. It's only a two-bedroom top floor flat of an end-of-terrace Victorian house in a relatively quiet road. The rest of the family only live a few streets away. Lola and me, Nonna and Rik, Mamma and Papa, Jenni and Franco, and Milana, a family that lives in a pentagon, less than a mile from each other. It's stifling sometimes.

Matt and I moved here just before Lola was born. We'd lived with Nonna and Nonno Nico for two years before that while we saved up the deposit. They helped us a bit too. They could have helped a lot more, but Nonna is of the opinion that us youngsters have to learn to stand on our own two feet. We were so happy living here, the three of us. But the evening of the day we attended the twelve-week scan for Lola's little brother, Matt went out and never came home again. And the guilt is like my shadow. It follows me everywhere.

Turning on the kitchen tap, I clean my hands, making a mental note to refill the soap pump. Didn't I do that before the weekend? Surely, I couldn't have got through a whole bottle since Friday? I can't remember. It is that time of year, though – five years next Sunday.

I uncork a bottle of Dolcetto – one of three Italian wines Nonna gave me to sample as part of the selection process to update the restaurant's drinks menu – and fill a glass to the brim. Some days call for it. Opening the corner cupboard, I reach around the top shelf, take out a packet of Marlboro Red and remove two cigarettes. On second thoughts, I grab a third. It's been a stressful day.

As I open the balcony door, a gush of cold air rushes into the kitchen. There's no mistaking it. The thick of winter is upon us. The temperature has dropped significantly this week. The security light comes on as I walk out onto the small balcony, which houses a metal table and two chairs, with steps leading down to my stretch of garden. It's too cold to sit, so I lean against the railings, take a large sip of wine and light a cigarette, feeling a snippet of calmness as my lungs take the first hit. The sound of trains clatter in the distance as I stare down onto the ground floor flat's garden. It's illuminated by a security light that my presence out here always sets off. I'm surprised Bob and Eleanor never complain, but then, they're not the type.

After I've washed my hands again, I refill my glass and take it to the lounge. The Christmas tree stands waiting for me to turn on its lights, but I can't find the motivation. I find the remote under a pile of Barbie clothes and switch on the TV; the remaining two episodes of *Grey's Anatomy* from the latest series are waiting for me to watch. But the programme begins with the surgical team performing heart surgery on a middle-aged woman who doesn't make it, and I turn it off.

Instead, I search for some music. Vivaldi, one of Nonna's favourites, will do. Not my usual go-to, but I want to feel close to her tonight. Her words have unnerved me. I mean, it's not every day a family member alleges someone is trying to kill them. She can't be serious. Nonna doesn't have enemies. She has tons of friends. Everyone in the local community looks up to her, admires her for the success she has had with De Rosa's and the expansion of her restaurant chain.

I slump into the sofa, curling my feet under me. All I want to do is sit and stare into space for ten minutes and collect my thoughts from the day. But my phone rings. No Caller ID appears on the screen. I consider ignoring it, but it might be the hospital.

I recognise the voice straight away. It's a voice I'll never forget. 'Sienna?' asks DS Durant.

'Yes.'

'How're things?'

My stomach churns. What does he want? I haven't heard from him for ages. I stopped speaking to him months ago. 'Don't call me unless you have an update,' was the last thing I said to him. I felt bad. He was a good bloke. I got on well with him, very well, but there are only so many times you can stomach hearing the words, "We've got no new leads."

'It's not a good time,' I tell him, relaying the afternoon's events.

'I'm sorry to trouble you when you have so much else going on. It's not ideal to be raking up demons at a time like this, but we have new information regarding Matthew's case that I'd like to come and talk to you about.'

A small gasp escapes me. I cradle the phone between my ear and shoulder and run my thumb along the third finger of my left hand. He doesn't understand. No one does. The unwanted anxiety that resurfaces along with the nightmares every time they think they have a new lead. It's happened a few times. 'What new information?'

He hesitates, probably choosing his words carefully to minimise the upset they may cause. 'We're still in the early stages of our new line of enquiry. Let's discuss more when we meet. You've enough going on. Perhaps I could pop by after you've dropped your daughter at school in the morning. Around nine-ish?'

'My schedule has changed. Lola goes to breakfast club, and I start work at eight.'

'How about after you finish, then?'

'I don't know.' I sigh deeply. It's taken a lot to try and deal with what happened. Talking about it doesn't resolve anything. It always turns out to be a journey down memory lane I regret making.

'I'll be going to visit Nonna after work tomorrow.' I twist the imaginary ring on my finger, staring at where my band of gold once sat. 'I'll call you.'

I pop to the kitchen and empty the dregs of the Dolcetto into my glass, ignoring the nagging voice telling me I'll regret this in the morning. My mobile rings. I rush back to the lounge. Zach's number flashes up on the screen. 'Hey, honey, I'm home. How was the party?' he asks.

I feel bad. I should have texted him and told him about Nonna, but with everything going on, I forgot. 'It was a disaster.' I update him. He is upset. I knew he would be. Nonna's got a soft spot for Zach. She has done since I first introduced them. 'Good to see you moving on,' she said. 'With someone as delightful as Matt was.' She had been trying to persuade me to meet someone new for a while, introducing me to a couple of friends' grandsons. 'You can't be single forever,' she said.

Oh, I can, I replied, but not out loud.

'Do you want me to come over?' Zach asks.

'Not tonight. I'm going to crash soon. How was your weekend?'

'As crazy as any stag party I've ever been on. Simon had a good time. Dublin was freezing.' He tries to make me laugh with stories of the groom-to-be, but I can't even fake the slightest amusement to hear about Simon being handcuffed to some railings, while wearing a mankini. He agrees to pick up Lola for me tomorrow, and I tell him to get some sleep.

I call Milana. My sister always knows everything that is going on at the restaurant. 'Who is Jovani Bachini?' I ask.

'Never heard of him,' she replies.

'What about Gianni Bellini?'

'Nope, never heard that name neither. Who are these men?'

'Nonna mentioned the name to Rik earlier. She sounded worked-up. I thought he might be the man who she went off with last week, when you were at the Islington site.'

'How do you know about him?'

'Mamma told me.'

Nonna and Milana had gone over to the new restaurant to interview some candidates to manage the restaurant when it finally opens. Unfortunately, the guy to whom they had originally offered the job, and who had accepted, subsequently found another position. Mamma accompanied them. It was her day off, but she has a friend who lives nearby who she hadn't seen for ages, so she spent the day unpacking all the new crockery that had arrived by the box-load before meeting her friend for dinner.

'What did Nonna say about him?' Milana asked.

'*He's got to be stopped*. That was all I heard her say to Rik.'

Milana snorts. 'When I asked her who he was, she wouldn't say. Told me to mind my own business, as she does.'

'She reckons someone is trying to kill her,' I say.

'She's well confused. Must be all the drugs. Listen, I'm off to bed. I'll see you in the morning.'

I grab my laptop from the coffee table and fire it up. My CV glares at me with a cold stare of accusation and neglect – as it has done for nearly a year. I tut and close the file. Might as well wait until January; no one hires permanent staff in December. I type the name Jovani Bachini into Google, but it returns no one by that name. Was Rik lying?

I replace Jovani Bachini with Gianni Bellini. I'm sure that was the name Nonna used. Two people of interest stand out from the crowd of men Google throws back at me. One, a good few years younger than the other – I'd put him in his early forties – is a restaurateur who owns a chain of Italian restaurants in London and the south-east. There's an article about him opening a new fifty-cover establishment in Epsom, near the racecourse. Does Nonna have connections to him? The other man, a distinguished-looking guy, mid-seventies, looks vaguely familiar. Where have I seen him before? Perhaps I'm confusing him with a customer. I read some more about him. He is a successful entrepreneur with his multiple eggs in several baskets. He once touted for high office in Italy before moving to the UK with his British wife to expand his empire of prestigious London properties. I download both men's photos and airdrop them to my phone.

SEVEN

'I don't want to go to school today. I've got a tummy ache,' Lola says as I try and get her up.

'And I've got a cracking headache. That doesn't mean I get to stay in bed.' Although, I could well have done. A call from Papa kept me awake until the early hours. He confirmed the levels of troponin found in Nonna's blood proves she has suffered another heart attack, and she will be having further investigative procedures today. I ended up on the balcony for another cigarette. Her heart has let her down again. 'What do you think Bisnonna would say?' I ask my sleepyhead daughter.

Lola sits upright, clutching the bear Nonna bought her when she was born. Snugglebug – the near-human teddy who causes the most colossal commotion when he can't be found at bedtime. 'Is Bisnonna going to die, Mummy?' I reach over and scrape my fingers through her tangled mass of blonde hair, combing it away from her face. A ripple of emotion flutters my stomach. She is the image of Matt, especially when she is upset. 'I saw her fall over yesterday.'

'She's poorly,' I say. 'But you know Bisnonna. She's as tough as old boots.'

'What does that mean?'

'She's a strong woman who doesn't let anything, or anyone get the better of her. And she needs us to be equally strong for her. She wouldn't be happy if she knew you'd missed school, would she? So up you get. Chop-chop. You don't want to be late, do you?'

'Do I have to go to ballet after school today?'

'Absolutely. You've only got tonight and next week. Then it's the end of term.'

'Who's going to pick me up?'

Nonna often ferries Lola around to her dance classes, parties, and playdates, jokingly complaining that her great-granddaughter has a better social life than her. That goes for the two of us. 'I've asked Zach to take you to ballet.'

'I want you to do it.'

'I can't, Lola. Not today. I need to see Nonna.'

'I want to come.'

'Children aren't allowed.'

It's a fight the whole way to school. A battle of obstinate hair, a lost cardigan and misplaced ballet shoes turns into aching feet as we cross the park. 'Slow down, Mummy. You walk too fast,' Lola says when we are only halfway through.

She's right. Lately, I can't wait to get across the park. I once loved this part of the twenty-minute walk from home to the restaurant – a far cry from the laborious commute I had to endure when I worked up in the City as a PA to a high-flying investment banker. The days when Matt was still here. But when life throws you your husband's death certificate, your options are pretty limited. I couldn't stomach returning to that job. I needed something more flexible. A job where some days, when the stupor of grief took hold and desperation dragged me back to bed, I could call and say, I won't make it in today.

Two entrances border the park on the home side. One by the tennis courts and another near the children's playground, and I used to alternate between the two, but now I only take the latter as it's the quickest. It's usually about a ten-minute comfortable walk from one end to the other, but lately, over the past few months, I've knocked that down to seven when I'm with Lola, and five if I'm on my own.

'Are you sure you're not being paranoid?' Milana said, her tone condescending, when I arrived at work one morning in the summer and mentioned I thought someone had followed Lola and me through the park the previous afternoon. The feeling had been so intense, so real, as if some assailant could be lurking in the shadows, that I'd picked Lola up and struggled home with her on my hip.

The feeling continued, not every day and not always in the park. A bookshop occupies one of the buildings on the road opposite the restaurant. A delightful independent, it sells an eclectic selection of new and second-hand books. Behind the frontage displaying books is an armchair for customers. One afternoon, I'm sure I saw a man staring at me from that spot. He had hollow cheeks and sunken eyes, a ghost of a figure that made me shiver. Once I had passed the shop, I turned. He was still watching me, but dropped his head to his chest as soon as our eyes met. A nauseating unease made me quicken my pace, and when I turned again, he wasn't there, leaving me wondering if he had been a figment of my paranoid imagination Milana often tells me I need to do something about.

Sometimes the feeling starts at the end of the road down from the restaurant; before I cross to the park. A pub dominates one corner. An independent supermarket dwarfs the other. You can't miss it. The outside display of fruit and vegetables is a riot of colour whatever the time of year. I sometimes stop there to supplement my weekend grocery shop. Only a few weeks back, I was buying a head of broccoli – the only vegetable I can get Lola to eat without a fight – and that feeling of dread shuddered through me once again. Since then, I can't rid myself of this all-consuming feeling of being followed.

Lola stops dead. 'Mummy, slow down.'

Her excessive fussiness doesn't stop until, with a sigh of relief, I surrender her to her favourite worker at breakfast club. The pounding head I have from polishing off the Dolcetto last night isn't helping. Usually, she is such a good kid.

When I arrive at the restaurant, the sweet smell of buttery pastry swathes the air like a warm blanket. My stomach rumbles. I'm hungry, but I can't face food before another coffee fix. We only do a takeaway service until mid-morning, selling hot drinks and pastries: chocolate twirls, cinnamon rolls, and apple Danishes. We used to allow people to sit in, but Nonna complained about the clientele this attracted. Some people took an hour to consume their drinks and left a mess when they departed. 'We're not an internet café,' she said, frustrated by the lingerers with coffee cups long empty. So, we switched to a takeaway-only service. According to Nonna, the profit margin on tea and coffee to-go is so high, we're better off this way.

It looks more Christmassy in here today. While I was at the hospital last night, Jenni and Lola furnished the place with more decorations. Garlands of shiny red baubles and gold-sprayed pinecones are dotted about. Boughs of ivy deck the bar. I usually man the coffee machine, but Lola has made me late this morning, and I'm surprised to see Jared has taken charge. 'Give me a minute,' I tell him as I pass.

He nods and tells me, 'No problem.'

I head to the office next to the kitchen at the far end of the restaurant. It's tight in here. We could do with a bigger office, but Nonna says it's not commercially viable. 'I need a word,' I say to Milana.

She swings around from the grey filing cabinet with a bundle of papers in her hand. Her silky hair swings with her. 'What's up?'

I close the door and take a seat on the swivel chair in front of one of the two desks. Nonna sprinkled some of her festive spirit in here last week with a mini, pre-lit Christmas tree which sits on the desk I'm sitting at. She decorated it with London-themed tree chocolates – mini

Big Bens, black cabs, and red telephone boxes – and told us to help ourselves. She loves this time of year. Unlike me. When everyone gets out their party hat, I want to burrow under the duvet and hibernate until it's all over.

Milana sits on the chair behind the desk, eyebrows raised, and picks up a pen, twirling it in her fingers.

'What's Jared doing here this morning?' I ask. 'He doesn't usually work the morning shifts.'

'I asked him last night if he'd do some overtime. Someone's got to run this show in Nonna's absence.'

'I'm worried about her.'

'Aren't we all. Another heart attack! Did you see my WhatsApp last night? To the family group,' she says.

I shake my head.

'I said we all need to stay positive.'

'What about the wedding? Should we cancel it?' I ask.

'Let's assume it's still going ahead. We must keep her spirits up for when she comes round. Anyway, Rik needs to make that decision.'

'He said she's been really stressed about work these past few months. Why won't you tell me what's going on?'

'What's there to tell? You know everything. We've been working towards the opening of the two new restaurants. The Islington one is behind schedule. It should already be up and running. Nonna was gunning for it to be open for Christmas, but that's not going to happen. And we've been busting a gut to get Highbury ready by Easter, but it's unlikely we'll meet that deadline either. It's been stressful.' She shrugs. 'That's business for you.'

'What's been the delay?'

'Something to do with the finances. I don't get involved in that side of things. You know Nonna won't allow me to.' She clenches her teeth. 'You wouldn't believe she supported me through a business and finance degree and is financing my MBA, would you? I mean, I've studied everything to do with running a business, finances, and all of it. I could take so much off her hands, but you know how obstinate she can be. It's like she doesn't trust me. I'm the Senior Business Development Manager here, for heaven's sake.'

This title cracks me up. The senior makes me laugh more than anything because there is no junior role. Milana came up with it a while back when Nonna decided it was time to expand the De Rosa chain and branch out beyond the current three East End restaurants. Milana is the type of person who needs a title, whereas Nonna couldn't care less. Probably because she is the boss of everything anyway.

Milana continues. 'I'm in charge of strategic planning – of all the new restaurants we plan to open over the next three years – so surely I should have access to the finances as well?'

I've heard this all before. Milana is a control freak. 'Tell me more about the man who turned up at the Islington site last week to speak to Nonna.'

She taps the pen on the desk three times. 'There's nothing much more to tell. Nonna knew who he was. She wasn't happy about seeing him; I could tell. She got flustered. He was quite demanding, said they had things to discuss. I got the feeling it was something to do with money, and, as I said, she doesn't involve me in the financial side of things. They went off somewhere. That's all I know. She texted me later to say she had a headache and was going home. When I asked her about him the next day, she told me to mind my own business. It was to do with a private deal she was involved in, and she would tell me more when the time was right.'

I reach into my pocket and remove my phone. Then, selecting the photos app and clicking the desired image, I turn the screen towards her. 'Was this the man?'

Squinting, she leans towards me. She shakes her head at the photo of the first guy I found last night: the younger Italian restaurateur. I flick to the second photo, the older Italian property magnate. 'How about him?' I ask.

She nods her head vigorously. 'He's the one.'

EIGHT

'But he looked different the day Nonna went off with him,' Milana adds.

'Different in what way?'

'Thinner.' She takes the phone from me and zooms in. 'Much thinner and older.' She pauses to think. 'He was dressed the same, though. Business casual. A bit like Rik dresses. You know. Chinos, tailored blazer, button-down shirt.'

'This picture was taken a few years ago at a cancer support charity ball. He generously donated to the raffle. The top prize of five thousand pounds in cash.'

'Not short of a bob or two then! What's his connection to Nonna?'

I shrug.

'Then how come you have his photo?'

I ignore her. 'Have you any idea where they went?'

'I've already told you, no.'

The door crashes open, and Mamma marches in,

harassed. 'What're you doing in here, Sienna? There are a ton of jobs that need doing out there. Franco called to say he has developed a cold and doesn't feel it appropriate to see Cara, so your papa has gone instead.' She sucks in air. 'There's always something with that man.' She beckons me. 'A crowd has appeared from nowhere. It must be the cold weather. Everyone wants a coffee. Help Jared behind the bar, will you?' She turns to my sister. 'You could help out as well,' she says, although I'm unsure why she bothered. My sister rarely dons an apron.

Milana tosses the pen on the desk. It swivels across the surface and bounces onto the floor. 'I've got enough to do in here.'

I take a space behind the bar and assist Jared in reducing the queue of customers snaking out of the door. Most days, there's a queue like this one. De Rosa's coffee is the talk of the community. Even the tiny coffee houses who specialise in the highest grades of beans can't seem to compete. 'Thanks for helping out,' I say.

'No problem,' says Jared. 'The extra cash comes in helpful this time of year when you have a kid with expensive taste.'

I laugh. 'Tell me about it.'

He laughs with me. 'My daughter wants a pony. "A pony," I said to her. "You've got about as much chance of Santa bringing you a pony as I have of him bringing me a winning lottery ticket. It ain't gonna happen." I mean, for starters, where are we going to keep a pony?'

He is serving a woman who is jiggling a double buggy with two wailing faces sticking out from identical blue covers. The noise is deafening, drilling into my sore head. Jared pours coffee into a disposable cup. 'You've got your hands full there,' he says to the woman, his eyebrows dipping in the middle.

The woman yawns. 'Tell me about it. I've hardly slept a wink all night. I've brought them out for a walk for some peace.'

Jared presses a lid on the cup and hands the woman her coffee, then walks around to the front of the counter. Squatting in front of the buggy, he places a hand on each of the babies. 'You going to give your mummy some peace today, little ones?' He starts singing. Brahms's *Wiegenlied*. A vision flashes before me. Matt used to hover his head above my bump every night and sing this lullaby when Lola was growing inside.

'They're so cute,' Jared says, smiling up at the woman.

'Can I leave them here with you?' she laughs, preparing to leave.

'Let me help you.' She follows Jared to the exit, where he holds the door open for her. Wind rushes through the restaurant. 'Thank you for your custom. Please visit De Rosa's again.' As he closes the door, he calls after her. 'I hope you get some sleep tonight!'

I stare at him. It's hard to think of Jared as a former criminal spending time behind bars. All because he wanted to feed his family and put a roof over their heads. He told me the whole story back in August at Nonna's staff summer barbecue, after we'd both had too much to drink.

His partner was pregnant, he got laid off, and their unsympathetic landlord kicked them out of their crappy one-bedroom rented flat because he was two months behind on the rent. 'Blimin' place didn't even have any heating,' he slurred, as he swiped another two glasses of Pimms and lemonade from a passing waitress. He lowered his voice. 'So, when the offer arose to drive a car with a boot full of goods, no questions asked, from London to Manchester, in exchange for the sum which would cover the deposit and a year's rent for a decent two-bed, I jumped at the chance. What could go wrong?' He handed me one of the glasses of Pimms. 'Everything, that's what.' He went on to tell me that when you find yourself sharing a cell with Paul Keys, a burly thug with a history of convictions, you either sink or swim. He found himself perfecting the front crawl at record speed. 'There comes a time in your life when there's no mucking about anymore. The time had come to get serious.' He was working towards gaining a City & Guilds NVQ in Professional Cookery in the prison's restaurant when Cara De Rosa walked into his life. She was dining with Angela Martin – a no-nonsense type in charge of the Prisoner Apprenticeship Pathway, and Jared charmed Nonna as he served her a plate of sweet potato katsu curry.

And here he is.

My phone beeps in my pocket. I slide it out and read the text.

need help. come when papa leave. on own. urgent. nonna

. . .

The hectic morning morphs into the lunchtime rush, which is crazy today – even more than the norm – especially with Papa at the hospital. Nonna's garbled message has played on my mind all day. I'm desperate to see her, but Papa phoned to say she is waiting to be taken to theatre. Her failing arteries need fresh investigation, and most likely further stents, is the consensus amongst the professionals.

Jared is running the kitchen in Papa's absence, leading the cooks to feed the variety of clientele who pack the place – ladies who lunch, mums with babies asleep in car seats, and friends, young and old, having a Christmas catch-up. Local entrepreneurs, also, escaping their desks for a bite to eat. I glance up at the chalkboard with the specials of the day. Jared has scaled it back from our usual four to only two, but being De Rosa's classics, this is sufficient. Chicken and chorizo tart, and vegetarian fettuccine, supplement our selection of salads and freshly baked herby focaccia sandwiches.

The local grapevine is in full bloom. People have been dropping by all morning, bearing cards and gifts and asking after Nonna. A harried-looking woman walks in. She looks familiar, but I can't place her at first; then her A-line, grey wool skirt and a hooded cape give her away. The type of clothes she stocks in her vintage clothing shop down near the canal. Scanning the restaurant until she spots me, she works her way through the tables towards me holding a gift bag. 'Helen, how are you?' I ask.

She doesn't look as spruced up as usual. Her mascara has smudged, and strands of her pink hair hang from what looks like yesterday's top knot. She gives a brief nod. 'I'm so sorry to hear about Cara. Can you give this to her for me, please?' Her voice is shaky. 'How is she?'

I take the bag. 'Not the best, but we're staying positive.'

'I've been so worried about her.' Her voice breaks as she struggles to talk. 'Please tell her I'm thinking about her.' She scrabbles around in her handbag. Staring at me, she pulls out a business card, which she places in my hand. 'There's my mobile number. If I can do anything to help you here, please call me. Any time.' Abruptly, she turns and darts towards the exit. And, like a flurry of winter wind, she rushes out of the door.

Perturbed, I take the gift to the office. 'Another present for Nonna,' I say to Milana, placing the bag with other gifts and numerous cards that have arrived today.

She glances up from the computer. 'Who from this time?'

'Helen. The lady who owns the vintage clothing shop. Do you know her?'

She nods. 'Nonna's friend. They've been spending a lot of time with each other lately.'

'She looked as if she was going to burst into tears.'

'I wasn't aware they knew each other so well,' she says.

'Me neither.'

NINE

It's growing dark when I leave. And it's snowing. Large flakes powder my face. I brush them away as I rush home across the park to pick up my car from home. I used to love the stroll across the park in winter, watching the kids pour out of school and into the playground to have a quick swing and slide and run around to expel their energy before darkness arrived. This winter, though, the stroll has transformed into a power-walk and often a run when I can muster the energy.

The snow appears heavy enough to settle. Lola will be happy. She loves the snow. I did too when I was little. When I was about seven or eight, Nonna bought me a sledge for Christmas. She bought one for Milana too, but Nonna should have known better. Getting mucky and cold wasn't Milana's thing. In the end, Nonna claimed it for herself and took me sledging in Mansfield Park in Chingford every year. Milana missed out big time on the prized memories of sledging alongside Nonna down the short sharp hill there. But the night I stood at the lounge window and waved Matt off for the last time, snow was falling, and it's never since had the same appeal.

I jump into my car, mount my phone in its holder and listen to a message of Nonna's croaky attempt to back up her insistent text to visit as soon as possible. My heart misses a beat as I negotiate the busy streets to the hospital. There's a demanding edge to her voice. The tone she adopts when those close to her sense we'd better do as we're told. I return the call and connect to her mobile, but it doesn't ring; it sings with her invitation to speak clearly after the tone.

I switch on the car radio and listen to the news warning us that hospitals are busy preparing for the imminent surge in winter demand, a reality I witness when I enter the ward. Nurses rush around, tired and stressed, and doctors yawn over notes at the nurses' station. I pass them, wincing as gel stings the sores on my hands, and head along the corridor to Nonna, only to find an empty bed. 'Cara De Rosa?' I say to one of the admin staff typing at the nurses' station, my voice cracking as the word Rosa leaves my mouth. I point across the way. 'She was in that bed yesterday.' The woman peers over the top of her glasses at a whiteboard and, with a nod, directs me diagonally opposite, where I see Papa sitting at Nonna's side.

I reach for more hand gel from the dispenser above the sink and take the chair on the other side of Nonna, letting my bag drop to the floor. 'What's happening?' I ask Papa.

'They can't understand why she won't wake up.' He attempts a smile, but it gets stuck in his anguish.

'She wasn't like this when she had her last heart attack,' I say. 'Do you remember us coming to see her after the stent surgery? Franco had already picked her up and taken her home.'

Papa stands. 'They found a small blood clot on her lung. Nothing to worry about, they said. They'll deal with it with meds. They're running more tests.' He tells me that after the angioplasty this morning, and the insertion of three stents, they had expected a quicker recovery, and her deterioration is a cause for concern. 'The doctor said this heart attack was as severe as the last one. She's not getting any younger, I suppose.' He shoulders into his puffer jacket and zips it up. 'I'm leaving now you're here.'

The smell of death hangs in the air. 'Stay for a while, Papa,' I say, scared to be left alone.

'I can't, love. I had a text from your mamma. It's going to be carnage at the restaurant tonight. We're fully booked, and the group of fifteen coming in for their Christmas party has added another two.'

I feel sorry for him as he plods up the ward, his head drooping with the weight of his worries. He has not been himself lately. He used to be so laid back, but he stresses at even the little things these days. Nonna detected the same. She suggested he and Mamma could do with a change, and offered them the management of the new restaurant in Islington, but Papa declined, claiming he is too old for such a malarkey.

I take Nonna's hand in mine. Firmly at first, but it's cold and clammy like a wet cloth, and it feels fragile, so I loosen my grip. She looks so old. I swallow my pain. It's too much to deal with. 'I can't lose you, Nonna,' I whisper. 'Nonna, squeeze my fingers if you can hear me,' I repeat.

Gradually, she opens her eyes, dazed.

'How are you?' are the words that slip from my lips. It's a silly question given the circumstances.

'I want you to know.' She stutters her words. 'I'm moving.' Her eyes close. I stare at her, unsure what to make of this. Does she mean moving beds, moving home? She adores her house, has lived there for my whole life. She splutters, and her eyes open slightly as if she hasn't the energy to open them fully. 'I've been waiting for Don,' she slurs, 'to leave.' For a woman usually so vibrant with life, it's upsetting to see the effort required for her to talk. 'I need to speak to you on your own.' She nods towards a jug of water on the overbed table. I refill the plastic cup and guide the straw towards her dry mouth. Her lips are cracked, her vibrancy lost. She looks so *wrong* lying there. Tipping her head forward, she takes a sip. 'So pleased you're here.'

'I'm worried, Nonna, especially after what you said yesterday. You do understand what's going on, don't you? You've had another heart attack.'

'Don't let Zach slip by, Sienna. He's a good man, perfect in every way. He's always there when you need him. You don't want to lose him. And you will if you don't let him in.'

I ignore her words, telling me what I already know. She's been ticking me off on this one for months. She says the train is at the station, patiently waiting for me, but I'm too stubborn to get on, and that's not a good place to be. It'll leave me on the platform with all my luggage. What she can't understand is that the guilt I harbour from Matt's death won't let me climb aboard. No one understands.

I blame it on the blame.

Because I was instrumental in Matt's death.

It could have all turned out so differently.

I wasn't well the night he died. Nothing serious, I had a head cold. It was a Monday and Papa's was birthday that week. Nonna had spent the afternoon preparing a feast to which she had invited the whole family. But when the time came to leave, I couldn't face it. More so out of laziness than because I felt ill, though. If only I had known the consequences of saying to Matt, 'I'm not going.'

'They'll understand. The last thing they all want is your cold,' he said. 'I'll tell you what. I'll drop off Don's present and card and stop off at the chippie on the way back. How does battered sausage and chips for two sound?'

If only I'd gone. Instead of him taking the detour to the fish and chip shop, we'd have tucked into Nonna's feast.

'Nonna, you need to tell me what you meant by someone wanting you dead. Do you mean Gianni Bellini?'

Her eyes widen. 'However do you know that name?'

'He came to see you in Islington last week. You went off with him, and no one saw you for the rest of the day.'

Her head moves a fraction from left to right. 'Don't worry about that for now.'

'But who is he?'

She grinds her teeth and expels her message with great effort. 'There're more important things you need to learn. Things I need to say. And you're the person to hear them.'

I can't bear seeing her like this. She doesn't deserve it.

63

This is the person who gives so much and takes so little. 'You need to rest.'

Huffing, she fists her hands. 'Bloody well let me talk.' I gasp. I don't think I've ever heard Nonna swear. She's too sophisticated. Women like Cara De Rosa don't swear. Or if they do, it's only silently in their head or when home alone. Her speech slurs. '… because I know… I know you'll help me find justice. I trust you. You'll stay calm.' She takes several deep breaths. 'I have three things to tell you before I die.'

I release my grip from her hand and hold a palm up in front of her face. 'Stop right there. You're not going to die.'

'You won't like what I have to tell you, but I'll never rest in my grave without you knowing.'

'Nonna. Enough of this. Stop.' I tap her hand. 'You're stronger than anyone I've ever known.'

'You must listen. Before it's too late.' Breathlessness slows her words even more. 'I should've told you this long ago. But it wasn't my story to tell. I was waiting for others to show some decency.'

I feel my cheeks pale, the blood rushing to shield myself from her words.

'The time's never been right. I wanted you to be an adult, but then life took over, and it has been so unkind to you.'

Hot tears well up, stinging my eyes. My hands reach up to cover my ears. 'Stop. Whatever it is, I don't want to hear.'

A health care assistant appears with an observation trolley. She stretches out a pair of latex gloves. 'I'll be back in a minute,' she says and wanders off.

'Firstly, Jared must go.' She pauses to catch her breath.

'Jared?'

She nods.

'Why?'

'Do as I say. And you need to organise the decorators.'

'Decorators?'

'Pilkingtons. I've arranged for them to come in the new year.' Her lips manage a brief smile. 'For the honeymoon.'

'Nonna, you're not making sense.' We only decorated the restaurant last year. She is confused. One minute she is talking of dying, the next of sacking staff and unnecessary decorating.

'You take charge of them. You're the only one I can trust.' She coughs and splutters, clutching her chest. Alarms sound from the surrounding machines, ringing in my head. 'What I'm about to tell you is going to upset you, but you need to hear it before I die.' Inner strength fights its way to the surface, and her words explode from her mouth like a time bomb detonating. 'Papa is not your real papa.'

TEN

I gasp and laugh. 'Nonna, you're being silly. Stop.' A smidgeon of doubt creeps into my tone. 'Don't be ridiculous.'

'It's true. I've lived with this secret for so many years, waiting for Bettina to come clean, but she never has. I don't want to die with this burden. Face her and decide how to move forward.'

I release her hand, shocked at her words. 'You can't be serious. Nonna, do you realise what you're saying?'

Her eyes widen. They look like the plastic eyes of a doll. She talks but doesn't see me. As if I'm not there. The left side of her face is drooping; she looks like she is growling. She struggles to talk, but she gives it all her effort. 'Sorry.' I have difficulty making out what she says next. Her words are garbled and slurred like those from a drunk, but she is determined to make me hear them. 'This is most important. Listen carefully,' she says, momentarily resting her eyes. I wait with bated breath, perplexed as to what she is going to come out with next.

But I don't get to hear further revelations. Monitors flash. Alarms beep. The young health care assistant returns and panics, staring at me as if I should know what to do. In her haste, she trips over her trolley. Her arms flail as she tries to steady herself on the overbed tray. Water flies from the jug, covering me, and the cup falls, bouncing along the floor. She reaches for the red button on the wall and smacks it with her hand. Doctors and nurses appear one after the other like a row of late buses.

A nurse asks me to leave the area. I back away from the chaotic scene, bumping into Rik as he catches my shoulder. 'Whatever's happened?' he asks. A nurse, who introduces herself as Paula, guides him away. She ushers us both to the visitors' room, reassuring us that the medical team will soon have everything under control. 'I'll come and find you when we know more.'

We wait on the synthetic sofa, staring at the scrapings of Blu-tack covering the walls where posters once hung. We don't say much – a few words of comfort and offers to fetch drinks to add to the empty disposable cups littering the coffee table. My guts are twisting, spinning with the turn of events and the news Nonna has delivered. She must be disorientated, the meds mixing her words into a moonshine of confusion.

Of course Papa is my papa.

Rik gets up and wanders over to the kitchenette. He flicks the kettle on and opens the fridge. Bending down, he removes a bottle of milk, swearing when he realises it's out of date. I need answers. I need to speak to Mamma. 'Are you and Nonna moving house, Rik?' I ask.

He frowns. 'Moving?'

I nod. 'Nonna said some things to me which don't add up. She said you're moving.'

He comes to sit back down beside me. Leaning his elbows on his knees, he stares at the floor. 'We've talked about it, but not for a while. I want to. She's not so keen.' He sighs and looks up at me. 'I don't mean to sound disrespectful towards your grandfather, but there's something uncomfortable about living in a house your partner has spent most of their life in with another man. I want us to have a fresh start, but she vows, the only time she'll be leaving Cara's Place is in a coffin.'

'That's what I thought.' I imitate Nonna's Italian accent at its strongest, "The only time you'll get me to leave this house is the day I move to heaven. Or to hell. Whichever will have me."

He manages a laugh, but only a brief one. 'Sounds about right.'

'She also said she has arranged for the decorators to come in.'

His face scrunches up with confusion. 'They've only just finished decorating the lounge.'

'She meant the restaurant,' I say, before adding, 'I think.'

'That doesn't make sense. It was only decorated last year. It doesn't need doing again so soon.' He takes a large gulp of air, puffing it out in bursts. 'She sounds confused.'

Confused. That's all this is. Confusion. Papa is my real papa.

Nurse Paula's reappearance interrupts our conversation. She smiles sympathetically. 'The doctors believe Mrs De Rosa has suffered a stroke. We're sending her for a CT scan. I'll update you when we have some more news.'

The journey home proves tedious. Snow has slowed the traffic. It's settling on the pavements, but the roads are a slushy mess. All I want is a soak in a hot bath and for this dreadful day to end, but the hazardous conditions have caused an accident. I'm sitting in a queue of traffic, absently tapping the steering wheel as I wait for the lights to turn green, when it occurs to me. My stomach convulses, spasming as if it's having a fit. Why have I only just realised this?

If Papa isn't my real papa, then Nonna isn't my real nonna.

ELEVEN

I find Mamma's number and press the call button. I need to confront her with this, but what if Nonna *is* confused? I can't do it in front of Papa. I'll have to go to their house when he's not around. As the line connects, a call comes in. It's Rik. I delete the call to Mamma, slamming my foot on the brakes. The car behind me comes to an abrupt halt.

'It's confirmed. Cara's had a stroke.'

Zach and Lola are having fun on his PlayStation when I finally arrive home, numbingly cold and disturbed. 'Time up,' I hear Zach say as a controller thuds onto the coffee table.

'One more, one more, Zach,' I hear Lola say from the kitchen as I squirt soap into my hands.

'Another time. Your mum's home. I need to get dinner, and it's past your bedtime. How about you get your PJs on, and I'll come and read you a story.'

Lola runs and pecks me on the cheek on the way to her bedroom. 'I beat Zach again,' she tells me, alternating pumping her biceps in the air.

'I've missed you,' Zach says, kissing me, as he comes into the kitchen. 'You look done in. Sit down, and I'll get you a drink.' He tugs at the collar of my coat, but I push him away.

'I'm popping out for a smoke.'

'I've cooked a fish pie.' He smiles. 'Red or white?'

'White, please.' There's no way I can face a glass of red after finishing that bottle of Dolcetto solo last night. I fetch my packet of cigarettes and unlock the back door. 'I've had a day from hell.'

Snow has settled on the balcony, and my foot slips as I step outside. I steady myself on the railing and pull up the hood of my coat, huddling in the corner to light a cigarette. Zach nips out with my drink. 'I'll read Lola a story while you have this, then I'll dish up, and you can tell me about your day.'

Nonna's right. He is perfect in every way.

But he's not Matt.

Bob McIntyre waves up at me from his garden. He's collecting logs from the log store he constructed from old pallets last autumn to replace the one that had decayed to a pile of rotten planks. 'You'll catch your death up there, girl.' I like Bob. He's a short, red-nosed, jolly-old-elf kind of man. I return his wave and watch him load logs into his arms before returning inside.

When Matt was still with us, Bob showed him how to make the same log store for us. Matt, who was partial to a real fire, took pride in keeping ours piled with logs. He loved nothing more than to share a bottle of wine and the latest movie in front of our roaring fire. I haven't lit one since his death.

Taking my phone out of my pocket, I call Mamma, only to listen to her instructions to leave a message. I don't. I can't think what to say. Ten minutes and two cigarettes later, I'm still out here when Zach reappears. It's taken me this long to say the words out loud. 'Nonna's had a stroke,' I say and gulp down the last of my wine.

He tells me how sorry he is, that Nonna is a fighter, and she will get through this. He takes my glass and returns with a refill, standing with me as I brief him on everything else that has gone on since his weekend away. Even though he hates me smoking and is shivering with the cold, he stays with an arm around me, listening intently. I start with the revelation about Papa.

'You sure it's not all the meds she's on?' he says.

I shrug. I can't bear to think about this anymore. I turn the conversation to Jared. 'You're not going to like this,' I say. Jared and Zach have become mates over the past year. They are members of the same gym, and when I introduced them, they acknowledged they already knew each other. Since realising they had a connection, their friendship grew to more than a nod from across weightlifting stations.

I tell him what Nonna said about Jared. 'I don't understand it,' I say. 'He is our up-and-coming chef. He's part of the De Rosa family now, as Nonna would have it. I can't begin to think why she would want him to go.'

'Jared would be so offended if he knew Cara had said that about him. She's his idol. He's told me loads of times he wants to own a chain of restaurants like her one day.'

'She went from talking about her honeymoon to getting the decorators in, to sacking staff. At one point, she even said someone was trying to kill her. Then there was all this about this Gianni guy. None of it makes any sense.'

'It's the drugs. I saw it with my mum in her final days.' He winces when he realises what he has said. He squeezes my shoulder. 'Sorry, I'm not suggesting Cara is going the same way. One minute my mum was high, the other begging me to tell her where I kept the key to the medicine cabinet so she could end it all.'

'That must've been hard for a fourteen-year-old boy to hear.'

'I try not to think about it.'

'And she swore. Nonna doesn't swear, does she? Never.'

He tightens his grip around me.

'She's confused,' I say. 'You're right. The meds have messed with her head. Papa is my papa.'

'You need to speak to Bettina. That's the only way you'll find out.'

'If she'll tell me the truth. Put yourself in her shoes. If someone threw that accusation at you, would you admit to it? If it is true, surely she would've said something about it by now? Especially with someone like Nonna on your case.'

'Fair point.'

'She's working tonight. It's flat out at the restaurant this week, what with Christmas.'

'I guess the wedding's off.'

'Who knows at this stage? Rik will have to decide that. I wonder what else she was going to come out with?' My stomach turns. I can't bring myself to express my thoughts of what if I never find out?

'Be positive. You know Cara. She'll get over this and will be back bossing you all about again in no time.' He laughs as he unhooks his arm from around my shoulder. 'Come on, let's go in. Dinner will be burnt.'

I ask Lola about her day as I tuck her up amongst her mammoth collection of teddies the family has bought her over the years. Being the only newborn since I came on the scene, everyone spoils her rotten, especially Jenni who sees Lola as the child she was never able to have. School was OK, her ballet lesson went well, but the best part by far was Zach picking her up and bringing her home via McDonald's. 'Why can't he move in with us, Mummy? Then his PlayStation would be here all the time.'

If only life were that simple.

As Zach dishes up the fish pie, he says, 'I need to tell you something. It's not a good time, I know, but it'll never be a good time.' He twists his lips as he hands me a bowl of peas.

'And?'

'I can't keep it from you.'

I pick up my fork and stab at the potato topping of the fish pie. 'Keep what from me? Come on, today can't get any worse.'

He runs his hands through his thick, spiky hair.

'Spit it out,' I demand with a nervous laugh.

'There's no good way to tell you this.'

'Say it will you?'
'I think your Uncle Franco is having an affair.'

TWELVE

'Let me rephrase that. Franco *is* having an affair.'

Stunned, I don't say anything at first. Then I burst out laughing. 'Is this a joke?' But his grim expression tells me to quit laughing.

'A few weeks ago, when I was out for a run, I saw him coming out of the salon with a blonde woman. A little older than us – thirty-something – they were larking about, and I thought to myself, I wonder what they're laughing at?' He looks awkward, as if he is a naughty schoolkid telling tales. Zach is the most diplomatic person I've ever met. Having this conversation won't be sitting comfortably with him. 'I didn't think much of it at the time. It must be someone who works for him and Jenni, I thought. Then, when I went to meet the lads up in town on Thursday night, you know, for those who couldn't make it to Dublin for the weekend, I saw them together again. I was coming out of Holborn Tube station. Franco was waiting outside. Strange, I thought, I wonder what he's doing here? I was about to call out to him, but the blonde turned up.'

I can't believe what I'm hearing. Franco is not the kind of guy to cheat. He likes women. We are all aware of that. He's in the ideal job, able to flirt with all the female clients. What Nonna is to the restaurant, Franco is to the salon. But he has always seemed committed to Jenni. They've been together years. I know they've had their issues. They desperately wanted kids, but, according to Papa, Franco's little swimmers weren't strong enough to make it to the shore. This put a massive strain on their relationship because he refused to do anything about it, declaring what will be will be.

'And they kissed.' He grimaces, his green eyes open wide. 'Like a proper, full-on tongue-down-throat job.'

I grimace. 'Poor Jenni.'

'Then I can't believe what I did next.'

'What?'

'I followed them.'

'Where did they go?'

'To the Holborn Premier Inn.'

'For Christ's sake.'

Zach doesn't stay tonight, although he wants to. 'I'm worried about you,' he says, leaning against the wall by the door.

'I'm fine,' I tell him. And I am, but I want to be on my own. I need to get hold of Mamma, and I've been itching to get on the computer to see if I can find anything on this

Gianni Bellini ever since I showed Milana the photos this morning. Nonna's words from the party, "There are plenty around here who would love nothing more than to see me take my last breath", keep replaying in my mind.

'I'll pick Lola up for the rest of the week.' He softly pecks the tip of my nose. I look into his eyes. I love them. A sharp green, they attracted me to him when we first met. He runs his own social media company from his small flat about a mile away from the restaurant and had dropped in for a coffee. An hour later, blushing, he left with my phone number.

'She has Street Dance tomorrow and Musical Theatre on Wednesday. Thursday –'

'Stop. I'll never remember all that. Put it all in a text. Tell me when and where I need to be, and I'll be there.'

When he's gone, I nip for a quick cigarette and wash my hands before slumping down on to the sofa with the dregs of the wine. I power-up my laptop and tap Gianni Bellini into the search engine. This good-looking guy – in a rugged kind of way – makes for interesting reading.

Gianni Bellini has silver-grey hair – and lots of it considering his age – goatee beard, and a distinguished scar running along the top of his right eyebrow. I flick through the information about him from several online articles, and facts and figures I gather from Companies House. Professionally, he has had a successful life. Using the inheritance from their late mother, Gianni Bellini and his brother bought some properties back in the mid-eight-ies. Three run-down, two-bedroom flats in Shepherd's Bush, which they refurbished with the leftover proceeds of their British mother's estate. Fast forward ten years, to the mid-nineties, after his brother lost his fight with cancer, Gianni sold the flats for a whopping ten times the amount they had paid for them. Given that his brother had no other family, Gianni used the proceeds, plus what he had earned from his other business ventures, to reinvest in several properties needing modernisation. And from then on, taking full advantage of the stream of Middle Eastern royalty and Russian oligarchs who were transferring funds and moving into the UK, his property empire exploded. With loans that would keep most of us awake at night, he purchased a prestigious piece of real estate in neighbouring Acton and commissioned an apartment-and-commercial complex that made him millions. Coupled with a break-through project in London's West End, he expanded into several other UK industries. His main company, Bellini Holdings Limited, has offices in Mayfair and, from what I discover, he is still actively involved, despite being in his seventies. However, little appears regarding his private life, other than he married a British woman some forty years ago.

Where does Nonna fit into all of this?

I need to find this man.

THIRTEEN

Jared is the first person I see when I arrive at the restaurant this morning. I'm late again, and he has stepped in, again, behind the bar, serving drinks to a queue of early morning customers. I throw my bag into the office. A habit of mine that winds Milana up. She is at the Islington site this morning, sorting out something or other, so it doesn't matter that my bag lands on her perfectly laid out desk, nudging her iMac mouse a few centimetres to the right. I tie my apron around my waist and join Jared. Nonna would not be pleased if she were here. She is never late for anything. I smile as her voice rings in my head. "Lateness is a sign of disrespect, dear girl. It's saying to the person you're meeting that your time is more important than theirs."

My laptop kept me up until the early hours. Once I had exhausted all leads on Gianni, I started my search on the man standing beside me serving customers with a smile. Why does Nonna want him gone?

Jared Kingston is not on Facebook, but I found him on

Instagram, proudly supporting the restaurant and regularly posting his creations. This man is undoubtedly fond of a dessert or two. Photos of mouth-watering cheesecakes, panna cottas, tortes, and various flavours of gelato served as sundaes dominate his feed. Scattered amongst the food images were old shots of him working out at the local gym, where he and Zach first met, and photos of his partner and daughter, who he clearly adores. He appears in some of the pictures; in others it is them alone. I remember Nonna telling me his partner nearly left him when he went to prison, but it is clear from these photos why she didn't. They look loved-up in every shot. His account gives nothing away other than a regular guy living a normal life. Why does Nonna want him gone, then?

It doesn't add up.

Mamma is in a particularly bad mood this morning. Two waitresses have called in sick for this evening's shift. 'You'll have to pitch in later. Can you get Zach to look after Lola? Even if it's only for an hour or two.'

'I need a word with you.'

'What about? I'm up to my eyeballs today.'

'It can wait.' It can't. Not really. But I guess we have enough happening at the moment. Besides, a family showdown in the restaurant is the last thing we need.

'I'll call Zach. I'm going to see Nonna when I finish this afternoon, though.' I'm not sure what kind of state I'm going to find her in, but I pray she will be awake and coherent. I need an explanation of her words yesterday. I can't fathom what's worse. The thought that Papa may not be my real papa, or she may not be my real nonna. It simply can't be true.

Mid-morning, I pop to the chemist a few doors down from the restaurant. My friend Maddie, who I met at a support group for young widows Nonna found the year after Matt died, recommended a new remedy for the cracks on my hands when I dropped in to see her last week. Maddie lost her husband in a motorcycle accident the day of their fourth wedding anniversary. The two of us met up outside the group and cried and cried until she started to laugh again and insensitively told me it was about time I did as well.

'You can't wash away grief, Sienna,' she said last week as she wrote down the name of the cream for me on the back of a packet of Marlboro Red I dug out of my bag. Had she been speaking to Nonna? They sounded exactly like the words Nonna uses. Except she attributes my obsession to guilt, not grief. Perhaps it's a nebulous blend of both.

She grabbed my wrist and winced. 'Look at these hands. They're getting worse. They'll get infected. You've got to stop with all the washing. Please, darling. Go and see someone. Talk it out. In the meantime, try this cream.'

It's alright for her. I still grapple with my grief daily. Shortly after Maddie lost her first husband, she met Tyrone at a nightclub. Somehow, she was able to deal with her feelings, and one year later, she married him. They now have three kids.

Death is universal, but grief is personal.

There are plenty of textbooks and websites advising ways to survive it, but we all have to find our own coping mechanism to deal with the pain. I read somewhere about a widow describing the trauma of losing her husband. She likened it to the cut from a sharpened knife, throbbing and intense in the early days, blunting to a dull ache as the months and years move on. But the scar remains as a constant reminder. I guess Maddie's knife was not as sharp as mine, her cut not as deep.

Even five years on, the sorrow will sometimes catch me off guard. I'll be delivering plates of food to a table in the restaurant, and a man will walk in wearing a denim jacket. Or, I'll be crossing the park, and I'll spot a guy riding a blue mountain bike.

Grief. An oppressive weight on my heart.

I weave amongst people sniffling and coughing, chatting and complaining, and grab the bits I need, before joining the queue trailing to the door. Is that Jenni two places ahead of me? I angle my head to confirm my thoughts. 'Jenni, hi,' I call out. She turns, dropping a tube of face cream from her crossed arms acting as a shopping basket. Clutching the other items closer to her chest, she asks the young lad between us for help. He picks up her cream and places it with her other supplies. She acknowledges me with a half-smile and quickly turns to face the front of the queue. A bit odd. Usually, she can't wait to strike up a conversation with anyone prepared to listen. When she gets to the till, I see her unfold her arms. Several items drop onto the counter. The face cream, cotton pads, a dispenser of hand soap, a tube of Colgate; and is that a *pregnancy* test? I shuffle a few steps sideways and tilt my head. I'm sure it is. Do they have some news soon to share with the family? Surely not after all these years. Or perhaps she's buying it for someone else. She drops her arms to her side and crouches over her purchases.

Once she has paid, she stops briefly. 'Terrible news about Cara, isn't it?' She glances at the clock on the wall above the shelves of over-the-counter medicines. 'Must dash. I've got a client at eleven-thirty, and I need to stop off at the card shop. I want to drop in for one of Don's sandwiches if I've time. I might see you there.' She hasn't taken a breath, and she zooms out of the door.

In the mid-morning lull, before the lunchtime rush revs up, I grab a coffee and pop outside for a quick cigarette. It's the only time I'll get before I clock off for the day. Even in the cold winter air with the hubbub of passing traffic and honking horns, this small, decked space is a calming place to be, thanks to Nonna's stylish flair. White-painted walls enclose the area on either side, and it is sheltered overhead from the elements by a manual awning. I pull out a seat from the four-seater bistro set of lime green table and chairs. It's freezing my butt, but my feet are killing me. I take a drag of my cigarette, staring at the numerous planters filled with shrubs asleep for the winter.

Nonna loves sitting out here, especially in the summer. On hot days, when she has the time, she insists I spend five minutes with her before I pick up Lola from school. I always oblige. Anything to dodge a wait at the school gates is fine by me. She will bring me a glass of her grapefruit and papaya juice. An unadulterated recipe she created herself that she gets her team to bottle, and she sells in the deli for a small fortune. We serve it in the restaurant as well. The taste is scrumptious, so it is hardly surprising people are willing to pay a fiver a pop. She will reel in the canopy, and we sit in the mid-afternoon sunshine, sipping our drinks and munching on truffle-coated arancini balls or other leftovers from lunch. I can hear her talking to me now, telling me the Latin names of the latest additions to all the shrubs and flowers she and Papa have planted in the borders contained by reclaimed railway sleepers.

Tears sting my eyes. I can't lose you, Nonna.

Grabbing my phone from my pocket, I google the number for Pilkingtons, the decorators. Sean Pilkington is an old friend of Nonna's. She has used his company's services for years, at home and in all her restaurants, but I'm bemused to hear she has arranged for him to come in again so soon after the recent refurbishment. It doesn't make sense. The call goes straight to voicemail, and I leave him a message to phone me as soon as he can.

A voice startles me. 'Mind if I join you?' Jared pulls out the seat next to me. 'It's getting crazy in there, and if I don't grab my chance, it'll be late afternoon before I get another opportunity.' He offers me another cigarette. I decline. His Silk Cut do nothing to satisfy my needs. I tap the base of my packet of Marlboro Reds and accept his offer of a light instead. 'Sorry to hear about Cara's latest setback,' he says. 'I'm gutted for you all.' Glancing up at the grey sky, he continues: 'I'm praying she'll be back here with us soon.'

He tells me about when Cara first brought him here to the restaurant. 'I was petrified of you all.' He sweeps his hand along the outline of his beefy body, from his number-one-all-over haircut down to his size thirteen Doc Martens. 'Strange to think a guy my size can be scared. But I was. All I wanted to do was impress Cara De Rosa.' He swallows. 'She's a good lady. A real good lady.'

Why does she want you to go then, Jared?

FOURTEEN

I stop in the restrooms before joining the lunchtime madness filling the tables. The staff toilets are out of action. We've been waiting over a week for a plumber, which Nonna is none too pleased about. I'm squirting soap into my hands from one of the chrome dispensers attached to the wall when Jenni walks in. I can see her in the reflection of the mirror, but she can't see me. Deep in conversation on her mobile wedged between her shoulder and ear, she marches directly into a cubicle. I lather the soap in my hands, listening, but I only hear mumbling until she raises her voice and says, 'Be patient. It'll all be OK, my darling,' before flushing the chain and heading out to the basin next to me. I can't help glancing at her belly. She is wearing a burnt red tunic, over leggings, which fits as perfectly as ever over her flat middle.

'Hey, sweetie,' she says. 'I didn't notice you here. You OK? You look like you have the weight of the world on your shoulders.'

'I'm worried about Nonna.'

'We all are. Have faith. She's a toughie.' She removes a large cosmetics bag from her handbag. 'I meant to ask you when I saw you in the chemist, can you come in tomorrow afternoon instead of the morning? Something has come up.' Taking out a gold tube, she unscrews the middle and coats her lips with red gloss.

'I'm not in the mood, to be honest.'

'Come on. Chin up. We should still run with our plans, despite everything. Cara would want us to. It'll do you good to get away from everything.' She reaches for a tissue from her bag and blots her lips.

'I'll see if I can work it with one of the other waitresses.'

'Of course.' She takes a deep sigh, throwing the lipstick back in her cosmetics bag. It clinks against the other items. 'I've ordered two of Don's caprese focaccia sandwiches, my favourite. Should keep me going until bedtime. These busy days running up to Christmas exhaust me. And what with everything happening with Cara.'

'Is Franco better today?' I ask.

'He's fine. Twenty-four-hour man flu.' She rolls her eyes. 'Always picks up a cold this time of year. It's the long hours he insists we keep. And he will continue his social life. You know what he's like, always out meeting someone or other.'

I want to tell her that her cheating husband is not the perfect man she thinks he is. But is it my place? I had this conversation with Maddie a while back when she found herself with the same moral quandary: to tell or not to tell. She caught her friend's drunken husband, as Maddie so politely put it, *snogging some slapper's face off*. If it were me, I'd want to know, I told her. But finding myself faced with this dilemma, it's not so clear-cut. Maybe Jenni knows, and she doesn't care, content to live in her fool's paradise. She could end up hating me for snitching on him. And Franco might never speak to me again. Perhaps the pregnancy test kit was for her, and, finally, they are going to have a baby. The need to have her husband around might outweigh her need to live with the truth.

'Franco will insist on slotting all our clients in for a Christmas fix, even if it does mean working late every night for practically the whole of December.' She gives a brief laugh. 'Like mother, like son. He won't be told, you know.' Closing her bag, she takes one last look at herself in the mirror and adjusts a few wisps of hair. 'Text me if you get any news on Cara, won't you, sweetie? Franco is popping up there later, but he has to meet someone tonight about the new salon. We're nearly there with signing contracts.'

For close to a year, Franco and Jenni have been negotiating on securing new premises to house another hairdressing salon. Nonna has told them many times that they should expand into the neighbouring areas.

'I thought Franco was ill?'

'Like I said, a dose of man flu. Plus, you know Franco, always got something on the go. Anyway, I'll love you and leave you.' She air-kisses me. 'See you tomorrow.'

Something on the go. Don't you mean *someone* on the go, Jenni?

· · ·

After work, I hurry home to fetch my car. There's no one in sight today as I rush through the park, not even a shadow teasing my peripheral vision. But I still race across as fast as the icy paths allow.

The drive to the hospital is tedious. Falling snow never mixes well with school pick-up time. When I arrive at her bay, Nonna's bed is gone. I skim the ward to find her, my body twisting from side to side, as are my guts. Perhaps they have moved her to another bay like the other day? Maybe she is in the mortuary.

A hand cups my shoulder. Nurse Paula's soft voice says, 'It's OK. She's been taken for a scan. She's only just gone, so don't expect to see her for at least another half hour.' Relief eases my rapid heartbeat. 'Go and get yourself a drink. No use waiting here.'

'How is she?' I ask, wanting only good news, but the solemn look etched on Paula's face tells me I'm not going to hear what I want.

'I'll ask a doctor to stop by and update you. You've missed Rik. He said you were on your way, so I sent him home for a while. He's been here all day.'

I head down to the hospital café and order a coffee. It's not busy, only a few doctors and nurses snatching a break, so I find a table easily. I plonk myself down and fish my phone out of my bag, clicking on Instagram to occupy my mind. Since speaking to Jared this morning, I haven't been able to stop thinking about him. Finding his page, I gasp. His account has been set to private. Why has he done that? What doesn't he want others to see?

I flick through to the restaurant page. Milana runs the

social media for the business, showcasing photos of delicious dishes on the De Rosa's Facebook and Instagram accounts, and tweeting news about the restaurant and food industry, plus ongoing progress on our plans to expand. It's a task she could hand over to Zach. He runs social media platforms for companies sizeably bigger than ours and is successful at it, but my sister is too much of a control freak.

She does a professional job, though, I can't deny that, rewarding the restaurant with the credit it deserves. Posting twice daily, she captivates a sizeable audience. She's not as active on Facebook, but manages a personal Instagram account with an impressive following and high engagement. She's always bragging about the thirty thousand people who follow her account @its_that_ms_milana, commenting on her enjoyment of life. I read her profile.

It's Ms Milana

Life is a challenge. Meet it.

Life is an opportunity. Capture it.

Life is a game. Play it.

Each line ends with an emoji: a red heart, an oncoming fist, raised hands, and a grinning cat with smiling eyes. Photos of her out and about, with friends and boyfriends, in bars, restaurants, pubs and clubs, fill her eye-catching feed. From what I can see, apart from when she has a coat on, and she owns several shades and styles of these, she is wearing something different in every single shot. It's a side to Milana I find hard to acknowledge. I was once the same.

She lives alone. At the moment. Hollywood-handsome men are constantly moving in and moving out. She sometimes brings them into the restaurant. 'Commitment issues,' Nonna says of her eldest granddaughter. I continue skimming through her feed, trying to redirect the truckful of jealousy riding through me in a more positive direction. How wonderful it is to see my beautiful sister living her life to the full.

But she's not my sister, is she? According to Nonna, Milana and I have entered the world of halves.

I switch to Facebook and pull up Nonna's account. She hasn't been on Facebook long, only a couple of years. She sent me a friend invite when she set it up. The request still hangs out there, along with the few hundred others I've ignored over the years. I find my page and accept Nonna's request.

Pinned to the top of her page is a newspaper clipping from the local Gazette dated five years ago: *No Update on Local Hit-and-Run*. A shivering chill engulfs me, despite the stifling hospital heat. Nonna added a simple comment.

A £25,000 reward is being offered to catch the spineless monster who failed to stop after driving my son-in-law into the path of an oncoming transit van.

I swallow hard.

It was Nonna who backed the financial reward for information leading to the arrest and conviction of any guilty party.

The article details the high-profile investigation that dominated the headlines for many days. I read through it. The cowardly act that left a young woman widowed and a small child fatherless. But a stolen car found burnt-out at a disused industrial site, ten miles north of the M25, gave the detectives working on the case little to go on. They were as desperate as the family to find the culprit, but sometimes, depressing as it is, the police have nowhere to go.

A welcoming call interrupts my browsing. 'Your grandma is back,' Paula informs me. I refit the lid on my unfinished coffee, drop it in the bin, and make my way back to the ward to find Nonna asleep, appearing worse than yesterday. If that is possible. Not only has the left-hand side of her face not recovered, but it's sagging worse today. 'Talk to her. She can hear you,' Paula says, fiddling with the clip on the drip line attached to an infusion pump. Part of the machinery keeping Nonna alive.

I perch on edge of the bed. Bruises discolour her frail hand I take in mine. When Paula wanders off, I start talking. 'Nonna, I need you to wake up. I have so many questions for you, but first I need you to tell me the other thing you were going to say yesterday. Can you remember?' I ask her several times, but each time, there is no reply. 'Hang on in there, Nonna.'

After about an hour of me talking to myself, it seems, a doctor stops by. He is much older than the one I spoke with yesterday. A straight-up kind of guy, he tells me how it is. 'The risk of stroke in the year following a heart attack is significantly higher in the first month. It's a medical fact, I'm afraid. Mrs De Rosa has been unlucky.' He skim-reads her notes. 'What we're concerned about, though, is for someone so relatively young, we would've expected a quicker recovery following the surgery yesterday. We shall continue to run further tests, which may or may not give us greater insight. Until then, she needs time to recover.'

Franco returns a little later, distress plastered across his face. He squeezes my shoulder. I cringe. He has no right to do that after what he has done to Jenni. He sits down but instantly gets back up, catching the pocket of his quilted pea coat on the arm of the chair. 'Damn,' he says, picking at a loose thread. He looks at Nonna, tuts, and paces up and down the length of the bed. 'What is going on here?' he says, stopping at Nonna's side. Pulling his coat sleeve aside, he glances at his watch as if he has somewhere he needs to be.

I need to leave. His company is more than I can handle. All I can see when I look at him is Jenni's despondent face when I tell her what her husband has been up to.

FIFTEEN

When I get to my car, I turn on the engine and trigger the wipers, shifting the layer of settled snow. I crank the heating on full, waiting for the windscreen to demist. Plugging in my phone, I dial the number I've been burning to call all day.

Something is amiss. It's like pieces of a puzzle are floating in my peripheral vision, but I can't seem to focus long enough to slot them together to form an intelligible picture.

'I'm sorry, but Mr Bellini has taken a leave of absence,' says the well-spoken gatekeeper at Bellini Holdings. 'He won't be in the office for the foreseeable future. Is there anyone else I can direct your call to?'

'My name is Tracey Williams.' I hate lying, but for fear he might not speak to me if I reveal my real name, I say the name of a friend of mine. 'I need to get hold of Mr Bellini as a matter of urgency. Please could you give me his mobile number?'

The woman hesitates. 'I'm afraid I can't give you that information.'

I try to persuade her into handing over the details, telling her it's in everyone's best interest, especially Mr Bellini's, but her skills of deflection allow for zero negotiation. 'What exactly do you want to talk to Mr Bellini about?'

'I can't say, other than it's urgent.'

'Leave me your details, and I promise to get him to call you at his earliest convenience.'

I relay my number. 'As soon as he can, please.'

Traffic is piling up on the main route back home, the weather causing all kinds of hassles. A broken-down bus blocks one of the lanes, so I negotiate a shortcut, only to find faulty traffic lights causing similar issues. Zach has agreed to mind Lola until eight o'clock. He would stay all evening, he said, but it's his gym night. 'If you're really stuck, I'll cancel, but we've only got one week left of the Tour de France challenge, and I'd be letting the other guys down.'

'I'll be back in time,' I told him. He would definitely stay all night if I needed him to, but I can't do it to him. Since September, he has shown unflagging commitment to this indoor cycling challenge, raising money for the local hospice. For the last ten weeks, a group of four of them have been competing against nine other teams to see which can cycle two thousand miles the quickest. I can't think of anything worse, but he enjoys these evenings. Jared is one of his teammates. Their team is currently in joint first place.

Bad moods prevail when I arrive back at the restaurant. Mamma is racing around, preparing for the Christmas party of twelve soon to arrive. Come the run-up to Christmas, Nonna usually chips in and manages these parties. From late November, after the lunchtime craziness has died down, the tables in the centre of the deli, home to Christmas hampers and gifts by day, are cleared to make way for the Christmas party bookings which occur every night, save Mondays, to the twenty-third of December. Every year, the restaurant closes for the first two weeks of January. According to Nonna, folk are broke, and new year resolutions ban pizza and pasta, so takings are low. 'What's the point?' she says, 'I'd rather spend two weeks in the sun.'

Opening the door to the office, I go to throw my bag in. A bark stops me mid-aim. 'Don't you dare.' Papers and files meticulously laid out cover Milana's desk. 'I'm drowning,' she says, lifting two pieces of paper filled with Excel spreadsheets and graphs. Her cheeks are flushed. It looks like she has been down to the gym. She jiggles her mouse, and her screen lights up. 'The leaseholder of the new restaurant in Stamford Hill is threatening to pull the plug.' She clenches her fists and gives a straight-lipped smile. 'The accountants have been trying to get hold of Nonna, but of course, they can't, so it's all fallen in my lap.' She drops the papers on the table and slams her hands on top of them. 'I managed to speak to the leaseholder. He said the deadline for Nonna to get the funds to him passed last week.'

She gets up and walks over to the filing cabinet by the door. She's wearing a short black dress and her mid-thigh leather boots, looking every inch the chic woman I wish I could be but don't have the nerve for. Or the figure. If only I could cut out the wine. And the cheese I sneak home from this place most weekends. Not to mention the constant flow of Lola's sweets I can't help picking at most evenings after I've kissed her goodnight. Milana flips through a row of drop files and pulls out one. 'This is the exact reason I've been telling Nonna for God knows how long, she needs to allow me to be involved in the finances. I'm trying to scramble together some reports, with only half the information, to see if the bank will give us a loan. What chance do I have?'

'Perhaps Rik can help.'

'I've already asked him. Zero help, he was. He said he doesn't get involved in any of Nonna's business. Luckily, I've found quite a bit out from some files I discovered in her office at home. There was a list of passwords in a note-book I found in one of the drawers.'

'You've been through her stuff?' I can't believe she has done this. Nonna won't be at all happy. 'Rik allowed you to?'

If she feels any shame, her face shows no sign of it. 'He doesn't know. Papa gave me the keys to her house. I let myself in.'

'I can't believe you did that. It's his home now, as well, Milana.'

She tucks her hair behind her ears. 'Whether you like it

or not, Sienna, we have to face facts. She may not be coming back to work.'

I gasp. 'Don't say that.'

'Needs must.' She gives a sympathetic half-smile. 'We have to face the fact she's not a well woman.' She shakes her head vigorously. 'I know it's wrong, but I feel cross with her. She's left me right in the lurch.'

It doesn't happen often, but I feel sorry for my sister at this moment. I sit in the chair opposite her. 'I need to tell you something.'

'Not more bad news, please.'

'When I was with her yesterday, Nonna was coming out with some weird stuff. She reckons we need to get shot of Jared.'

'Sack him?'

'You got it.'

'You've got that wrong.'

'She said he needs to go.'

'That's ludicrous.'

She tries to carry on, but I interrupt her. 'She also said she's arranged for Pilkingtons to come in and redecorate when we close in January.'

'What?' she laughs. 'That's bonkers.' Her face turns serious. 'She's really not in a good way.'

My phone rings. I rummage around in my bag. Turning the screen to Milana, I snigger. 'Talk of the devil, it's Sean Pilkington.'

The call lasts less than thirty seconds. Sean Pilkington hasn't heard from Nonna since his team painted her lounge in the summer.

SIXTEEN

'See, I told you,' Milana says, sitting upright. 'That's what happens to some people before they have a stroke. Sheridan's mum became confused when she had her second one. Remember? She thought Sheridan was her sister.' Her lips downturn. 'Her sister died five years earlier. It was so upsetting for the whole family. Anyway, listen, I need to get back to this lot. Otherwise, we're going to lose the Stamford Hill premises. Nothing will upset Nonna more. It's been a pain, this one. It's caused her sleepless nights.'

I follow the thyme and rosemary aroma flowing from the kitchen to where Papa is stirring a large stockpot of his heavenly De Rosa winter soup. His own concocted recipe he refuses to share with anyone proves a popular menu item. 'Do you recognise the name, Gianni Bellini?' I ask him.

He shrugs. 'Should I?' He grabs a teaspoon and dips it in the soup to taste. 'A bit bland. Something's missing,' he mumbles and rummages around in a drawer under the worktop for a pair of scissors.

'No. It's someone Nonna mentioned.'

He snips a stem of basil from the plant on the side. Tearing it into pieces, he throws the torn leaves into the pot. 'In connection to what?'

'Nothing in particular,' I say, and leave him stirring.

After the Christmas party in the deli is under control, I race home. It's busy in the park tonight. I pass workaholics heading home from the station and tipsy people getting into the spirit of the season, serenading passers-by with *Jingle Bells*. I walk as fast as the snow will allow. Not only do I feel uneasy, but I also don't want Zach to be late for the gym. As I pass the public toilets, I take the left turn. Not my usual route, but hairs are prickling on the back of my neck. The feeling someone is following me is spooking me. My legs feel wobbly. I need to get home fast. It feels like a pair of cold eyes are piercing the back of my head like daggers. I spin around. A tall man strides a foot or so behind me. Fear chases through me. 'What do you want from me?' I yell, surprising myself.

He stops dead and raises his hands. 'Sorry. Who are you?' The park lights illuminate his shocked face. He shoves his hands in his coat pockets and drops his head, giving me a wide birth as he hurries past me. A couple of young kids hanging off a bench, stare at me, smirking at my irrational behaviour.

I need to get a grip.

Arriving home, I'm climbing the stairs, breathless from running, when my phone buzzes. His gatekeeper has kept her promise. An austere male voice with an Italian accent says, 'Gianni Bellini here. You called my office this morning. What can I help you with?'

I sit on the step in the middle of the stairs. Now I've got him on the phone, I feel awkward. 'I need to speak to you about a woman named Cara De Rosa.'

'What about her?'

I hesitate before uttering, 'I'm not really Tracey Williams. My name is Sienna De Rosa.'

There is a pause for a few moments before he speaks, his tone circumspect. 'How did you find my details?'

'That doesn't matter. I need to understand what your connection to Cara is.'

Another pause. His tone changes, becomes softer. 'I'm at home tomorrow. Why don't you come here for a chat?'

I hesitate again, wondering who I could get to accompany me at such short notice.

He gives me his address. An exclusive road in North West London. I tell him I'll see him tomorrow afternoon.

I end the call and miss my footing on the next step. I've pushed myself so far out of my comfort zone, I'm tripping over myself.

SEVENTEEN

Despite Mamma protesting that I'm leaving her in the lurch, I quit work early today and head to Hair by De Rosa. I'm not in the mood. Nothing feels right or normal without Nonna around. But I haven't had my hair cut for so long, there are at least two inches of split ends, and if I don't take this opportunity, there won't be another one for at least a month. Franco and Jenni are meant to be heading off to the Canary Islands in the new year. As well as the restaurant, Nonna insists the salon shuts for the first two weeks of January. My last hair appointment consisted of a date with the kitchen scissors accompanied by a large glass of red, for which Jenni has never forgiven me.

A bell chimes as I push open the heavy door. Franco acknowledges me with a big smile from behind the reception desk. Gesturing for me to take a seat on one of the leather sofas jazzed up with brightly coloured cushions, he tells me Jenni had to pop out but will be back any minute.

'Where's she gone?'

'Doctors.'

'Is she OK?'

'Women's stuff,' he says with a shrug. He walks over to the sofa in his uniform black trousers and shirt, and hands me a selection of magazines. 'Thank you,' I mumble, finding it incredibly difficult to look him in the eye. It's too hard to remove the image Zach so eloquently presented to me the other night of Franco's tongue down some woman's throat.

He perches on the arm, invading my space. 'You OK, la mia bella nipote?' I nod. I wish he wouldn't call me that. Not now. I once loved hearing him address me this way. But now I know what I know, it doesn't sing with the same appealing tune. We have always got on so well, Franco and me. When Milana and I were growing up, he and Jenni were always taking us for days out. They had the time. I think they saw us as the kids they could never have. Franco is supremely loyal to his roots, much more so than Papa. He used to take Milana and me around all the art galleries and museums, educating us on everything Italian. His favourite is the Estorick Collection in Islington: Britain's only museum devoted to modern Italian art. I stare at the framed poster hanging from the wall behind the reception desk. A colourful abstract he purchased when he took me there one day. On a few occasions, before they invested in the salon and worked in hairdressers in the West End and Papa and Mamma were flat-out in the restaurant, Jenni and he took us to Italy during our summer holidays. I have fond memories of those happy times. Days packed with sandy feet and never-ending gelatos.

I open one of the magazines and flick through the glossy pages.

'Drink? A Christmas Prosecco?' he suggests, standing with his hands in his pockets, rattling the change at the bottom of one of them.

'I'm driving later.'

'I'll get you a coffee, then,' he says, not bothering to ask how I like it because he already knows. Franco makes the best flat white this side of the Alps.

I glance around the salon. A stylish establishment, it has Nonna's mark of elegant quality stamped all over it. Not a big place, but they sure make use of every inch of space. Mirrors cover the back wall behind a line of washbasins. An optical illusion that makes the place appear twice its size. A few feet in front of each washbasin, hairdressers are combing and colouring, cutting and cropping before full-length ornate mirrors draped with strings of warmly-lit bulbs.

Jenni arrives, flustered, apologising profusely as she stamps snow from the pumps on her feet and dusts flakes from her hair. The pumps match her pine-green jumper dress and red bauble earrings. 'Silly shoes. What was I thinking in this weather? Give me a sec to put my stuff away, and I'll be with you, sweetie.' She calls out to one of the staff. 'Nancy, gown and wash my client, could you, please?'

I've never met Nancy before; she must be new. She is an all-hips-and-hair kind of woman, the blondeness of which could only have come from a bottle. Is she the member of staff having an affair with Franco? Including part-time and

Saturday staff, twelve other women and two guys work for Hair by De Rosa. Four of the women, besides Nancy, are blonde. I've met them all and can't imagine it being any of them.

I pop to the toilets before Nancy starts on my hair, squirt a mass of Frankincense liquid soap into my palms and rub it into a lather. I stare at myself in the glitzy mirror, asking how I am going to spend the next hour or so with Jenni without blabbing what I know about Franco?

When I join Nancy, she has a towel at the ready. She slips it around my neck and leans me back in the chair. As she shampoos my hair, I learn she can talk at much as Jenni, as she launches into a monologue of her life history. Then, as she settles me at the first station in the row of eight and combs my hair, she continues her chat with her plans for Christmas Day, but I'm not listening. It's lively in here. There is a vibration of chatter, along with white noise from hairdryers buzzing and Christmas songs belting out from Heart FM. Two young apprentices dash around, sweeping up hair and delivering trays of Prosecco and the prawn vol-au-vents Jenni makes this time of year. Nancy taps my shoulders. 'Jenni will be with you soon.'

I sit, admiring the artificial Christmas tree. Nonna and Lola decorated it at the end of November. Neon-coloured ornaments hang from the tinsel branches – miniature candy canes, fairy tale shoes, stockings, and chandeliers. Beside me, the hairdresser and her client are exchanging pleasantries about the gifts they've bought for their families. When Jenni arrives, she toys with the scissors in her hand and candidly advises me my hair needs a good trim.

'These split ends will only get worse,' she says and suggests doing away with a good few inches. She pats the crown of my head. 'The bulk of the length is what's causing this flatness. Shame to lose any of these beautiful curls, I know, but shall we go with some layers and four inches off these ends?' She flips up a section of my hair. 'I'll straighten it and tong it afterwards. Give you some corkscrew curls. It'll suit you.'

'Do what you think best.'

'Vol-au-vent? Bubbly?' she asks. 'Come on, it's Christmas. You love my vol-au-vents.'

'Go on then. Only half a glass, though.'

She disappears, returning with the Prosecco and two of her prawn vol-au-vents. I take a sip of the bubbly, and bite into the flaky pastry. 'Delicious,' I say.

'They're better than usual, aren't they? Fresher. I've started making the filling at home and keeping it in the fridge here. I find the pastry less soggy that way.' She gets to work, her scissors and comb working perfectly together like a choreographed dance. I ask. 'Franco said you had to see the doctors. You OK?'

Her cheeks blush. She lowers her voice, telling me about her troublesome menstrual cycle.

'Jenni,' I say, lowering my voice even further. She looks at me in the mirror, and I mouth, 'Are you pregnant?'

She stops cutting and places a hand on each of my shoulders, the blade of her scissors pointing towards my ear. Her cheeks turn as red as the bauble earrings dangling from her ears. A small smile on her face answers my question.

'You are! Congrat–'

Dropping her head to my ear, she whispers, 'Shh… shh, don't say a word to anyone. Please. Franco doesn't want to announce it until after the twelve-week scan. We've sworn each other to secrecy. He'll kill me if he knows I've told you.'

I mimic zipping my lips. 'Call me Santa. Your secret's safe with me.'

She glances over each shoulder, checking if anyone could possibly hear our conversation. 'Did you see the pregnancy test kit in the chemist yesterday?'

I nod.

'I thought so. I've got such bad morning sickness. I'll talk to you more later,' she whispers in my ear. 'Please, not a word to anyone, especially to Franco.'

'Stop stressing. It's not my news to share.'

She makes it clear; the subject is no longer one for discussion. When she has dried my hair and applied a finishing product to the ends, she dances the handheld mirror behind my head – 'See what layers do for the hair' – and picks up one of the expensive tubs of intensive conditioner from the display cabinet next to the mirror. 'Use this twice a week. It'll do those curls a world of good.' She searches through a line of tubes of hair masks and picks one out, thrusting both products into my hands.

'I can't afford these,' I say, pushing them back towards her.

'Call it an early Christmas present.' She winks at me. 'Don't tell Franco.'

EIGHTEEN

I'm a package of haggard nerves for the entire journey to Gianni's house. I can't believe I'm doing this. And especially not alone. Troubling thoughts play games in my head. A vigorous match of table tennis of 'What if he's a mafioso,' to 'That's a tad far-fetched.' *Now you are being paranoid.* Sat nav reported a journey of thirty-five minutes when I started, but traffic hampers my progress. 'Bloody roadworks. They're everywhere,' I mutter to myself, trying to navigate a three-point turn in a narrow street, resulting in a nine-point shambles by the time the car is facing the opposite direction.

My heart is racing when I arrive an hour later at the main road that leads to his house. I watch the comings and goings of the chic eateries and high-end boutiques as I tail the traffic before turning left into his road where five-storey, Italianate terraced houses surround a small park and residents-only parking bays line the pavements. The smell of wealth charges the air, and I haven't even got the window open. I circle the park, conscious I'm late. Luck is not on my side for a space, so I head to an adjacent street, where I find an empty metered parking spot. Annoyingly, I need to download an app to pay by card, which only adds to my exasperation.

I race around to Gianni's house. Taking the stone steps up to his front door, I press the buzzer. There's no answer. I peer over the iron railings into the window of the basement next door. A twenty-something woman, dressed in a smart trouser suit, sits at a table tapping away on a tablet. She reminds me of my sister. I should have told Milana, or someone, I was coming here, but everything has moved so quickly. I buzz again, and an older woman wearing a black dress and a white apron comes to the door. Her hair is scraped back into a tight bun.

'Gianni not here,' she says in a strong East European accent when I introduce myself.

'Where is he?' I ask, frustrated. 'He agreed for me to meet him here today.'

'Mr Bellini at hospital,' she says.

Has he has gone to see Nonna? 'Which hospital?' I ask.

'He call me. Complications. He not coming home today,' she says and tries to close the door.

I wedge my boot between the door and the frame. 'Which hospital? This is important.'

'Royal Hospital.'

Not the same as where Nonna is being treated. 'What's wrong with him? Has he had an accident?'

She shakes her head. 'Very ill man.'

'He's got my number. Please make sure he calls me as

soon as he can.' I retract my foot. She nods and the door clicks closed.

I stamp my foot on the floor. What a waste of time.

I call Gianni's number on the way back to the car. It goes to voicemail, so I tell him how disappointed I am to have missed him and please could he call me to rearrange our meeting. A text comes in as I'm talking. It's from Jenni.

Thanks for your understanding. You mustn't tell anyone. Not even Milana. Franco will kill me. Love you. Hugs. Jen.

It takes me ages to work my way through the traffic to see Nonna. Sleet follows a falling of snow and then it rains, as if the weather can't make up its mind how it feels. A bit like me.

When I get there, Mamma is sitting beside Nonna, texting on her phone. 'Where the hell have you been?' she asks.

I can't stop looking at Nonna. Never have I seen someone look so deathly grey. Machines drone, beep, and flash, providing running green and red lines to indicate her frail body is still with us, but for the first time since this fiasco began, I'm scared. Really scared.

'I had some errands to run.' I place a bag of tangerines, Nonna's favourite fruit, on the overbed table.

Mamma glances at her phone and stands up. 'You were meant to be here an hour ago. One of the chefs has phoned in sick, so Papa had to stay at the restaurant.' She picks up her bag. 'She's been like this since I got here. I've tried to give her a drink, but she's not taking anything.'

'What're they doing for her?' I look around the ward, searching for a doctor, or at least a nurse.

'I haven't managed to speak to anyone.'

'Why not?'

'There's no one around.'

I take the chair she has vacated, but stand straight back up. I must have this conversation. 'Before you go, I need to talk to you about something. I can't see when I'm going to get the chance otherwise.'

She glances at her phone. 'Make it quick. I really must get back.'

The words catapult out of my mouth before I have the chance to change my mind. 'Is Papa my real papa?'

She jolts back. Her lips form a tentative smile. 'Wherever has this come from, Sienna?' She draws her bag to her chest.

I glance over at Nonna and back to face Mamma. 'You have to tell me–' Visitors of the surrounding beds turn to stare. I reach over and yank the curtain around the bed. '– the truth,' I whisper vehemently, not wanting to broadcast our family drama to the listeners on the other side of the curtain.

She doesn't need to speak. Her shaking hands, and the colour draining from her cheeks, tell me all I need to know. 'Cara should never have said that.'

NINETEEN

'It's not true,' Mamma says, as an alarm sounds. A nurse appears and presses a button on one of the machines, flashing a quick smile before she disappears. 'Simply not true.' Her hand flies out in Nonna's direction. 'She must've been confused.' Mamma flicks her hand towards the drip stand feeding a concoction of medication into Nonna's bruised arm. 'It's the illness.'

The relief is overwhelming at first, but it soon starts to dissolve as doubt creeps in. I stare at her. Is she telling me the truth? I ask her what Nonna could have possibly meant, but she stonewalls me with excuses until her phone rings. She glances at the screen and promptly stabs the end call button. 'Let's finish this conversation another time.'

'Did she mean Milana, then? Is Papa Milana's real papa?'

'Stop this. We don't need all these unnecessary theatrics, Sienna. Not here. Don't you think we have enough going on? We are all the same family.' She lances through the gap between the curtains.

I chase after her, calling her name, but the doctor I have spoken to a couple of times has finished with the family of the patient in the next bed. She is heading towards Nonna. I retrace my steps to speak to her. 'What is going on?' I ask. 'She should be showing some signs of improvement, shouldn't she?'

The doctor flicks through Nonna's notes. 'She's a poorly lady. Anyone who has gone through what she has – and, let's face it, a second heart attack and a stroke is a pretty big deal – is going to take a considerable time to heal. The body is a remarkable machine. Give her time.'

I'm shaking as I pick up one of the tangerines and peel the skin, the smell refreshing in the staleness of the stagnant air. Tearing off a segment, I waft it under Nonna's nose.

'Nonna, please wake up for me.' Her eyes spring open like a jump-scare from a horror movie. 'Nonna,' I whisper, taking her hand. I love her hands. They are usually so warm and soft, but today this one is so cold to the touch. Even to my hand which hasn't warmed up from the freezing temperature outside.

Her breathing is shallow. 'I've been waiting,' she pauses to take a few breaths, 'for you to come.' She's finding it difficult to talk. Her facial muscles are drooping, slurring her words as if she has been to the dentist and had a filling.

Tears spring from my eyes. I wipe them away. 'It's so good to speak to you.'

She manages a smile. 'You're wearing your halo.'

I frown. 'Halo?'

'Every time I see you lately, you've got a halo of light around your head. You're an angel.'

I squeeze her hand, dismissing her comment with a laugh. Everyone is right. The drugs are in control of her now. *But halo?*

'It's not my heart.' She shakes her head before returning her gaze to me. Her words spill slowly, like a dripping tap. 'I know my heart.' She takes another deep breath before she gives her final outburst. 'I've been poisoned.'

'Poisoned?!'

'And I know who by.'

TWENTY

'Who, Nonna? Don't go back to sleep.' I tap her hand. 'Tell me.'

Her eyes open momentarily.

'Who has done this to you?'

She tries to speak, gives it all her effort. I can tell by the weak grunts she expels. But she can't find the strength to turn them into words. Her eyelids quiver, and she emits a shuddering breath before surrendering to the stronger forces of her wretched condition.

Is it the drugs talking here – hallucinations declaring poisoning? All test results point to another heart attack and a stroke. Who did she mean? Rik is the first person I think of. Surely not? Is this a case for the police? DS Durant's freckled face appears in my thoughts, reminding me I haven't returned his call. We've played telephone tennis since we last spoke, and the ball is in my court.

I stay talking to her for an hour, begging her to wake

up, but my efforts go unrewarded. Rik arrives around seven. 'She looks worse than earlier,' he says.

'I agree.' I stare at him, trying to imagine him poisoning Nonna. But how would he have done it? And wouldn't she already be dead?

'I'm going to speak to a doctor,' he says.

'I already have. They said to give her time. She woke up for a while.'

'Really?' he says.

Do I detect doubt in his tone? I go to tell him what she has claimed but what she said to me at Lola's party makes me stop. "Some would love nothing more than to see me take my last breath."

I bite my lip.

Who did she mean?

I stand up, preparing to leave. 'She opened her eyes, but didn't say anything.'

Why am I lying? I'm not a liar. Nonna taught me never to lie. Liars never prosper. Lies always return to bite you in the rear. One lie is enough to question all truths.

When I arrive home, Lola is already asleep, and the classic smell of winter comfort food suggests one of Zach's flavoursome casseroles is bubbling in the oven. I'm hanging up my coat when he comes to the door and kisses me. 'I like the hair.' He crouches down to lace his trainers. I'm later back than planned, and he is keen to get off. 'Suits you shorter. How's Cara?'

'Not good.' I want to add she's more than just not good, and neither am I, but don't want to hold him up.

He stands and kisses me on the lips. 'Do you want me to come back after the gym?'

I lean against the wall. 'I've had a day of it. I think I'll get an early night. Tomorrow?' I'm lying again. Plans are already in place for the night ahead.

He kisses me again. 'Sure. I promised Lola I'd take her to the cinema after school.'

I absently agree, unable to think so far ahead. 'Thanks for everything,' I shout after him as his muscular body flies down the stairs. He waves a hand, but doesn't turn around. 'I'm lucky to have you.' But he doesn't hear these last words, because I whisper them.

I grab the bottle of Chianti I slipped in my bag on the way out of the restaurant and pour myself a glass, conscious I should give the drink a miss for one night. It's been far too long since I saw a night through without a glass of something or other. But Dry January is not far off. I pick at the sausage casserole Zach has cooked to perfection. But the day has stolen my appetite and replaced it with a stomach full of confusion. I throw my fork on the plate and search for a cigarette.

Usually the neighbour's security light comes on when I'm outside, but it must need a new bulb. Instead, settled snow reflects light off the clouds, allowing me to see into the ground floor flat's garden where Purdy, the McIntyre's cat, is in a stand-off with a fox – a deadlock of wills. My head is in a spin. Nonna knows what she has been saying. Mamma was lying. I'm sure of it.

Back inside, I pick up my phone and try Gianni Bellini, only to hear his voicemail message again. Why doesn't anyone answer their phone? I fire up my laptop and google paternity tests.

It's time to find out the truth.

I peruse several sites claiming more than ninety-nine point nine per cent accuracy and twenty-four-hour turn-around from their award-winning laboratories. I read the procedures. It's a simple process – if you are doing it legally. I can forge Papa's signature on the forms and get a copy of his ID. All I need to work out is how to obtain a sample from him and decide whether I'm up for breaking the law.

I go for another cigarette, conscious this habit is getting as bad as my need for a daily fix of wine as another puff of smoke hits my lungs.

After washing my hands, I return to my laptop, spending a while trying to add to the information I've already gleaned about Gianni Bellini. What *is* his connection to Nonna? Could he be the person who has poisoned her? If she has been poisoned. And if so, how? Or was it all the medication talking again, the same as when she instructed me to sort the decorators and give Jared the boot?

I hunt for the photo I found of Gianni at the cancer support charity ball. This one photo leads to more articles about the night. The glitzy affair made the headlines because of the disappearance of one of the waitresses after-wards. CCTV caught twenty-seven-year-old Karina McNaught three streets from the rented flat where she lived with her husband. Her body was found four days later in secluded woodland in Epping Forest. A shiver tingles through me, raising the hair on my neck. A couple of people she was seen talking to after the ball were questioned, their names not made public, but no one has ever been charged with her murder.

Another criminal walking the streets, escaping justice; another innocent victim. I think of Matt, flinching at the cruel sense of injustice that must pain Mr McNaught every moment of every day.

The heating clicks off, and the temperature quickly drops. I shudder. This is not the warmest of rooms, even in summer. The more I search, the more images of the spectacular night, attended by some high-profile footballers and local dignitaries, I discover. I'm captivated, flicking through photos of sparkly dresses and tables set for royalty, until I come to one that steals my attention. Enlarging the image, I gasp as I realise my eyes are not deceiving me. At table number ten of twenty-six sits Rik with his arm around a beautifully dressed woman. She is wearing a gown embellished with tiny gems, and a string of diamonds circle her slender neck. Who is she? And, more importantly, what is her connection to Gianni? Or is it a pure coincidence they were at the same event that night?

I move to the lounge and fling my throw around my shoulders. A soft fleece Matt bought me for Christmas that he never got to see me open. I re-examine the photo of Rik at the charity ball, realising I know little about this man Nonna adores. And vice versa, or so I've always thought. He and Nonna have been together for two years, and, by all accounts, he makes her happy. Doesn't he? When Nonna talks about him, which is a lot, the tone of her voice *smiles*. The feeling is mutual, it appears from how I've seen him react since she was taken ill on Sunday.

I look at the date of the ball, calculating it was held roughly six months before Nonna had her first heart attack. Six months before Nonna and Rik first met. Suspicion leads me to google his name. Rik Spartans, or Frederick, as Nonna calls him when she's cross with him, has a Facebook account, but, unfortunately, like Nonna's, it's set to private. He is a scientist, an epidemiologist. A detective like DS Durant, but Rik searches for the causes and effects of viruses and diseases. He holds a senior position working in the tuberculosis unit of the NHS in North London. Nonna has mentioned it before, but I wasn't paying enough attention to remember the details. He has a daughter, but I've never met her. Fiona Spartans has lived in California for the past ten years. I was in Italy with Lola when she came to visit Rik last year. I type Fiona Spartans into the search bar and find her almost immediately. She is a fashion blogger and vlogger, a successful one. Known as Fashion Fi, she's all over social media, collaborating with large-name designers. I scroll through her Facebook page, focusing on the intermittent photos of her private life at parties and fancy restaurants rather than the professional posts of the latest designer gear hitting the market.

Shivering, I wrap the throw around my body as I carry on scrolling, abruptly pausing when I find what I'm looking for. If you search hard enough, these things can't hide for long. I click on a photo Fi Spartans has been tagged in, amongst a crowd posing on a yacht sailing in the Mediterranean. The photo originates from the Facebook page of a Jane Marcia – the daughter of Silvia Marcia. I keep searching. Silvia, I discover, was Rik's fiancée when she died of a heart attack. I gasp as I realise she was the lady Rik was with in that photo taken at the charity ball. She died not long afterwards. It strikes me as odd, so I continue exploring until the strands of mystery start to unravel. Silvia Marcia was a very wealthy woman, owning a successful chain of online boutiques for curvy women. Upon her death, Frederick Spartans inherited the vast sum of her estate, despite the uproar from Jane Marcia and her younger sister Amelia.

TWENTY-ONE

Is Rik still at the hospital? I don't want to speak to him, but I need to know if he is still there. When I call him, he answers promptly . I apologise for disturbing him. 'It was a pocket call,' I say. 'How is she?'

'Still the same.' These are the words I don't want to hear, but they could be worse. 'A nurse is changing one of the drip bags, and then I'll call it a day.'

I find Maddie's number. She only lives a few streets away, and she owes me a truckload of favours. Lola and I often pop over there late afternoon on a Saturday. I babysit her kids while she and Tyrone venture out to dinner. 'I need your help. Could you come over for half an hour?' I ask.

'I'll be right there.'

Nonna's house is a double-fronted Victorian detached she always knew she would own one day. Situated on one of the more exclusive tree-lined streets of the local area, a short stroll from the park and the railway station, it sits back from the road and boasts the almost unheard-of luxury of off-street parking for not one but two cars. When she first came over from Italy with Nonno Nico, over forty years ago, they rented a small flat in the same street. Once they had their first restaurant up and running, Nonna insisted they put down a deposit on the Victorian rundown house in need of a new roof and central heating, among other bank-account-breaking expenditure. A mess, but she restored it to its former glory, adding a porch and erecting signage to tell the world this is Cara's Place. She has an album of before and after photos of the refurbishment, which took them over ten years. I browse through them often. It's one of the most prestigious houses in the local area. At today's prices, unless she liquidated all her assets, she'd never be able to afford to buy it.

It feels strange being here in the circumstances. I know Rik lives here as well, but it's hard to think of it as his home. It was, and always will be, my grandparents' home. Nonna gave me a key years ago.

I've got about fifteen minutes, twenty max, to be on the safe side. The aroma of her Dior perfume hits me as I walk into the large hallway, where I disable the alarm. Actually, the hallway is not that large. It appears so because it's void of the collection of coats, shoes, school bag, PE kit and ballet tote, I invariably trip over in my hallway every morning in my rush to get out of the door. The only furniture is a giltwood console. Fixed to the wood-panelled wall, it rests on two legs constructed of golden mermaid figures. Their beautifully carved fish tails join to form the base. Nonna loves this console. She came across it at one of the antique fairs she adores visiting in her spare time. On top sits a large glass vase with a bunch of wilted flowers – lilies and roses, Nonna's favourite. Their malodorous smell would upset her. She replenishes this vase weekly from her florist friend who runs her own small business in the neighbouring road.

I aim for the small study, off the lounge. As I open the lounge door, I glance to the right, where two steps lead up to a carpeted platform, like a stage, housing Nonna's pride and joy – a magnificent baby grand piano. I pause, imagining her sitting on the black stool, effortlessly rendering her favourite piece of music: *Dawn* by Dario Marianelli. Her natural grace extends to her lithesome fingers, which glide over the keys like a flowing stream. As soon as Lola was able to sit still on Nonna's lap for longer than a minute, Nonna started teaching her to play. It soon became apparent Lola shares her gift.

I panic as I hear a car pull up outside. Rik can't be home already. He should still be at the hospital. Did I miscalculate the journey time? I've planned what excuse I'll use if he turns up. Lola left a toy behind when we were last here. My heartbeat quickens. That excuse seems lame. He won't fall for it. Quick, think, Sienna! But I can't. The slam of a car door makes my heart beat even faster. I need to hide. I dart up the two steps and crouch behind the piano, immediately regretting my actions. What am I thinking? I should have turned the lights on and stuck with my first excuse. My stomach churns. The crunching and scraping of footsteps in the snow tells me he is approaching the front door. Shaking, I wait for the sound of the key in the lock. The doorbell rings. It can't be Rik. It rings again, and then I hear the scraping of a parcel being rammed through the letterbox. Thirty seconds or so later, the car engine restarts.

No time to waste, I dart into her study. I don't know what I'm looking for, but I begin at her desk. A framed photograph of Nonna and Rik, taken at the beginning of this year at a beach bar in the Bahamas, sits by her computer screen. Rik's arm is draped across her shoulders, and he is looking at her adoringly. My stomach turns. It's the same way he was looking at Silvia Marcia in that photo of the ball.

I hunt through the drawers, but nothing untoward captures my attention, so I focus on the mound of papers and unopened letters overflowing from her filing tray. A confirmation from the town hall of the forthcoming registry booking tops the pile. I think back to when Nonna announced her and Rik's engagement and that they were getting married soon. I was happy for them, wasn't I? My congratulations to them were genuine, unlike the thin smiles faking delight from Papa and Franco. And what about Mamma and Jenni? They appeared pleased. Or were their good wishes for a happy-ever-after also artificial? Along with their husbands, were they thinking about the health of their future bank accounts as a result of Nonna saying, "I do."

Halfway through the pile, a letter from Nonna's solicitor attached to a wad of papers secured with a paperclip piques my attention. I speed-read the opening paragraph of the letter thanking Mrs De Rosa for her instructions to change her will. Flicking through the sizeable document, I hunt for the changes, but they are not apparent, and I don't have time to read them in detail.

I flip through the other unopened letters, but they all appear to be an assortment of utility bills and credit card statements. At the bottom of the pile, I discover an unsealed envelope with *PRIVATE AND CONFIDENTIAL* in block capital letters stamped across the front. I remove the contents. It's a copy of Jared's contract of employment. I leaf through the sections on pay and performance review, probationary period and pension, until I get to part twelve: Termination of Employment. Two large stars in fluorescent yellow pen accent this title. The first section details the length of notice each party is required to give, depending on years of continuous service. The first line has been highlighted with the same yellow pen. Between one month and two years' service requires one week's notice. I pull my phone from my pocket and snap a shot of the page. Replacing the contract in the envelope, I shove it back in the filing tray. I pick up the documents from the solicitors again, but another car pulling up outside disturbs my attention. My heart pounds. I quickly bang the papers on the desk to shuffle them together and shove them into my bag. Tip-toeing over to the window, I lower one of the slats of the blind, relieved to see a man negotiating the path of the house opposite.

Enough is enough. I'm out of here.

When I get home, Maddie is watching TV. 'What's going on, Sienna? You look like you've had a run-in with a zombie. Fancy a glass of something?'

I shake my head. 'Not tonight. Thanks for coming over,' I say, hoping she will get the hint.

'Crap ain't half as mucky if you share it,' she says, raising a tattooed eyebrow. 'What's up?'

'I need to sort some stuff out. I'll share another time.'

'I'm worried about you. Let me take Lola for a few hours on Saturday, give you a break.'

'Thanks, but my aunty and uncle are throwing a small party for her in the afternoon to make up for Sunday.'

'Next week, then. Call me if you need me. Anytime.' She pecks me on the cheek on her way out.

I rush to wash my hands, then dash outside for a cigarette. As soon as the smoke hits my lungs, I feel a little calmer. But not for long. My phone beeping in my pocket sees to that. It's a text from Sean Pilkington, Nonna's decorator.

Sorry to confuse matters. My son made arrangements with Cara to decorate her garden room and replace the surrounding decking. Starting Jan 6 when she goes away. Sean P.

So, Nonna didn't mean the restaurant. She was talking about her garden room being redecorated. The sickening thoughts circling in my mind since Lola's party turn my stomach again. Nonna hasn't been confused at all. She mentioned when the leaves began to fall this year, the slippery decking was a hazard, and some of the boards have rotted.

Drugs can't be blamed, neither can a stroke. She fully comprehended what she told me.

TWENTY-TWO

I search for DS Durant's number. 'How did you know I was on nights?' he says, sounding pleased to hear from me, I think.

'I didn't. But something has come up, and I need to speak to you.'

'About Matthew?'

'Yes, and another matter.'

'I could pop over. Give me half an hour.'

'I'll put the kettle on.'

While I wait for DS Durant, I pour another glass of the Chianti. A large one. Something is needed to calm my nerves while I revisit the bundle of papers from Nonna's solicitors. Nonna has never hidden the contents of her will from the family. She has always made it clear it is split between her sons, with provision for Milana, me and Lola. A copy sits with her jewellery and passport in a small safe in her study at home. The code is her date of birth, followed by mine.

But she has left it all to Rik.

All of it. Every last penny. What made her change her mind? The same thing that made Silvia Marcia change her wishes to leave her fortune to Frederick Spartans instead of her daughters? Silvia died of a heart attack. Was that a result of poisoning? Did Rik poison Silvia Marcia as he hunted for his next victim: Cara De Rosa? Questions hurtle through my mind. None of which I have the answer to.

DS Durant takes his tea strong with two sugars. I should know. I poured him enough cups in the months following Matt's death. He spent more time here than he should have done; we both knew that. For me, it started as a comfort, having another male around. I wasn't in a fit state to heed the feelings he started to develop until it was too late. At that point I stopped calling him Craig.

'You remembered. I'm impressed,' he says, stirring his tea.

'Milk with two, of course I remember.' We exchange familiar smiles. It's been so long, yet it seems only days since he dropped by every evening, whether he was on shift or not. Even if it was for a quick five minutes, he would always pop in. 'I could fix you a helping of casserole if you want?'

He sips his tea. 'I ate earlier.'

'You've grown your hair,' I say. He used to sport the military look, but now his red hair holds a trendy quiff.

'I'm flattered you noticed. And yours is shorter. It suits you.'

He looks older. Five years of pressure from the job has lined his forehead and crinkled the skin around his eyes. I remember him telling me – late one night when he dropped by, and I asked him if he ever slept – his work was not a job, it was a passion. A way of life that lived with you seven days a week, fifty-two weeks a year. "You don't join the police if you can't cope with eating, living, and breathing, your career for the next however many years."

'How's Lola?' he asks.

'A diva, as they all are at eight years old these days.' I laugh. 'She's gorgeous. Quirky, loving, full of life.' I inwardly sigh for how I once was. 'You won't recognise her. It must be close to four years since you saw her.'

'Has it really been that long?'

I don't need to answer him. The pain is still evident in my downturned lips and the slow nod of my head. 'And how's life with you? Married yet?' He once told me about a girl who had swept him off his feet and his near brush with marriage. She cheated on him with his brother. Marriage was a game best left to others to play, he concluded, as he always ended up the loser in relationships.

He answers my question with a dismissive chuckle and asks me what I called him for.

'Tell me about Matt, first.' My late husband's name slips from my lips in a whisper of the grief forever within me. 'What's this new information you were talking about when you called the other day?'

'I don't work in the Serious Collision Investigation Unit anymore. As you're aware, I transferred to the local CID last year, but I've kept hold of Matthew's case. I don't want to get your hopes up, but I know you'd want me to tell you. Someone has come forward with new information through Crimestoppers. We've tracked a woman down in Northumbria.'

'Northumbria?' Is this it? After all this time? He told me he would never quit looking for the person responsible for Matt's death. He promised me. I believed him for such a long time. 'What new information?'

He removes his notebook and asks me, 'Does the name Jackie Blackstone mean anything to you?'

I shake my head. 'Who is she?'

'She used to live around here.'

'Whereabouts?'

'Stoke Newington. Crocus Road.'

I stare at him blankly, then quiz him some more.

He reassures me, tells me he's following up every avenue and reminds me he has never broken a promise to me. 'So, tell me, what did you call me here for tonight?'

I try to keep calm as I relay the events since the party on Sunday. There are certain things I omit. He doesn't need to learn about Mamma's possible infidelities or my uninvited visit to Nonna's house an hour ago.

'It could be confusion, but not necessarily. Can you think of anyone who might want to poison her?'

I shake my head and tell him all about my nonna, the unique Cara De Rosa. 'Cara will do anything for anyone, but she can be outspoken at times. It's the Italian in her. She's not afraid to tell people what's what, which some find offensive.' I pause before adding, 'But never enough for someone to want to kill her.'

Hearing Lola sobbing, I turn to the doorway to see her leaning against the frame. I rush over to her, scooping her up like a baby. 'Whatever's wrong, darling?'

'I dreamed Bisnonna died.' Her body shudders in my arms. 'Is she dead?'

'No, darling! I promise. She's OK.'

She hauls herself up in my arms, looking over her shoulder then back at me.

'This is my friend. His name is Craig,' I say, gesturing with a flick of my head over to DS Durant.

Strangely, she won't look at him. He gets the hint and politely asks to use the toilet. With promises not to leave until she is asleep, I coax Lola back to bed. 'Is Zach still your boyfriend, Mummy?' she asks with the confusion only a child could have over the complexities of relationships. Or am I underestimating her? Has she spotted the fondness DS Durant still carries in his eyes for me?

'Of course, darling.' I caress her shoulder. 'What makes you ask?'

'Sometimes, I worry.'

'Why?'

'Because,' she pauses, as if choosing her words cautiously, 'you don't love him as much as I do.'

'Stop worrying that beautiful little head of yours.' I stroke her hair. 'Sleep tight, my darling.'

Was I so astute at eight years old?

I wait for her to drop off before returning to the kitchen.

'Run through the people who work at the restaurant,' DS Durant says.

I tell him as much as I can about every member of staff, from the team of chefs to the bank staff of waiters and waitresses. When I get to Jared, I add, 'He was on the Prisoner Apprenticeship Pathway at Brixton prison.'

'I've heard about it. It's been a successful project.'

I give him Jared's backstory. 'Everyone was dead against the idea of her taking him on, especially Papa. Not necessarily because Jared had been in prison, but because Papa believes we should only employ Italian chefs. According to him, it's one of the ten commandments of running a successful Italian eatery. Only pure-blooded Italians can cook authentic Italian food. It's the way they nurture the dishes, knowing when to add an extra pinch of salt or a specific herb, he says. Nonna insisted, and to be fair to Papa, he came around pretty quickly. Jared is an endearing character. Everyone adores him.' I sigh heavily.

'So, what's the problem with him?'

'Nonna told me he has to go.'

'Go?'

I shrug. 'I thought she meant we needed to sack him. She was coming out with a lot of stuff at the time, but then I found this.' Reaching across the table for my phone, I locate the picture I took earlier in Nonna's study and turn the screen to him.

He squints at the photo. 'May I?' he asks, holding out a hand. I pass the phone over to him, and he enlarges the image. 'Appears as if she was looking into his official notice period.'

'I have no clue what Nonna's beef is with him.'

'I'll check him out. What about your family?'

'She's recently changed her will.'

'And?'

I hesitate. 'She's left it all to Rik. I should probably mention, last week, they announced their engagement, and they're supposedly getting married in the new year.'

He raises an eyebrow as I relay my suspicions about Rik and what I found out about Silvia Marcia. I also mention Gianni Bellini.

'You should join the force. You'd make a good detective.'

'There are so many unanswered questions.'

'And we will find the answers.'

'What will you do?'

'I need to make a call to the station. Then I guess I'm off to the hospital. We'll need to get some bloods. If she has been poisoned, then there's a possibility it could show up.'

'Only a possibility?'

'All depends on what she has been poisoned with. Routine toxicology tests won't show up all poisons. More detailed and focused tests are required, which can take weeks, I'm afraid.'

'But we don't have weeks.'

'It sounds like she has been on a cocktail of drugs for a long time. This will complicate matters. Leave it with me.'

Like I left Matt's case with you? When five years on, you still haven't charged the vermin who drove the car that stole my daughter's father and ripped my life in two?

No, DS Durant. I may need your help, but I will not leave this entirely up to you.

TWENTY-THREE

The following day, when Lola and I are midway through our morning bolt through the park to breakfast club, DS Durant calls. I'm dog-tired, having stayed awake for hours after he left last night, trying to make the connection between Jackie Blackstone, Stoke Newington and Northumbria, but nothing.

'I forgot you never sleep,' I say, my breath steaming the air. In the early days of Matt's case, he always seemed on-call, whatever time of the day, whatever day of the week. Sometimes, I would contact him in the early hours. Even when he wasn't at work, he would pick up the phone. 'I'll have to call you back,' I tell him. I want to get out of this park as quickly as possible. The faces in the trunks of the trees appear extra menacing today. The fierce eyes forming in the knots of the bark are staring at me, the mouths chanting like a chorus of creeps telling me they are after me. I will myself to calm down and focus ahead. After last night's episode, I don't want to unsettle Lola anymore. She referred to it again this morning as I was pouring milk onto her Shreddies. I understand how she feels. Zach is the Polaris of her universe. He treats her as if she's his own. The three of us make the perfect little family in her sheltered world.

After I've dropped her off, I don't head directly to work. At three o'clock this morning, unable to sleep, I hatched a plan. I need to find the courage to carry it through. I'm not good at doing that – seeing things through. I used to be. My ability to get things done once matched Milana's. Miss Efficiency, that was me. But that was life before Matt. I make a detour to Boots. If Mamma won't tell me the truth about Papa, I'll have to find another way.

En route, I return DS Durant's call. He answers immediately. 'I thought I'd give you an update. When I left yours last night, I spoke to my DI and headed straight to the hospital. I saw Cara.'

'Did she speak to you?' I ask, hoping he can shed some light onto this plight of darkness.

'I see what you mean when you say she's in a bad way. I spoke to her, but she didn't acknowledge me, I'm afraid. I managed to speak to one of the doctors. Mr Happy wasn't forthcoming in divulging information. What's that expression? Blood. Stone.'

'I know what you mean. They're all too busy.'

'He was insistent. A heart attack and a stroke are the cause of her condition. All the tests carried out, along with her medical history, back up the diagnosis. On the bright side, he said the stroke was caught early. She couldn't have been in a better place. So it is possible for her to make a full recovery. I managed to get some bloods ordered. Forensics will pick them up sometime this morning.'

'How long will that take?'

'I'll do what I can, but I doubt we'll see anything this side of next weekend.'

I don't add my thoughts. He knows what I'm thinking. *She could be dead by then.*

'Even then, they might not reveal anything. Are you at the restaurant all day?'

'Until three, then I'm going to the hospital.'

'I have to head over to Bethnal Green this morning. I thought I'd stop by on my way back. I think it's time to throw some pebbles.'

'Pebbles?'

He informs me he is going to assess the ripples that flow from letting everyone know about Nonna's accusation.

I'm on the computer, completing an order for incidentals, when Milana rocks up a little after ten-thirty. The smell of coffee drifts in with her as she hands me a flat white. 'Heavy night?' I ask, tutting with a smile at her deathly pale face. 'Which party did you choose in the end?' Forever the social butterfly, she had invitations for two events last night. How she could party until all hours at a time like this, I don't understand.

Slowly, she slips off her jacket as if it's a real effort. 'Both.' Switching on her computer, she adds, 'And don't I feel it.'

'And don't you look it.'

'Thanks for the encouragement. I woke up about two with a head from hell and spent the next hour throwing up. I drank far more than I should've.' She hooks her jacket over the arm of her chair, but, shivering, she changes her mind and slips it back on. 'God, I wish it were Sunday.'

'Well, if you will party on a school night.' I pause, empathising. 'Shouldn't you have stayed in bed?'

'I've got too much to do in this place. I'd best not come to see Nonna with you this afternoon.'

'There's a sickness bug going around Lola's class. Loads of kids are off. You sure you haven't got something like that?'

She shakes her head. 'No. I'd still be throwing up.'

I click on the *complete order* button. 'Have you sorted this short-term loan with the bank yet?'

She sighs heavily, picking up a file. 'That's another complication. Nonna had already applied for a loan for the Islington site. They want more figures before they'll consider another. I don't know what's going on. I think we're going to have to let the Stamford Hill site go.' She shakes her head, quickly regretting it. 'Ouch.' She rubs her temple. 'I think I need some Alka-Seltzer.'

She rushes out, and Mamma bursts into the office as I'm logging off the computer. 'That's the fifth complaint we've had this week,' she says. 'We need to get some agency staff in. We can't cope anymore.' Mamma tugs at a section of hair on each side of her head and mocks trying to pull it out. 'A table of four walked out last night. They left the worst ever one-star review on Trip Advisor. Do you know what they said?' She doesn't wait for me to reply. *'Food was excellent, as always. Service was shocking.* Cara will be livid.'

She is right. This kind of stuff never happens on Nonna's watch.

'While you're here…' I say, reaching into my bag. She looks at me wearily, a flicker of distrust in the blink of her eyes. I dig out my purchase from Boots and place the paternity test onto the desk, sliding it into her view. I'm shaking and surprise myself with the boldness with which I deliver my ultimatum. 'If you've got something to tell me, I'll give you until the end of the day tomorrow. If not, I'm going to ask Papa if he wouldn't mind helping me out with the Christmas present I'm working on for Nonna, and give me the sample I need to trace her family tree.' I can't believe these words have left my mouth. This is more Milana's style than mine. I've always been the quieter one. The non-confrontational one, who will always give in rather than face an argument. But the moment has come to find my voice and make it loud.

Mamma's jaw drops, her brow crinkles. 'Are you threatening me, Sienna?'

'I'm afraid so,' I say and walk towards the door.

When I enter the restaurant, I'm surprised to see Zach standing at the bar in what looks like a serious conversation with Jared. I walk over to them, startling Zach with a poke in the ribs. They stop dead as if their conversion was one for their ears only. 'What are you two scheming?' I ask.

'That's for us to know and you to find out,' Zach says in

a teasing tone.

'Tactical planning for our Tour De France challenge,' Jared pipes in.

Zach looks at him and winks. 'That's right.'

'You're lying,' I say. I glance at my watch. 'You never stop by at this time of day.'

'Would I lie to you?' Zach says, feigning a hurt face and slamming his open hand onto his chest. He picks up a take-away cup a waitress has plonked in front of him. 'Catch you both later.' He kisses me on the cheek and heads for the door.

'What were you two talking about?' I turn and ask Jared, but he is already making his way to the kitchen. I follow him, but he detours into the toilets.

I stop to wash my hands, then enter the kitchen, where it's manic. 'Spare me half an hour, will you?' Papa says as I pass through on my way outside for a cigarette. He is sweating like he has a fever. What is wrong with everyone today? 'I need someone to prep that lot.'

I follow his nod to a mound of onions and tomatoes waiting on the worktop. 'Not onions, Papa. You know I hate chopping onions.'

He shakes a hanky from his apron pocket, dabbing sweat dripping from his forehead. Nonna's absence has raised his stress levels to the rafters. 'I'm so behind this morning.' He stirs a pot of his garlic-infused Bolognese simmering on the stove. 'Would you believe it? Paulo has called in sick. On today of all days. Useless. I need to find myself another kitchen porter. It's all I need. We have Franco and Jenni's lot coming in for their staff Christmas party tonight. And leave the door open, will you? I'm roasting in here.'

Outside, flakes of snow spatter the table and chairs. One of the reclaimed railway sleepers retaining the borders has broken away. Nonna is always telling the staff not to sit on them. A pile of earth has spilt onto the decking, along with a couple of plants. I pick them up and push them back into place. My hands are shaking, not only from the cold, but also from the conversation I've just had with Mamma. I can't believe what I've said to her. Nonna says my people-pleasing behaviour is the only trait of mine she finds annoying. She'd be pretty chuffed with me today.

I light up and take a long drag on my cigarette, thinking how sad and neglected the courtyard looks in the depths of winter. Nonna's absence has stamped its mark everywhere this week. Nothing is running smoothly. As if someone has put diesel into the engine of De Rosa's when they should have used unleaded.

I dig my hand underneath my coat and scoop my phone from my jeans pocket, trying Gianni's number again, but to no avail. I call the hospital, but there's been no change. Nonna is not responding to the prescribed medication, so they are trying a different tactic. I consider having another cigarette when Papa comes storming out as white and green as the lime-coloured table and chairs scattered with snow. He throws his hands in the air. 'A bloody detective has turned up. What's going on?'

'Calm down, Papa.'

'He wants to speak to all of us. Whatever for?'

'Nonna has said someone has been trying to poison her.'

My words sound so bizarre, so harsh, as I voice them in the cold winter air.

Mamma appears. She stares at me, nodding her head sideways in Papa's direction. 'Has he told you?'

'Told me what?'

She paces up and down the courtyard. She doesn't get far. It's too small an area. 'The police have turned up. I'm sure it's that chap who was involved in Matthew's case.'

Papa sums up our conversation.

'That's ridiculous,' Mamma says. 'How do you know, anyway?'

'Because I'm the one she told,' I say.

She gasps. 'And you didn't think to tell us first?'

'I called the detective who is involved with Matt's investigation.'

'Why would you do that? He was never any good. How long is it? Five years, with no success?'

'I don't need reminding.'

'Why didn't you say anything to us?' Mamma looks from me to Papa and back to me. Her top lip curls, or has it been like that all day? 'Why go to the police?'

'Exactly what I said,' Papa adds.

'I called DS Durant for advice,' I say.

'What were you thinking?' Mamma asks.

I shrug.

Mamma says, 'Come inside, Sienna, will you? Milana has scarpered, and the police want to speak to me.'

'Where's she gone?' I ask.

'I told her about the police arriving, and she grabbed her coat and ran out.'

TWENTY-FOUR

I hurry inside like a small child who has been ticked off. When I reach the office, I call Milana. Three attempts and she still doesn't answer. What is she playing at?

Mamma appears. 'The agency is sending a bank waitress, thank God. Find her an apron when she arrives, can you? Then help Papa in the kitchen with his onions. I've never seen him so stressed out.'

You neither, Mamma. What *is* wrong with all of you?

In the kitchen, I see Jared photographing a tray of his lip-smacking tiramisu. Not even Papa can match his recipe. I often take a slice home.

'Is that for Instagram?' I ask.

His face beams. He turns the screen to me. 'How's that for a shot?' I nod my approval. 'I'll send it over to Milana to post.'

'Don't you post these pictures to your own account?' I ask.

'I do, but my account is set to private, so Milana posts

everything on the De Rosa business page. More exposure for the restaurant.'

'Why did you set your account to private?'

'Had some weirdo start following me. Wouldn't leave me alone,' he says nonchalantly and tucks his phone back in his pocket. 'Wouldn't take a slice of this up to the hospital for Cara, would you? She loves my recipe.'

'Sorry, she's not up to eating at the moment. As soon as she is, I'll let you know.'

'What's with the detective?' he asks.

I slide closer to him. 'Nonna believes she has been poisoned.' The more I voice it to people who know her, the stranger it sounds.

He grips the worktop, his bulging eyes piercing into mine. 'You kidding me? How?' He clears his throat. 'Why? Who would do that?'

'That's what the detective is trying to find out. Before she had her stroke, Nonna told me she knew who was trying to poison her.'

'Who?'

'She didn't get to tell me who.'

'And the cops think it's someone here?'

I shrug. 'Who knows?'

'Cara's too lovely for anyone to want to do that to her.' His hand slaps against his chest, his fingers spread out like a fan. 'You've really shocked me.'

I'm preparing the onions and tomatoes the way Papa likes them – onions thinly sliced, tomatoes finely diced – as DS

Durant casually questions Jared, telling him he is looking into all angles of Cara's accusation. The kitchen grows busier as more orders arrive, and by the time I've finished with Papa's onions, not a table is free when I go and serve in the restaurant.

I meet DS Durant coming out of the kitchen on my way back in with another order. 'Anything?' I ask him.

'Everyone's on edge, aren't they? Tell me about the other people Cara mixes with regularly.'

I lean against the wall by the office. 'There are the people at the dance club where she and Rik go on a Wednesday night, and people she meets in the park when she's walking her neighbour's dog. She knows so many people around here.'

'Who?'

'The list is long. She's well-known in the community, always popping out for a coffee with someone or other.'

This is no exaggeration. Nonna always endeavours to help people out. The local area has seen a rise in co-working spaces over the past few years. Membership clubs for workers who want to avoid the commute into the City or West End or those living in small flats like Zach who want somewhere to work other than the kitchen table. Like kids to Nutella, Nonna's sweetness has a way of drawing these people in. Or maybe it's her astute business acumen because they invariably end up as De Rosa clients, whether for a Friday night meal with their partners or a complete restyle at the salon.

'Anyone in particular?' DS Durant asks.

I pause to think. 'There's a woman, Helen Myer. She's

recently set up the vintage clothing shop near the entrance to the canal. Nonna and she have become friendly. She's been in here asking after her a few times. She's really upset about what has happened. Maybe have a chat with her? Oh, and there's the woman who owns the Asian bakery at the end of the street. I can't remember her name. Nonna met up with her last week.'

He jots down particulars in his notebook. 'Anyone else?'

'Not that I can think of. Milana would be the best person to ask.'

'What about family?'

'There's Franco – Cara's son – and his wife Jenni.'

'I remember you mentioning them before. Where can I find them?'

'They still own Hair by De Rosa. The salon up the road. Well, I say they own it.' I cross my arms. 'Nonna owns a large chunk of it. She forked out the funds to get the business off the ground.'

He smiles. 'I recall her being a rather controlling character.'

I shrug. 'Some might put it like that. I'd say more a generous character than a controlling one. She loves helping people succeed. She just doesn't like people taking advantage of her.'

'I'm almost done here. There are still a few of the waiting staff I want to talk to, but I'll come back later. I want to pop into the salon on my way back to the station.'

'They'll be busy. It's their work's Christmas party here tonight.'

'I'm sure they'll find a minute or two to speak to me. What happened to your sister?'

'She had to go home.'

He raises an eyebrow.

Is he thinking what I'm thinking? How strange that when he appeared, Milana shot off. Or am I being too mistrustful? 'I'm not sure if she has a hangover or is unwell. She was up in the night being sick.'

'I'm going to Rik's house later.'

'I want to come.'

'That's not appropriate, Sienna.'

'I don't have to turn up with you. I could already be there. I'll know if he's not telling you everything.' Where has all this boldness come from? It's as though Nonna's absence has bestowed on me a gift of bravery.

On the way to the hospital, I call Zach. 'Something's come up. I'll explain later. I'm going to collect Lola. Would you mind her later?'

'That would help me, actually. Work has been bonkers today. She won't be happy, though. I said I'd take her to the cinema, remember?'

'You could do that tomorrow if you're free.'

'OK. Tell me where and when.'

'Could you get to mine for six? I'll go back to work for a couple of hours and bring dinner home for us.'

'This all sounds rather mysterious.'

'I'll fill you in later.'

'Don't worry about dinner. I'll cook for you.'

. . .

Nonna is no different today. I sit with her for three-quarters of an hour, struggling to find stuff to chat about. There's only so much positivity you can inject into a one-way conversation when life is so grim. When I've exhausted my updates about Lola and work, I ask again the question I desperately want answered: 'Who did this to you, Nonna?'

But there's nothing.

I dash to pick up Lola, racing across town faster than I should in the icy conditions. Nonna's words echo in my thoughts: "Slow down, my girl, you'll have an accident."

'I don't want to do piano practice,' Lola moans when I tell her where we are going. 'I want to go to the cinema with Zach. He promised me.'

I bend down, so we are at eye level, and fasten the toggles on her duffle coat. 'Listen, darling. You know sometimes I tell you Mummy needs you to do something without questions.' She nods reluctantly. 'Well, this is one of those times.'

'Why?'

'No questions, I said.' I secure another toggle, stifling a smile at her indignant scowl. 'Zach will take you to the cinema tomorrow night.'

'What about Sunday? Are we still having our day out together? Will you still take me Christmas shopping?'

I stroke the top of her head. 'Of course.'

Obediently, she follows me to the car, as I say a silent prayer.

How different Rik appears tonight. Weary-looking. He meets me in the hallway, perturbed, I think, because I let myself in without ringing the bell first. I didn't want to give him the chance to turn us away.

'Hi, Rik. Did you get my text? I hope you don't mind us dropping by. Nonna will be so disappointed if Lola misses her Thursday piano practice.' Lola tugs my hand. I give her a sweet smile begging her forgiveness for my shameful fibbing.

Rik gives an absent nod. 'I'm in the kitchen if you need me. I've got someone coming around in a bit. The police want to speak to me about Cara. Do you know anything about this?'

I hesitate. How much should I reveal? I thought DS Durant would already be here. I can't deny what has gone on today, but I don't want to alarm Lola. The doorbell rings. Rik turns to answer it. 'Off you go,' I say to Lola, breathing a sigh of relief. I steer her into the lounge, where she skips up the steps and takes the stage on the mini grand piano. Pulling out the black stool, she lifts the lid and resumes her playing position. Like Nonna has taught her: spine as straight as a ruler, neck as long as a giraffe, arms relaxed. Lola shakes her shoulders and fills the room with the life Nonna's absence has left, her body swaying in time to the music.

I peer around the room. It's not as tidy as usual.

Nonna's touch is missing. She would be huffing and puffing at her treasured cushions strewn higgledy-piggledy across the sofa, not to mention the one thrown on the floor. Several cups and a plate with a half-eaten bacon sandwich clutter the usually clear glass coffee table.

Climbing the two steps to the piano, I sit on the stool next to Lola, swallowing the wedge of sadness blocking my throat. The elegance with which her fingers glide along the keys reminds me of Nonna.

Please come home soon, Nonna. I miss you so much.

Lola glances up at me. 'Why does a policeman want to speak to Rik?' she asks. I stare into her doe-like eyes seeped in vulnerability, overcome with a maternal wave of sadness. The passing months are stealing her childhood innocence far too quickly. I shrug because I can't find the right words to answer her. She flashes a smile before returning to the keys. 'That's beautiful, darling. Keep playing. I'm going to get a drink,' I say.

The kitchen door is ajar. Luck is with me for once. I peer through the gap. DS Durant and Rik are sitting on stools at the centre-island – an enormous chunk of granite topping a variety of cupboards and shelves that dominates the centre of the room. It houses the hob and the sink and seats four comfortably along the length. Rik, propped up against it, is drinking a bottle of beer, DS Durant a glass of water.

'What exactly can I do for you, then?' Rik asks. 'You're obviously not here to discuss what I do for a living.'

'Just making conversation,' DS Durant says. 'I'll be frank

with you, Rik. I'm worried about Cara. I'm speaking to all the family, trying to cover all bases.'

Rik scoffs. 'Not as worried as I am.'

'Not only her current health, but recent events, from what people are telling me, they don't add up.' DS Durant glances at his notebook. 'I have some questions, but I'll start with telling you about a few puzzling things Cara has said to her granddaughter. And, please understand, these are routine questions. I'm asking others close to her the same.'

Shuffling forward, until he is sitting on the edge of the seat, Rik places his beer on the island. He rests his elbows on his knees and clasps his hands together. One of his knees starts bobbing up and down. 'Which granddaughter? What things?'

'Cara said everyone was wrong about her heart condition. Rather, someone was trying to poison her, and, what's more, she knew who.'

If his jaw could open any further, it would reach his chest. His elbows straighten, and he sits upright, clearly shocked. 'Who?'

'That's what I'm trying to figure out.'

'She mentioned something similar to me.'

'Can you elaborate?'

'I didn't take her seriously. She's been really confused lately.' He scratches his head. 'This past week, in fact.'

'In what way?'

'The family stress her out. Work has been stressing her out.'

'Why would that be?'

'She takes on too much. I keep telling her to slow down, but Cara is a woman with her own mind. That's one of her endearing qualities; she's a unique human being, in charge of her own destiny. She should be taking it easy at this time of her life. Let's face it, she could be drawing from all the pension plans she has paid into over the years and leading a life of luxury, but no, not Cara De Rosa. She's opening all these new restaurants and has no plans to retire.'

He swipes his bottle from the side and swigs his beer. 'She's also been complaining about her vision, saying everything is blurred. I've been on at her to get an optician's appointment, but she said she hasn't had the time. So, I arranged one for tomorrow, but, of course, I had to cancel it. She also told me she had run into some financial difficulties. Nothing sinister, from what I could make out. Some money she was expecting didn't pan out as planned, so she had to shuffle around some funds. I don't get involved in her business ventures, other than listen and offer what advice I can when she asks. We try to keep work and home separate. Otherwise, you know how it ends up. Work's all you talk about. And that's not good for Cara's heart, her mental health, or our relationship.'

'Who is Gianni Bellini?' DS Durant asks.

The silence, and the way Rik stares at the floor, tells me he knows precisely who DS Durant is referring to. He looks as if he is trying to think of how best to answer the detective's question. His eyes dart from side to side, his thoughts spinning the lie he is about to tell. 'I've never heard that name.'

TWENTY-FIVE

DS Durant pulls a piece of paper out of his file. I can't tell what is on it. He holds it towards Rik. 'You ever seen this man?'

I guess it's a photo of Gianni.

Rik stares at the paper, shaking his head. 'Never. Who is he?'

'That's what we're trying to work out.'

'What's the connection to Cara?'

'He appeared at the Islington restaurant last week. Cara went off with him.'

'How do you know?'

'Bettina told Sienna.'

'Do they know who he is?'

DS Durant shakes his head. 'We've managed to track him down, though, and I will be going to see him.'

Rik stands, quickly, as if DS Durant has hit a nerve. 'That's what I mean about her not being herself. She'd never go off with a stranger and not tell me about it.' He heads to the fridge and fetches another bottle of beer. 'But I guess I was wrong.' He takes a large gulp of air, puffing it out in bursts. 'Do you think she meant it? About being poisoned?'

'It's something we need to look into. Any idea what she could've meant? Why she thinks someone is out to poison her?'

'No idea,' Rik says, sitting back down. He crosses his arms over his chest and stares intently at DS Durant. 'You don't think I'm involved in all of this, do you?'

'I'll be talking to the whole family and everyone she has been in contact with recently.'

'You didn't answer my question.'

'Like I said, Rik. I hope you appreciate I have to speak to everyone who has a connection to Cara.'

Rik's arched eyebrows form two curves of consternation. He takes another large gulp of his beer. 'What else did you want to ask me?' His tone has changed. It's more guarded.

'Jared Kingston.'

'What about him?'

'Cara wants him sacked.'

'That's absurd. Jared is Cara's favourite. Do you know the story about him? His background.'

'I've been briefed.'

'Cara is really fond of him. He's a big supporter of the restaurant. Always pulling in clients. He's a great chef. Reliable. Cara gushes over him. Far better than some of the others they employ.'

'You have no idea why she would say this, then?'

'No idea at all. She was clearly confused.'

'Some of these are pretty damning statements.' Glancing at his notebook, DS Durant says, 'Tell me about Silvia Marcia.'

Rik's jaw drops again. 'What's she got to do with anything?' A hint of hostility edges his tone.

'I'm doing my homework, Rik–'

'I can't see the relevance to Cara.'

'–And I'm covering all angles.'

Rik hesitates, his nostrils flaring like a panicked horse. 'I was engaged to her before I met Cara.'

'Why did your relationship end?'

'Why are you asking? You obviously know.' Silence. Then, 'She died.'

'How?'

'A heart attack.' His words are a murmur. I barely hear them.

'I'm sorry to hear that. Were you with her when she died?'

Rik leans back in his chair. 'Why are you asking me questions you already know the answer to?' Rik waits for DS Durant's answer, but it's not forthcoming. Rik looks to the floor. 'Yes, I was with her, and I couldn't save her.'

'I'm sorry.'

They both remain quiet. The only sound is the tick-tock of the large gold-framed clock hanging on the wall. Nonna loves this clock. I was with her when she found it years ago at an antique fair in Alexander Palace. She bought me a set of Russian dolls at the same time. Lola still occasionally plays with them. I nip back to the lounge to check on Lola, who's still performing her melodious tunes.

When I return to my spot at the kitchen door, I can see DS Durant peering around the room. 'Nice kitchen you've got here, Rik. Tell me, who does the cooking in this house?'

'Me mostly. As you know, Cara's a busy person. She's not always here for an evening meal. Sometimes, she brings food back from the restaurant.'

'Must be great to live with someone who owns a restaurant. All that lovely food.'

'Sometimes she eats there, or she grabs a bite to eat with friends.'

'Which friends?'

Rik shrugs. 'Cara knows lots of people in the local area. Ask her family. They'll know more than I do.'

'Tell me about Cara's relationships with her family.'

He scratches his head. 'You got all night?'

DS Durant remains expressionless.

'Where do you want me to start?'

'Let's begin with her sons.'

Rik curls a cupped hand over his lips as if he is scared words he'll regret will spill from his mouth. 'Look, I don't want to speak out of turn, but we don't get on. Not really.'

'Why's that?'

'They haven't liked me from day one. I got it, at first. They loved Nico, their father. You'd think grown men would act a little more maturely, but not those two. I made massive allowances for the pair of them. Don's okayish. He has his moments. But Franco. Well, I keep out of his way whenever possible and when not, I stay shtum and suffer him for the sake of Cara. *Suffer* him.'

'I have reason to believe Cara has recently changed her will.'

Rik bites his lip. A phone rings. He jumps up. 'That could be the hospital.' He rushes from the room.

I stand watching the DS making notes. I've never seen Rik treat Nonna with anything other than the respect she deserves. He apparently loves her, adores her. Why, then, is he lying about Gianni Bellini? Unless the loving way he looks at her, compliments her, talks about their future together, is all for show. Let's face it; he has landed himself a comfortable position with Nonna by his side.

Rik returns, frowning.

'All OK?' DS Durant asks.

Rik shakes his head. 'That was the hospital. I need to go.'

DS Durant snaps shut his notebook. 'No problem, Rik. We can continue this conversation another time.'

TWENTY-SIX

Christmas partygoers pack De Rosa's tonight. Italian folk music belts from the speakers. Fervent chatter fills the air. Mamma shouts orders to the staff, sounding more like Nonna than is comfortable. Like me, she has grown braver with Nonna out of the way. Milana hasn't shown up since her abrupt departure following DS Durant's appearance, so I guess Mamma considers herself in charge tonight. A position she appears to be relishing.

Braver until DS Durant drops in again around seven. This time a woman accompanies him. She is pretty – shoulder-length blonde hair, dimples, and a dainty nose. I wonder if she's his girlfriend, and I'm staggered by how much I dislike the thought.

I still haven't heard from Rik. My nerves are frayed. I'm taking an order from a noisy group of thirty-somethings celebrating at the table by the door when I hear DS Durant say to Mamma, 'We were just passing, and I know you don't get a better pizza in this part of town.'

A quick smile flickers on Mamma's stressed face. Sweat glistens on her forehead; her cheeks are flushed. What is wrong with her? She sweeps her arm around the restaurant. 'We're fully-booked, I'm afraid.'

'I know it's impossible to get a table in here without booking first. Especially this time of the year. We were thinking takeaway.'

'Everyone in town seems to have ordered pizza tonight. Our delivery guy didn't show. We had to call in backup, so we're behind. I can't even ask Milana to chip in. As you know, she's off sick.'

'We know what we want. A large hot and spicy for me. A small four-cheese for my colleague. This is Charlie, by the way. Charlie, meet Bettina.'

Mamma hesitates, clearly uncomfortable. Why is she so keen to get rid of them?

DS Durant doesn't allow her time to refuse. 'We'll order a drink while we wait.' He looks over to me, and we exchange nods and smiles.

I deliver the table's order to the kitchen, where organised mayhem produces a cacophony of shouting, sizzling food, scraping knives, and clinking spoons. Papa is flipping alternate pans on one of the cookers. Jared is beside him doing the same. The pizza chefs are shuffling pizzas from the oven to wooden serving boards and boxes ready for takeout. Others are plating-up food ready to be served. I quickly pin the order alongside the row of others, leaving swiftly for the bar.

Collecting a tray of drinks, I head to the deli where the Hair by De Rosa team is enthusiastically enjoying the party.

Franco and Jenni occupy either end of the large table. Seven members of staff sit between them on either side. Jenni is joining in the spirit of the occasion, whereas Franco looks troubled, stifling yawns as though he'd rather be somewhere else. They had a case of Prosecco after work, Jenni told me when they arrived. 'A whole twelve bottles.' She winced. 'I'm not in a position to partake,' she whispered, patting her stomach and winking. 'Franco isn't drinking, and Mandy and Debbie are dedicated drivers, so you do the math.' I search the table for Nancy, my teeth grinding when I spot her occupying the seat next to Franco. She is wearing a sparkly, low-cut top, her voluptuous shape testing the buttons to the max. Mamma is taking orders. It's a set menu. Choice one, two or three, it shouldn't be difficult, but it proves to be with so much Prosecco bubbling in this many people.

Nancy has ordered a vodka and tonic. I have to stop myself holding it above her head and pouring it over her perfectly-styled Farrah Fawcett feathered flick. How dare she do this to my aunty? As I place the drink in front of her, I dig deep and whip out a fake smile. A chore I should be accustomed to by now, but still find challenging.

'What is this, tonic?' she asks, sweetly. Squinting at the bottle, she shoves it back at me. 'I asked for vodka and soda.'

'I'll change that for you,' I say through another feigned smile I have to dig even deeper to unearth. At record pace, I distribute the other drinks. The quicker this group gets dessert, the faster I can get out of here.

After the mains are served, I encounter Nancy again,

this time in the ladies. She is propped up against the sink, staring in the mirror. Lyrics to a Britney Spears song from yonks ago – I can't even remember its name – jumble from her mouth as she concentrates on reapplying her make-up. Unsteady on her feet, she must have moved on from the vodka and soda, and is clearly enjoying the house white, free-flowing as part of the deal. One of the heels of her killer boots buckles, and she grasps the sink to anchor herself.

She doesn't see me. I enter a cubicle, and, as I'm taking a wee, I hear the door slam and someone else enter. They must be from the party, as I hear Nancy strike up a conversation with a woman with a squeaky voice who has evidently also taken full advantage of the free drinks their bosses have provided. The two of them complain about the food before slagging off one of the other stylists. Their discussion grows trickier to comprehend as they both keep talking over each other. But there's no mistaking Nancy's parting words. 'He will leave her, you know. After Christmas, when he has everything sorted, he'll be all mine.'

Knowing I need to think this through, it takes every ounce of self-control not to storm out of the cubicle. This isn't the time or the place for a downpour of rage and emotions. I drop my head in my hands. It's sad when you start to see people in a different light. Franco has always shone so brightly in my eyes, blinding me to the cheating rat he is. I wait for their voices to fade into the din of the restaurant and the door to close before leaving the cubicle to wash my hands. 'It's time for that conversation with Jenni,' I say to myself in the mirror.

TWENTY-SEVEN

It's chaos at the restaurant again this morning. Milana doesn't appear. I call her, but she doesn't answer. Instead, she texts to say she is still sick and won't make it in today. I respond, saying I'll pop in to see her later and ask if I can bring anything, but her reply tells me not to bother. She's not in a fit state to face anyone.

'Mamma is running late,' Papa informs me as he dashes about the kitchen assembling a large dish of his tasty chicken cacciatore, one of my favourites of his recipes. 'She didn't sleep well. Up all night. I don't know what's up with her.'

Our Friday waitress, reliable Rachela, who has worked for De Rosa's for years, has phoned to say she won't make it as she has been up all night being sick. Staff are dropping like dominoes. This place is falling apart.

Mid-morning, Nonna's friend Helen appears, catching me arranging a tray of drinks at the bar. She doesn't look well either. Her usually peachy complexion is washed-out, her eyes dark and her nose red as if winter flu has taken a hold. She orders a glass of Nonna's special grapefruit and papaya juice. 'I can see you're busy, but I was wondering how Cara is?' she says when I deliver her drink. 'I'd like to see her.'

'I'm so sorry, but she's not up for visitors,' I say, reaching out and touching her elbow. Her bottom lip quivers, so I add, 'I have your number. I promise to call when she's up to seeing people.'

'When will that be?' she asks, shivering despite the heavy tweed coat she is wearing over a polo neck jumper. She drinks the juice in one.

'I can't say. Are you OK, Helen?'

She nods, throws a fiver on the table, and excuses herself, disappearing as quickly as she arrived.

Nonna's absence has affected so many people.

While I'm sneaking a quick break before the lunchtime flurry, Papa returns from his bi-weekly trip to the wholesalers. I stub out my cigarette and help him carry bags bursting with flour and fresh produce from his car into the kitchen. He dumps a load on the worktop. 'The wholesalers was rammed, took me forever to get through the checkout. Then the car wouldn't start. I need to get that damn thing booked in for a service. I regret the day I ever bought it.' He needs to learn to order supplies online, Milana keeps telling him, but he won't have it. He insists his careful selection of the best ingredients is what has earned De Rosa's its reputation.

Jenni appears at the kitchen door. What is she doing here? She unbuttons her coat, displaying a jolly Christmas jumper. 'I could kill for one of your legendary caprese focaccias, Don,' she says, walking towards Papa and pecking him on the cheek.

'Your wish is my command,' he says with a big grin. Nothing pleases Papa more than people praising his food.

Walking over to me, she mouths, 'Can we have a quick word?' She clasps my arm and guides me to the stock room. 'I know this isn't the best place to talk,' she says, looking around at shelves packed with giant bags of pasta and semolina and jars of anchovies and capers, 'but I want to thank you for not saying anything.' She joins her hands across her belly. 'Franco would never forgive me if he knew I'd told you. We'll announce it as soon as we get the scan results, I promise.' Her voice falters. 'I'll be devastated if we lose it.'

Why is Franco running around with that bimbo then? I remain silent. My stomach turns for the news I had every intention of delivering, but how do you utter the words no wife ever wants to hear? That their husband, who they adore, is a two-timing creep.

'It's all I've ever dreamed of. You know that. A baby of my own. I still can't believe it's finally happening.' She bites her lower lip and grasps my shoulders. 'I'm going to be a mother, Sen. Finally! I'm going to have a child of my own.'

I think back to the years when I was growing up. Tears followed Jenni around like a rain cloud. Mamma told me she was a manic depressive until Nonna explained the real reason. It took several miscarriages before Jenni finally faced reality. She was never going to be a mother. She's so excited. That's the real reason she's ushered me in here. She knows I won't say anything to Franco. She wants a reason to express her excitement with someone. I can't spoil this for her, not at this moment. It's a conversation for another time. 'I'm so pleased for you, Jenni. You, more than anyone, deserve this.'

I wish I could say the same for that husband of yours.

Back in the kitchen, Papa has wrapped her sandwich. 'Extra rocket, just as you like it,' he says, handing it to her.

She takes the package from him. 'Perfect. This'll keep me going.'

'You take care,' Papa says, as he pecks her cheek before she heads out.

When she has gone, I pick up an order of courgette and saffron risotto marked for table five. Jared calls out to me. 'Table eight will be ready in two mins. Four and seven will be shortly behind.'

Table five are proving tricky. One of them complains their cutlery is dirty. She is right. I apologise and grab her a new set. A guy from table six flags me down. 'This latte is lukewarm,' he grumbles. 'I asked specifically for it to be extra hot.'

This wouldn't happen on Nonna's watch. The waiting staff are getting sloppy.

While I'm delivering a fresh latte – extra hot – to table six, Mamma shows up, red-eyed. Papa saying she didn't sleep well wasn't an understatement. She doesn't even acknowledge me. With her head bowed, she disappears into the office.

I follow her. 'You look terrible,' I say. 'You're not coming down with what Milana's picked up, are you?'

She throws her bag on the floor. She is shaking. What is wrong with her? Sliding her trembling hands into the pockets of her jeans, she looks at me. 'We need to talk.'

Guarded, I take a step back, knocking into the wastepaper bin, sending it crashing to the floor. She collapses into a chair, her hands above her head in defeat. 'You're right.'

I gasp. 'It's you? Did you poison Nonna?'

'What? How can you think that of me?' She drops her hands into her lap. Her chin falls to her chest.

'Mamma. What *is* going on?'

She glances up at me. 'I can't keep this to myself any longer. Papa is not your real father.'

TWENTY-EIGHT

I gasp. 'I knew it.'

She shakes her head, blanching. 'I was so stupid. So goddamn stupid. A drunken fumble that cost me so dearly.'

I listen in shock as she tells me about her mistake, and the misery it has caused her every day of her life since. 'I thought I'd be able to put it behind me and get on with my life,' she says. But she couldn't. Because the shame buried itself so deep inside her core, she has never been able to bring it to the surface for her to properly deal with it. And only by freeing yourself from the guilt, can you reach the crux of the problem to enable you to move on and deal with the depression and shame that forms part of the package. That is her take on it all anyway, from what she has learned over the years. Name a video, she has watched it twice-over. Suggest a self-help book, she has read it cover to cover. Propose a podcast, she has listened to it time and again. Mindfulness and meditation, she has ticked both those boxes. 'I've sat opposite many a professional, claiming they could cure me as well,' she says. 'I'm a good person, I did a bad thing. I should move on.' She emits an uncontrolled moan. 'But I can't forgive myself. Because I didn't only do something bad. I did something unforgive-able. I betrayed your papa.'

She tells me that at the beginning of every day, when Papa says, "Morning, love," he might as well add, "How would you like your guilt dished up this morning? Poached, scrambled, or boiled?"

'It wasn't even fun,' she says, screwing up her features and shaking her head in disgust. 'I was caught at a low moment: fed up, stuck at home alone every night while your papa worked. Work, work, work, that's all he did in those days. Because he could never say no to Cara Bloody De Rosa. Then a friend invited me out one night. It was the sixth or seventh time she'd asked. I couldn't put her off anymore. I'd used up every excuse under the sun. It was only meant to be a few drinks at a local pub which should've ended in time for me to be home long before your papa finished work for the night. Our neighbour babysat Milana. "It's good to see you getting out," she said. "Spending every night on your own at your age is not good." People were noticing. It was when I went to the bar to order another round, he approached me. He asked me to let him buy my drink.'

'And?' I say.

'One thing led to another.' She groans loudly. 'I can't even bring myself to tell you any more.' She lowers her head. 'I'm so ashamed.'

'You need to explain yourself, Mamma.'

'I can't, because I still can't understand what made me do what I did. Ever since I can remember, all I ever wanted was a family.'

I always knew she was the impatient child who couldn't wait to grow up, so she could have a family of her own. She has often told me the story of when, on her fifth birthday, her parents bought her a Tiny Tears dolly. It had pale blonde hair and a white nylon dress and came with a bottle with a pink teat. From the moment she unwrapped her gift, she fell in love. She called it Dorothy because she was a fan of *The Wizard of Oz* and thought Dorothy Gale was the most beautiful girl in the world. They became inseparable. Her family knew how much she adored this plastic human she treated like a real baby, so the following year they bought Dorothy a sister she christened Daisy.

'My dream was to get married and have two children, like my Dorothy and Daisy. And that's what I was blessed with. As soon as I met your papa, I knew he was the one. The day my brother walked me down the aisle, I was the happiest girl on this planet. I was barely eighteen. So young, I know, but it didn't matter. You know how that feels.'

I do know. I was only eighteen when I married Matt. Everyone advised me against it. "Wait a while," they said. "What's the hurry?" they asked. Matt wanted us to be married before our baby arrived. He was a little old-fashioned. Not that I hesitated for a moment when he dropped down on one knee.

Mamma continues. 'Money was scarce, but I didn't care. Money was never on my agenda. Your papa placed a big tick in every other box. He was a family man and a grafter. Traits he inherited from Cara. It could've all been so perfect. I could've been so happy.' She shakes her head, looking at me with desperation. 'So, why I screwed it all up, I'll never understand.'

She tells me that nine months after their wedding, Milana slipped out as easy as a kid out of a water flume. Mamma was blissfully content. Life was good. No, life was perfect.

Then it was as if the author of her life switched from penning perfect romance to writing sickening horror.

'Your birth was a completely different story. As if God was punishing me for my sins. I was in labour for three days, then it all got complicated, and they had to slice me open to get you out. Cara took over, because I couldn't get out of bed. It was only a matter of time before I realised why. Whenever I looked at you, the overwhelming guilt and sadness reminded me of my sleazy mistake.'

Cara went to stay and help. A temporary arrangement to help her over the baby blues, Mamma tells me. But the baby blues turned into depression, graduating from blue to grey to the darkest black, and Cara wouldn't leave. Instead of Mamma bonding with me, it was Cara who stole that entitlement, and by the time I was able to walk, and Mamma was able to care, it was way too late.

'Cara guessed. At what point exactly, she couldn't say when she finally confronted me. She sat on the edge of the bed and stated, "She's not Don's baby, is she?" My tears answered her question.'

I take a large gulp of air. 'Nonna knew! All this time, she

knew she wasn't my real nonna? How could she keep this from me?'

She frowns, fidgeting in the chair. 'Don't judge her. It's complicated. People do what they think is right at the time. She said I should've been honest from the beginning. I should've confessed as soon as I found out I was pregnant. She's been on about it again lately, saying it's never too late to come clean.' She sighs deeply. 'Cara had so many wise words for me. You know what she's like. "Something or someone will eventually expose you," she said. "Living with this kind of deceit will kill you in the end. It's how cancer manifests itself. It's what weakens the heart and damages the immune system. It's what makes you drink too much whiskey."'

I'm finally understanding why Mamma was never around for me. She couldn't help it. Her toxic mistake destroyed her nurturing nature and replaced it with a self-destruct button.

Her chin drops to her chest. 'But how do you admit to your husband that you have committed the most immoral of crimes, and the daughter he cherishes is not his?'

TWENTY-NINE

'He doesn't know?' I ask. 'Still? After all this time?'

The divulgence of her secret has rendered her speech-less. Her shoulders are slumped as if she wants to curl into a ball and roll back in time.

'How do you know for sure, then? You and Papa must've still been sleeping together.' My voice trembles. 'He could be my real papa,' I add in hope. 'Answer me!'

I startle her out of her trance. Her head jolts up to look at me. 'Of course, we slept together, but not often. Working at De Rosa's is not exactly conducive to a healthy marriage, especially in the early days. Your papa worked such long hours. I didn't know for sure at first, but I had a pretty good idea from the dates. And then, the second they put you in my arms, I knew.'

'How?'

'I just did.'

'Then how come Papa never guessed?'

'He was so busy back then, Sienna,' she says.

'He still is.'

'I hardly saw him.' She raises her hands towards the office door. 'This place was taking off. Cara and Nico had your papa working all hours. Don't get me wrong. We did well from it. He brought home a healthy paycheque every month; significantly more than he would've working anywhere else. That's one thing I can say for Cara. She's always been generous. We had a nice home. I didn't need to work, but I would have swapped the money any day to spend more time as a family. By the time your papa had cleared up for the night, he often didn't arrive home until the early hours. The only day he had off was Monday. And upon Cara's insistence, we invariably went to her house for dinner. Then, when you were older, and I knew it was possible to arrange the same paternity test you're considering, well, of course, I did it.'

My stomach is churning. I'm finding this vomit of truth hard to digest. I think I'm going to be sick. 'How could you keep this from us?'

'Because I love you. Believe me, Sienna, you're all my world. I know I don't always show it, but that's what guilt does to you.'

I feel sorry for her at this point. I know more than anyone what it's like to live with guilt.

'I made a dreadful, dreadful mistake. But your papa would leave me if he found out the truth, I know he would. I don't want to break up my family. We belong together.'

'Is Milana Papa's real daughter?'

'Yes.'

'How can I live with this information and keep it from him? You can't expect me to. I'm not that kind of person.'

'You have to.'

'I can't. No way.'

But the look in her eyes tells me I must find a way.

'What are the benefits of him knowing this now, Sienna? It'll hurt him dreadfully. And what will it do to your relationship with him?'

A knock at the door halts the conversation. Mamma turns her face from view as a waitress pops her head around the door. 'It's swamped out here,' she says. 'We need some help. Customers are complaining about the service.'

'We'll be right with you,' I call out to her. As she closes the door, I turn to Mamma. 'We need to continue this conversation. Freshen up and get back to work. We have a business to run.'

That's what Nonna would say. She would tell everyone to don their coat of bravery and soldier on. I can hear her voice as if she is standing in the room saying, "Come on, people. We have a business to run."

I feel numb, emotionally pummelled, like I've gone twelve rounds in a boxing ring with a heavy weight fighter striking emotional blows. I rush out of the office to deal with the complaining customer, placating her with twenty-five per cent off the bill. It's what Nonna would have done. 'See you again soon,' I say with the best smile I can manage. After organising the other waitresses with encouraging words that we *will* get through the day, I rush to the kitchen to fetch another order.

'Sienna.'

Jared is holding a plate of bruschetta out to me. 'Your favourite. I even added a splash of balsamic vinegar just for you.' I stare at the thumb-sized slices of rustic bread topped with oily slivers of baby tomatoes, shreds of basil, and the optimum sprinkling of salt and pepper. They look so appetising, but I'm not hungry. Mamma's revelations have ruined my appetite.

'Have one,' Jared says. Picking up a serving spoon, he scoops up a bruschetta and presents it to me.

'Another two orders,' a waitress shouts, rushing into the kitchen. 'Sweet Jesus, it's a madhouse out there today.'

I pop Jared's offering into my mouth and take a second one that he holds out to me. I stand eating as I stare out of the back door. Beyond the courtyard garden, through the open gate, I can see Papa kneeling at the boot of his car, still dealing with his trip to the wholesalers. A bag must have split; he is gathering items from the ground and throwing them in another bag. I watch him struggling up the path with two boxes under his arms and two bags in his hands, muttering to himself. If I could hear his mumbles, my guess would be, he is expressing how fed up he is with life. There is a heaviness to his shoulders I've never noted before, drooping with the weight of Nonna's absence. Poor Papa. Mamma's right. How can we crush him with any more at a time like this? What's the point?

He steps into the kitchen, frowning, and rests the heavy bags on the side, trying to catch his breath. The boxes have proved too much of a challenge. One of them falls to the floor. 'What a day! I'm so behind.' He looks like he might break down – a sight that makes me feel even sicker. I've only ever seen Papa cry once. The day Nonno Nico died. They shut the restaurant, and he came home sobbing.

Tears prick my eyes. For him. For me. For us – the man I've called Papa my whole life. When I handed over the money for the paternity test kit to the cashier yesterday, I said a silent prayer. Please let me be wrong. But I knew I wasn't.

I start shaking. It must be the cold, although I feel hot. An uneasy feeling sits in the pit of my stomach like the aftertaste of a bad meal. I don't feel good. My hands are clammy. I need to get back to work. 'Want some help, Papa?' Am I slurring my words? The bruschetta repeats on me. The room spins. Something feels wrong. I want to sit down.

I make my way through the kitchen and into the restaurant. It's noisier than before as if one hundred drunk people have arrived and are shouting for service all at once. A thumping sensation grinds my belly. Again, I think I'm going to be sick. The sharp taste of tomato shoots up into my throat. I'm certain someone is trying to pull my legs from under me. I spin around. What is happening? 'Someone help me,' I try to shout out, but the words cling to my throat, unable to leave my mouth. My blood is boiling, bubbling through me. Why is it so hot in here? Mamma beckons me over to her, nodding towards a table of customers who have recently arrived. I try to shout out again, but the obstinate words cling to my throat like blisters. Panic rises from my gut, fear twisting and turning inside me. I swallow hard. A man jumps up in front of me.

Are there two of him? The room is spinning. My hands are cramping up, my heart beating faster and faster.

I grab the back of a customer's chair, catching the handbag hanging over the back, which falls to the floor. The woman jolts around, kicking her handbag under the chair. The bruschetta repeats on me again. I'm tired, so tired. I must lay down.

I've been poisoned.

Jared has poisoned me.

THIRTY

When I come round, Mamma and a waitress help me to the office. We pass a busy table of customers, where the empty plate of Jared's bruschetta sits amongst glasses of wine. They have demolished the lot. One of the guests has a Santa hat on. He is digging into a sack and presenting small gifts with a ho-ho-ho. Mamma says to the waitress, 'Get Sienna a glass of water, please.' She turns to me, 'I hope you haven't picked up Milana's bug. That's all we need.'

I want to ask her if it's any surprise I blacked out given the bombshell of secrets she has exploded in my face, but instead, I tell her, I'm fine. 'I haven't eaten today, and I came over light-headed, that's all.'

'That's ridiculous. There's a whole kitchen of food out there.'

She leaves to fetch me a sandwich. I find my phone and search for DS Durant's number. 'I have nothing on the guy, Sienna. I questioned him extensively,' he says when I relay my suspicions about Jared. 'We need to wait until your grandma's bloods come back. In the meantime, I'll speak to him again when I get the chance. See if I can get anything else out of him. Is there any of the bruschetta left?'

'No. It was served to one of the tables.'

'And they ate it all?'

'Yes.'

'And they are all still OK?'

'Yes.'

'As I said, let's wait for the bloods.'

Wait for this. Wait for that. I've heard it all before with Matt's case. I waited so patiently as each excruciating minute evolved into hours and days, then weeks and months. Until finally, the years smothered the last of the hope I had managed to cling to that they would ever find who took my husband from me.

DS Durant continues. 'I've spoken to the hospital again. Your grandma has had more tests. All results confirm she's had a stroke and a heart attack. Are you sure you're not being paranoid?'

Is that how I appear to those around me? Some pathetic misery who is suspicious of everyone? I end the call and throw my phone across the desk.

Mamma returns with a sandwich. 'You're looking better. Eat this up and get going. I'll get Jared or someone to walk you home.'

'No,' I say, sharply. 'I'll be fine on my own.'

'I need to get back out there,' she says, patting her pocket. 'I have my phone on me. Call me if you feel bad again.' I tell her to give me five minutes, and I'll come and help. 'We can't have you blacking out on us again. We'll cope somehow. Lunchtime will soon be over.'

'Has anyone heard from Milana?' I ask, looking at the sandwich. Any other day, I would have wolfed it down, but the smell is turning my stomach.

'I spoke to her yesterday, but I haven't been able to get hold of her today.'

When she leaves, I place the plate on the desk. Composing myself, I head to the toilets to freshen up. I stare in the mirror as I'm washing my hands. Circles of worry blacken my eyes, and my cheeks are pale. 'Hurry back here, Nonna,' I whisper. 'I need you. You wouldn't tell me I'm being paranoid.'

As I'm gathering my things in the office, papers Milana has left on the desk distract me. I thumb through them, shocked to discover a personal application for a bank loan. The next page reveals the details of a lease to another restaurant up for sale. Is she getting a loan to branch out on her own? I call her, but there is no answer.

The sun is low in the sky as daylight fizzles out far too early on this bleak day. Despite the cold weather, the park is busy with local workers escaping for a late lunchtime stroll, and mothers with prams and kids on scooters. I don't take my usual route. I bear left towards Milana's instead. She lives on the west side of the park in a two-bedroom mews house that Nonna gave her a small deposit towards, at the same time she helped Matt and me with the deposit for our flat. The biting wind penetrates through me, whipping my hair and stinging my face, as I hurry along. Full of unease, I focus on the exit of the park nearest to Milana's house.

I pass a family running around, a mother and father with two small kids playing football, makeshift goals made from their coats. Scenes like this are so hard to stomach. That could be Matt and me now, with Lola and her little brother. The baby I miscarried the day after Matt died.

Further along, a group of youths are hanging out on a bench, music thumping from a chunk of metal sitting on a youngster's lap. They stare at me, so I pick up the pace, glancing back when I've passed; but none of them is looking my way. I turn to catch the glance of a man behind me. Is that the same man who I saw leaving the pub before I crossed to the park? Is he following me, like the stranger who sometimes does? My heart skips a beat. Faster, faster, I quicken my stride. A feeling of dread grips my stomach. Who is he? I'm sure I've seen him before. But how many customers have I served in the restaurant? He has sped up. I can hear his footsteps getting closer. He coughs. I turn, cowering, and he strides past me, comments on the extremity of the weather, and bears off right in the opposite direction.

DS Durant's words repeat in my head. "Are you sure you're not being paranoid?"

Despite ringing the bell three times and banging on the window, no one comes to the door at Milana's house. I try calling her again, but there's no answer. I'm getting worried now. What has happened to her? I drop her a text asking where she is.

I skip the park and take the road back home through the streets where chimneys are smoking, and people are pulling closed their curtains. The orange glow of the streetlights leads the way. It's a longer route, but I feel safer. Then I panic. There are more people in the park. Surely that route would be safer? I scold myself for how crazy I sound.

When I arrive home, I wash my hands before nipping out for a quick cigarette. Bob is in his garden, collecting logs. He waves up at me and tells me, as he often does when he catches me out here smoking, 'Those things'll kill you in the end, you know. Knock 'em on the 'ead, girl.'

When I arrive at the hospital, Franco is sitting by Nonna's side, texting on his mobile. I don't recognise the corpse-like figure lying in the bed. A lump appears in my throat. A reminder of the helplessness I felt when the surgeons were trying to save Matt's life all those years ago, or perhaps an indication of how much I adore this extraordinary woman. Probably a bit of both. What Mamma told me today changes nothing. Nonna will always be my beloved nonna. But how she managed to keep quiet about this all these years, I still can't understand.

Her skin is sallow, her pallor ashen. She would be devastated to see herself like this. This is a woman who takes pride in her skin-care routine, encouraging others to follow her daily ritual of cream applications and facial exercises.

'No change,' Franco says, as I wash my hands. 'I've

spoken to the doctor. Same old, same old.'

I can't look him in the eye. The ugly face of infidelity has masked the man I have loved my whole life. I don't know if I even like him anymore. I want to have it out with him, scream at him. His wife is pregnant. He is going to be a papa. But what good would that do? I'd break my promise to Jenni. I could split them up when it's not an option either want. Not deep down. Franco still loves Jenni. I'm sure of it. 'You go,' I tell him, unable to bear sitting here with him for even a couple of minutes. 'Zach is sorting Lola, so I can stay for a while.'

'Are you OK, la mia bella nipote? You've been off lately.'

I shrug. 'Too much going on.'

He tousles my hair which makes me cringe. He glances at his watch. 'I need to get back to the salon. Rik is coming up here later. Probably best I'm not here when he arrives. I'm not in the mood.' He hooks his coat over his shoulder. 'Any change, call me.'

Nonna's mouth is so dry. Her top lip has cracked. Taking one of the glycerine swabs from the table, I soak it in the sterile water from a plastic bowl and gently clean the inside of her mouth. Blood stains one side of the swab from the ulcer a nurse told me about yesterday. I root around in my bag, searching for the beeswax lip balm which I brought along. With my pinkie finger, I scrape a smidgeon of the balm from the base of the small tin and smooth it over her lips.

There's a new occupier of the adjacent bed, a lady who is whimpering in pain, her soft moans clangorous in the bleak surroundings. I glance her way, but wish I hadn't. She is hooked up to as many machines as Nonna, and her deathly pallor resembles my nonna's ghost-like shell. I turn back to Nonna. 'I'm here,' I say. 'Please wake up. I have so much I want to talk to you about. Life's not the same without you. So much happened this past week. You'd know what to do. And I want you to tell me who has done this to you.'

She doesn't move a millimetre.

I talk to her for what feels like hours, pausing as nurses arrive to monitor the machines and register their findings. I look at my watch, dismayed to find that only twenty-five minutes have passed. Seeing her so frail, a fraction of the tenacious woman I know her to be, is unbearable. I kiss her forehead, cold to my lips, assuring her I'll be back tomorrow.

Back at the car, the tears I've saved for behind these locked doors stream down my face as I sit at the wheel, waiting for the windscreen to demist. I pick up my phone to call Milana again, but she has got in first with a text.

Starting to feel a bit better. Sorry I missed you today. Asleep all afternoon. Talk tomorrow. Mx

I drop a text to Zach, telling him I'm on my way, only to lose my grip on the phone as I press send. The phone bounces off my knee and falls to the floor, as does my jaw. I pull the sleeve of my coat over my hand and rub the windscreen, faster and faster, but it doesn't make what I can see any clearer. There's no mistaking the number plate on the Audi TT by the payment machine: R1K 1000. A woman occupies the driver's seat, and Rik has just embraced and kissed her before getting out of the car.

THIRTY-ONE

Thankfully, Zach is already up when I wake this morning. I couldn't face him. Not first thing. Hesitating, I reach over to the bedside cabinet. I open the drawer and remove the photo of Matt and me on our wedding day. I run a fingertip over his smiling face. 'Five years,' I whisper. 'I still can't believe you're gone. I'm so sorry.' I voice the regrets I'm still tangled in, like I often do. How I wished I'd gone with him that night to Nonna's house; that I never took his name; that I removed my wedding ring, because my fingers were swollen from the pregnancy, and gave it to him, never to see it again. And the biggest contrition of all – that I lost the life growing inside me, the child who would carry on his family name, because I couldn't pull myself together.

Stuffing the corner of the pillow into my mouth, I let out a tortured roar.

I drag the duvet over my head. The past week has let the air out of my tyres, and the thought of having to get through today's anniversary has left them completely flat. A week ago, I was at the restaurant with Nonna, happily decorating the table and preparing the food for a party to remember. Now Nonna is on her death bed, Papa is not my papa, and my uncle is having an affair. And so is Rik, by the look of things.

I tried following Rik's car when leaving the hospital, wondering who the woman was with him, but when I got to the exit barrier, I realised I had forgotten to pay for my ticket. Is she another Silvia Marcia, another Cara De Rosa? Is this his game? Have the next one lined up as he does away with the current one? Surely not. She must be a friend or work acquaintance. But how many colleagues do you allow to drive your car and embrace you like that?

I want to stay under the covers all day, but hearing Lola shouting from the kitchen, yelling at Zach to hurry up, I drag myself out of bed. Unhooking my dressing gown from the back of the bathroom door, I wrap myself up and make my way to the kitchen.

I wash my hands, then prepare a cafetière and pour myself a large coffee, stirring it for longer than is necessary. Fresh snowfall overnight has covered everywhere with a blanket of white. From the window, I watch Lola and Zach hurling snowballs at each other. My gaze is drawn to a line of terracotta pots. I've promised myself for the last five summers to bring those pots to life. Matt had been a keen gardener. He grew vegetables in a small patch at the end of the lawned area and planted annuals in those terracotta pots to jazz up the decking area. He was one of the upcoming new generation of men who wasn't ashamed to admit they enjoyed tinkering in the garden. The most love this garden receives these days is when Nonna drops by in the summer months to tidy up the borders while I get out the lawnmower.

When I step outside on to the balcony, I shiver. The sun has fought its way out of the deep well of winter, but it's still savagely cold. 'Come and join us, Mummy,' Lola calls out, scampering through the snow. She aims a snowball in my direction. Her face is rosy from the cold and the energy she is expending trying to defy Zach's nifty dodges. 'Ouch,' she screams as a snowball pelts her face. She spins around to Zach. 'I'll get you back, you meanie.'

Zach looks up to me, laughing, and beckons me to join them.

'Give me five,' I call out and take my cigarettes back inside to go and get changed. As I'm passing by the kitchen table, I hear Zach's phone beep. I glance down and see a message from Jared.

All sorted.

What's all sorted?

In the bedroom, I pull on a pair of joggers and an old hoodie. As I'm shuffling into my coat, I hear the unmistakable sound of breaking glass. I grab my boots and run to the back door to see Zach standing on tiptoes, peering over a fence panel into the McIntyres' garden. I sigh heavily. Not Bob's greenhouse! Lola, open-mouthed, turns and runs towards me, panicking. I hear the McIntyres' patio door whoosh open.

Zach and I exchange wincing faces. 'Whatever was that?' I ask, carefully negotiating the slippery steps.

'Sorry, sorry,' Lola wails. 'I didn't mean to.'

'Whatever did you throw?'

'I made a stoneball.' She points to three large stones along the edge of the decking area. Matt brought them back from a field trip to the Isle of Arran as part of his A level Geology course. I remember laughing at his choice of gift. But that was Matt, always full of surprises.

'Lola! That's dangerous.' I wiggle my index finger at her. 'You've got some apologising to do.' She obediently follows me down to a broken fence panel where we can slip into the McIntyres' garden. I really must get that panel fixed. It's been broken since we moved in. Bob and Eleanor have never complained, so it's never risen to the top of my agenda. Matt and Bob used to use it to pop into each other's garden for a chat.

Lola and I make our way up to the greenhouse, where I leave her to explain her actions. She dusts snow from her clothes where she has brushed past the extensive number of shrubs filling the borders. 'I'm sorry, Eleanor,' Lola says, embarrassment reddening her face even more.

Eleanor shakes her head, her arms wrapped around her slender body, massaging her shoulders. 'What will Bob say?' She winks at me.

'I'll sort the damage,' Zach shouts out from over the fence.

'Accidents will happen. Don't worry,' she says to Lola.

'Best stick to making a snowman next time,' I say to Lola. I turn to Eleanor. 'Let me clear up the glass.'

'Not to worry. I'll do it later.'

'I insist,' I say, opening the greenhouse door. I want to at least get that stone back.

'It's about time Bob replaced this old thing, anyway,' she says to Lola. 'It's had its day. Shall I tell you a secret?'

Lola nods her head.

Eleanor raises a finger and taps her lips. 'You mustn't say anything, but our children have clubbed together and bought Bob a new greenhouse for Christmas. One with toughened glass.'

I step inside. It's so organised in here. My eyes follow the vast array of potted plants crowding the three-tier shelves along three sides, and a line of bigger shrubs in large containers running along the middle. 'What a collection,' I say.

'You know Bob. Loves his garden.'

As soon as we moved here, Matt and Bob sparked up a relationship. I remember Matt telling Bob all his plans for our little plot of land: the deck he was constructing for the new table and chairs he had his eye on in the local garden centre; the greenhouse he was contemplating building; the shrubs he was going to plant. And, although our garden is way too small, he even talked about digging a pond and breeding koi carp.

Oh, Matt.

Eleanor throws her slim hand in the air, flapping it like a sparrow's wings. 'Move away from those two in the centre, dear. Beautiful plants, but they're poisonous. Come on, come inside. You'll catch your death of cold.'

'I'm so sorry, Mummy. Can we still go shopping?' Lola

says from the door. She is apologising for the broken glass, but I don't acknowledge her. Instead, my eyes gravitate to the poisonous plants, as an uncomfortable feeling consumes me.

THIRTY-TWO

Lola and I visit Matt's grave, as we do monthly, on special occasions and always on this day of the year. Nonna usually accompanies us. Today we take flowers and a personalised Christmas tree ornament I found on Etsy. It's wrapped in cellophane, but clearly shows my message: *forever in my thoughts*. Afterwards, we take a train to Seven Sisters then hop on a Tube train down to Oxford Circus. The zing in Lola's voice won't allow me a second's peace the whole way. But that's no bad thing. It's a day for distractions. I often wonder what life would be like if I didn't have her. I also wonder what it would be like if I could rewind five years, and I hadn't let Matt drive Papa's birthday present around to Nonna's house that night.

Lola's feet dangle over the edge of the seat, kicking the metal boarding, as she tells me in detail about the pampered princess party Jenni and Franco threw for her and her friend at the salon yesterday evening. She is wearing a red beret and the patent lace-up boots Nonna bought her a few weeks ago because they "suited her". As did the dozen other items packed in the stuffed shopping bags they returned with from their day out in the West End. Butterfly glitter tattoos cover each of her hands. 'You should've stayed, Mummy. You could've had a tattoo as well.'

'I needed to see Nonna,' I lie. Something I'm finding myself having to do more and more lately. The truth is, I couldn't bear to be around Franco and Jenni, too worried about news of Jenni's pregnancy, or his sleazy behaviour, leaking from my mouth. But how can I explain this to my daughter?

When we arrive at Oxford Circus, it feels arctic cold. The windchill factor isn't helping. I wrap Lola's scarf around her neck, and we zig-zag our way through the hustle and bustle of stressed shoppers. New Christmas lights this year form LED curtains that run from Marble Arch to Tottenham Court Road. They display festive symbols and messages of goodwill, which Lola reads out each time they change. 'Can we get some of them, Mummy?' she says, pointing to a street vendor roasting chestnuts. Their nutty smell turns my stomach. Matt always grabbed a bag of these when we came shopping up here this time of year.

'You won't like them,' I say and whisk her past.

We spend quality time together choosing gifts, and then Lola wants to head to Covent Garden. 'That's about a twenty-minute walk,' I say, shuffling shopping bags along my arm. 'Can't you get what you need in the shops here?'

She unfolds her Christmas shopping list which she must have updated only this morning, as the picture of the placard printed with *My grandmother is the one who brings out the best in me* wasn't on there when she showed me last night. 'There's a stall in the market that sells these. Tiffany showed me online. You can get them personalised. She got one for her granny. I want to buy one for Bisnonna. Please, Mummy.'

Hailing a cab is a tempting thought, but in the December traffic, it would take forever and cost a fortune, so I abandon the idea and head for the Tube. It's only three stops and one change. At least I'll get a chance to rest my feet.

Covent Garden is even busier than Oxford Street. Shoppers surge us along towards The Piazza, the wind stinging our faces, bags banging against our legs, where we find a small café tucked away in a side street. I take Lola to the ladies. We use the toilet then wash our hands. I give mine a good scrub. They feel extra dirty today. We order drinks and turkey sandwiches and find a seat at one of the wooden tables with metal chairs dressed in paper chains of festive colours. A young family occupies the table next to us – a mum and a dad with a daughter about Lola's age. The mum is pregnant. I stare blankly into my cup, listening to them chatting about granny coming to stay. Lola is listening along with me. 'Do you think you'll ever have another baby, Mummy? I want to be a big sister,' she says.

'Maybe. Want a donut?' Usually, I wouldn't encourage the extra sugar, knowing all the crap food she is exposed to at this time of year, but I've just seen the owner replenish the cake stands. Lola will want one of the reindeer donuts with pretzels for ears, for sure, and the need for comfort food is overwhelming. I leave her gobbling her sandwich while I go and order two.

We eat our food and chat about her Christmas list, school, and the snow. Anything other than the family next to us.

'Mummy. What's a bastard?'

I stop mid-bite. 'Wherever did you hear that word?'

'Jenni called Franco it yesterday. I heard her in the kitchen at the salon. They were arguing.'

'What else did she say?'

'She said he was a bastard, and he was as bad as his mother.'

What did she mean by that?

Lola prods my hand. 'What does the word mean, Mummy?'

'It's a child whose parents are not married to each other.'

'Am I a bastard?'

'No.'

'But you and Zach aren't married.'

'But Matt was your daddy.' She has the vaguest recollection of him. I do my best to keep the memories alive. The day she asked me who the man was in the photo pinned to the fridge was nearly as sad as the day I found out Matt was never coming back to us.

She frowns. 'So, if you marry Zach, will he be my daddy?'

Why is everything so complicated?

'I was married to your daddy, who was Matthew. If I marry Zach, he can be your daddy as well. You can have two daddies.'

'So, you are going to marry Zach?'

'Eat up. We need to go. And I never want to hear you say that B word again.'

The afternoon sky is darkening. Snowflakes swirl around us, appearing to glow in the icy wind like we are walking through a snow globe. We make our way along to Jubilee Market, dazed by the sensory overload of the crowds, noises, and smells. 'I'm going to get one of those bath bombs for Zach,' Lola says, stopping me at a stall of luxury handmade bathroom products, where the ambrosial smell of vanilla wafts from a burning candle. 'The sea-salt one. What are you buying him, Mummy?'

Swallowing hard, I say, 'I've seen a shirt he wants.' I cringe at how boring I sound. Our first Christmas together should be more special.

'He's bought you loads of things, you know.'

I glance across to the stall opposite selling handmade topsy-turvy dolls. Their beady eyes cast disparaging looks. 'You need to do better than that,' their V-shaped mouths seem to yell. 'You're a lousy girlfriend, Sienna De Rosa. An irrational, boring, lousy girlfriend. You don't deserve Zach.'

I wish I could be happier this time of year.

'I need to stop at the restaurant,' I say to Lola on the way back.

She protests. 'I want to go home.'

'I need to pick some papers up from the office,' I lie. Again. 'I'll be quick.'

Mamma is sitting wrapping knives and forks in napkins when we arrive. I see her through the window. I haven't spoken to her since her revelation on Friday. She has tried to call several times and sent numerous texts, but I couldn't find it in myself to respond to any of them. Remorse overwhelms her, shame mushrooming the lines above her furrowed brow. As much as I detest her for all the lies she has fashioned over the years to protect her secret, sadness overwhelms me for the mess my family is in. Nonna needs to get well soon. Everything is falling apart without her. The seams of our family have come undone, and only she has the thread to sew them back together.

The restaurant is unusually quiet. Then again, I rarely get to see it in the early evening and especially not on a Sunday. When we enter, the bell tings and Mamma looks up. Her bottom lip quivers when she sees it's us. A hint of forgiveness softens my tone, surprising her. 'I left some papers here on Friday.'

'How are you both?' she asks, putting an arm around Lola, but staring at me.

I'm tired, so tired. I can't believe a week has passed since Nonna was last here, proudly showing off Lola's ballerina birthday cake and ordering Papa to get a move on with the food. 'Bearing up,' I reply.

I leave Lola helping with the napkins and hurry to the kitchen, where the pizza chef is kneading dough, and Papa is sampling a pan of his indulgent chocolate dessert.

'Smells good,' I say.

'Not quite sweet enough,' he says, dulcifying the mix with a sprinkling of sugar.

I march out the back to the courtyard garden. Under the cover of the awning, along the back of the border, are a couple of plants. Are they the same as those in Bob McIntyre's greenhouse? I walk over to take a closer look. I'm almost certain they are. I whip out my phone and take a photo.

When Lola is in bed, I nip for a smoke, then, back inside, I wash my hands. I rub cream into them. I must pop to the chemist tomorrow and get some more of this stuff. It's helping. I'll get a few tubes to last me over Christmas. I squirt another blob into my hands as I plan.

I unwrap the box of biscuits Lola has wrapped for her class teacher and grab the note of apology I made her write before bed and nip downstairs to the McIntyres' flat. I press the bell, making a mental note to replace the biscuits as I wait on the front doormat. WELCOME is written across it with the O replaced with a big red heart. Bob appears. 'I'm so sorry for this morning,' I say, handing him our offerings. 'I will, of course, be paying for the replacement glass.'

'Don't you go worrying yourself. I'll sort it. Mishaps will happen with kids around. Having had five of the rascals myself, I should know.' His shriek of laughter makes me genuinely smile for the first time in days. 'It's about time I replaced the whole thing anyway.'

'Bob, can I ask you a question?'

'Fire away.'

'When I was in the greenhouse, Eleanor mentioned that one of the plants is poisonous. What's the name of it?'

'You mean the oleander plant?'

I dig out my phone and show him the picture.

He nods. 'The oleander. Beautiful flowers.'

'How poisonous is it?'

'Very. You shouldn't even touch any part of them. A viper lives in these beauties. A single leaf can kill. Why do you ask?'

'I'm interested. We have some plants like that at the restaurant.'

'Well, don't you go putting it in any of your customers' food.' Another holler of laughter booms from his mouth. 'You can die from ingesting it, you know! Any part of the plant.'

'Thanks, Bob,' I say, stepping backwards with a wave of my hand. 'Be sure to send me the bill for the new glass.'

I race back upstairs to my flat, my stomach in my throat. Firing up my laptop, I type oleander plant into Google. Images of the plant I saw in Bob's greenhouse, and in De Rosa's courtyard garden appear. I click on an image and study the text.

An evergreen, in summer, the oleander plant produces beautiful pink flowers.

This plant is highly toxic. A single leaf can kill a person. It can cause weakness and lethargy, dizziness and stomach pain, sleepiness and headaches.

The most serious side effect is cardiac abnormalities.

I continue reading, shocked at what I'm learning. Has someone been trying to kill Nonna with this plant? I read on, and what follows pretty much answers my question. In some cases, people speak of vision issues. Most notable are experiences of seeing halos of light.

THIRTY-THREE

Every piece of information leads to the same conclusion. Nonna was right. Someone has been trying to poison her.

Milana! Has the same happened to her? I find my phone and select her number.

'How are you?' I ask.

'Much better. I'll be back at work tomorrow.'

'What was it? What was wrong with you?'

'Food poisoning.'

Another call comes in. DS Durant's name flashes across the screen. 'I'll call you right back,' I tell Milana, end the call, and answer DS Durant.

'Can I come over?' DS Durant asks. 'I have some news for you.'

'What kind of news?'

'To do with Matt's investigation. I'd rather tell you in person.'

'Come right away.'

I press the end call button and notice a waiting voice

message. It's Gianni Bellini, apologising profusely for not being in when I called the other day and would I please return his call at my earliest convenience. I call him. He answers on the second ring.

'I'm most dreadfully sorry to have wasted your time the other day, Sienna. I'm not sure how much my housekeeper told you, but I was taken ill the day you came here. I can explain more when I meet you, which I am most keen to do. How about tomorrow?'

He tells me he's not well enough to travel, so I agree to go to his house again in the afternoon after I've finished work. I try to call Milana back, but I get her voice message.

I pour a large glass of wine and nip outside for a cigarette, my stomach turning like the drum of a washing machine. My head is spinning. Everything is mixed up, like the whites have been thrown in with the darks, and every-thing is a murky mess. One cigarette leads to two. Only the ring of the doorbell saves my lungs from a third.

After I've washed my hands, I go to the lounge, where, sitting in the chair by the empty fireplace, DS Durant delivers the words I've been waiting five years to hear. I've been dreaming of this moment. Not a day has passed when I haven't imagined hearing it. 'We've charged a forty-four-year-old woman with Matthew's death,' he says.

My hands grab the edge of the sofa cushion, my knuckles white. A woman! I'd always thought it would be a man. 'How sure are you?'

'Remember me telling you that we were given an anonymous tip-off? A message with a woman's name and an address in Northumbria. She's married with three kids.

She denied it at first, but broke down and confessed during interview to causing the accident that killed Matthew.'

Leaning my elbows on my knees, I cradle my head in my shaking hands, and the sobs commence. DS Durant comes over and sits on the sofa beside me. He puts his arm across my shoulder, pulling me towards the comfort of his fisherman's jumper, where he stifles the uncontrollable sobs of grief and relief that have been waiting to be released for five years.

'What happened to the car?' I ask, when I can finally speak.

'That we still haven't worked out. She won't tell us. I will find out. I promise you.'

I eventually go to the bathroom and splash my face with water, still in disbelief this day has finally come. The day I would hear someone is going to pay for what they did to my little family.

Once composed, I return to the lounge. 'I need to tell you something.'

'Fire away.'

I relay my thoughts about Nonna, telling him about the plants in Bob's greenhouse – the same ones in De Rosa's outside area. 'I'm certain Nonna knew exactly what she was talking about when she said someone was trying to poison her. You have to help me find out who has done this to her.'

His jaw tenses. 'I'm so sorry, Sienna, but I can no longer get involved.'

'What do you mean?'

'Things have got serious here. This is a potential

attempted murder enquiry. Another team will have to take it over from here. An investigation team more experienced in dealing with this kind of crime.' He tells me how deeply sorry he is.

'You need to speak to Rik. He has something to do with this. I'm sure of it.'

'I will pass on everything you've told me. I promise you.'

Grief and frustration, mixed with exhaustion, don't make for a tasty cocktail of rationality. 'I'm telling you, she was poisoned. Rik has something to do with it. Or Jared. Did you speak to him again? And what about the plants? Surely this puts a completely different light on things.'

'That's exactly why it needs to be raised. I'll make sure you get your chance to hand everything over to the MIT. This must be done properly, Sienna. You can't accuse people without proper grounds.'

'The what?'

'The MIT. Major Investigation Team. They are specialists in this kind of crime.'

'I see. But will you do something for me?' I ask. He raises his eyebrows. 'I've arranged to visit this Gianni Bellini tomorrow. Will you come with me? I don't know if he has something to do with it, but I intend to find out.'

There's a pause as he twists his lips. 'I want to, believe me, I do, but I can't. This is no longer my turf.'

'Please. I know he is somehow involved. I must see him, but I don't want to go on my own.'

'I can't.' At least there is a hint of regret in his tone. 'If he is implicated in your grandma's condition in any way, I'd get into serious trouble.'

'I can't go on my own.'

'No, Sienna. You don't go at all. The new team will arrange to question him. Leave it to them.'

I vent my frustration at him. 'What about Rik? Have you spoken to him again?' I tell him about the woman I saw driving Rik's car. 'You need to do something.'

'The new team will contact him. You need to leave this to the police. You've had a lot going on, Sienna. I've seen how this has all got to you. Why don't you get some rest?'

Through clenched teeth, I politely tell him it's time for him to leave. I've waited five years to find out who killed my husband. I can't wait another five years to discover who has tried to do the same to Nonna. I may never find out.

THIRTY-FOUR

The call from Rik arrives as I'm hurrying to the restaurant. I've dropped Lola at breakfast club. 'Cara's taken a turn for the worse. She's slipped into a coma. You should come to the hospital. I'm not sure how long we have left.' His voice is matter-of-fact. As if this hasn't come as a shock. Or perhaps this is his way of dealing with the situation.

The news has stolen my breath, as if a hefty weight has crushed my chest. I'm hyperventilating. I turn one-eighty. Back through the park, I dodge dog walkers, mothers taking their kids to school, and workers heading for the station. This can't be happening. Focusing on my steps pounding the ground, I speed up and run as fast as the slippery path will allow. As if I believe running faster will stop the beast of grief from catching me. But I should know better. I've been here before. Grief is a mighty force that will ensnare you in its trap however fast you run. As I unlock my front door, it catches up with me, pulling me to the floor as I scramble into my hallway. I try and resist until it beats me on the back with its invincible strength and brings me to my knees, where I curl into a ball and sob like a child.

Nonna's going to die.

My chest burns.

I can't go through this again.

My phone beeps. Messages to our family group chat fill the screen. Wiping my eyes on the sleeve of my coat, I read them.

Papa: *We should close the salon and restaurant for the day. I'm certainly not in the mood to work.*

Papa, always so sensitive.

Milana: *I'm here now. Nonna would want business as usual. Besides, what about the group of seventeen we have in for their Christmas party tonight? Let's take it in turns to visit her. I'll call the agency and arrange extra cover.*

Milana, always so practical.

Jenni: *We should pay Cara the respect she deserves and close. Sienna, you can't be on your own at this time. Where are you? Jx*

Jenni, always so kind and considerate.

Franco: *We can't close. We would let our clients down. We can't all be there at once. Let's take it in turns and keep business as usual.*

Franco, always thinking of others – or perhaps the pound coins.

Mamma: *We're already here, customers already in. Let's keep open. It's what Cara would want. I'm OK holding fort.*

Mamma, you surprise me. It's not like you to happily take charge.

I consider going to fetch Lola, but decide to leave her at

school for the day. Give her a few more hours in ignorance. Is that the right thing to do? I can't think straight.

What to do? What to do?

I make it to the kitchen, pain still heavy in my chest. I stare out of the window. Snow is falling again. I'm so cold, as if the thought of Nonna dying has tampered with my internal thermostat and set it to zero. This is how I felt after Matt died. So bitterly cold. I want to see her. 'Who did this to you, Nonna?' I cry out, smacking the kitchen sink until my hands won't take another bashing.

Another message pings.

Mamma: *Don has gone to the hospital. He's in pieces. Jared agreed to stay as long as we need him.*

I add a message: *I'm making my way up there now. Sx.*

I call Zach. I can't manage more than a whisper. 'Nonna's not good. I need to go to the hospital.'

He is gutted. I knew he would be. 'Give me an hour. I have a client call, but then I could take the rest of the day off. We can do whatever you want. We can pick Lola up and spend the day together.'

'I have to keep going,' I say.

'No, you don't.'

'I do, Zach. I do.'

'Whatever you need me to do, call.'

'Can you pick Lola up as planned? There's some stuff I need to sort out. I'll be home as soon as I can.'

'I'll do whatever you want me to. Keep positive, darling. She's still with us.'

I end the call and sob until the rage of grief thunders through me. 'I will find out who did this to you, Nonna.' I smack the kitchen sink again. 'They won't get away with it.'

Franco and Papa are at the hospital when I arrive. Nonna has been moved to the ICU. There should only be two visitors per patient, but the curtains are pulled around her bed, and I slip in unnoticed. A drip line has been inserted in her neck, and apparatus with a tube to her mouth is providing her breath. Papa is crying, a terribly upsetting sight. Franco is silent. Both stare at their mamma in what could be her final hours. They both acknowledge me with a nod. Franco stands to give me his chair. He rubs my shoulder as he updates me on what he believes is Nonna's gradual passage towards heaven. 'I still can't believe this has happened,' I say. 'Someone has done this to her, you know.'

'Sienna. Calm down,' Papa says. 'She's really sick.'

'Your papa's right.' Franco pats my shoulder.

I'm shaking, fear and grief and anger tensing my muscles. The curtains swish open, and a nurse appears wheeling another machine of doom. Two other nurses follow. 'I know these are difficult times, but only two to a bed, please,' one of the nurses reminds us. 'Perhaps one of you could take a break in the visitors' room.'

'I'll go,' Franco says.

'No. I will,' Papa says, jumping up.

'Both of you stay. I've got stuff I need to do. I'll be back later.'

I can't be here. I shouldn't have come. The fear and grief

are still pumping inside of me, but the anger is directing me to find out what the hell has happened.

En route to Nonna's house, I call Zach again. 'You know you said to call if I need anything. Well, I do.' I tell him about going to see Gianni. 'Will you come with me?'

'Are you sure this is a good idea? You know nothing about this man. He could be dangerous. Why don't you leave this to the police?'

'He's old, and he's not well. I'm not scared, but I don't want to go on my own.'

'What about Lola?'

'I'll get her sorted.'

'I'll meet you at yours.'

I'm on the phone with Maddie, arranging for her to pick up Lola from school this afternoon, when I arrive at Nonna's house. Seeing Nonna's Mini on the drive causes more tears. She loves this car. Papa said it doesn't suit her; she should be driving something bigger. Franco said she needs something more robust like his Range Rover – a king of the road. But Nonna loves how she can nip around town so much easier in a small car. I ring the doorbell, but there's no answer. Rik's car is in the drive. Where has he gone?

I let myself in, shocked to see a cabin bag at the bottom of the stairs. Where's he off to? 'Rik, are you here?' I shout out, but apart from the odd creak from the central heating, it's creepily silent. With trepidation, I hurry to the kitchen. It's a mess compared to the usual standard of neatness. The bin is overflowing, and dirty cups and glasses clutter the sink, alongside Nonna's lilies and roses, looking as dead as her, in the glass vase full of murky water. Seeing them angers me more. Someone is responsible for this.

I wander through to the lounge, which is equally as messy: the sofa unmade, cushions on the floor, and the pieces of Rik's antique chess set that Nonna bought him last Christmas lay horizontal on the board as if they've all been knocked over. The Christmas tree sits sadly in the dark corner, its lights switched off. It's so quiet in here, so different. It's the same way I felt after I arrived home after Matt died. Death hangs in the air like an unpalatable aura I can almost reach out and touch. I try and think back to happier times. Sitting in this room with Nonna reading me a story, playing backgammon with Nonno Nico, while he regaled me with stories of his youth.

Movement outside sends me over to the patio doors. The shed door is open, and I can see Rik. What's he doing in there? I raise my hand to knock on the glass, but stop. He won't hear me from here.

I turn back to the room. Papers on the coffee table catch my eye. It looks like the letter from the solicitors I found in Nonna's study the other day. The one about her changing her will that I took home with me. How did they get back here? Confused, I pick them up. The letter is dated two days before Nonna collapsed. She must have changed her will again. Pounding on the patio doors startles me. Cold air rushes in as Rik drags a door open. Awkwardly, I throw the papers back on the table; the paperclip flips off, and they scatter across the floor. 'What exactly are you looking for, Sienna?' he asks, stamping snow from his feet. He's wearing a turtleneck jumper and jeans, so different to his usual shirt and trousers.

'Nothing.' My voice cracks. Shivers race down my spine, freezing me to the spot.

His eyes are red. He is scaring me. I can feel my heart beating in my chest. 'It doesn't look like nothing to me,' he says. I flinch as he slides the door shut with a clunk. 'All you need to do is ask me, you know.' Striding towards me, he bends down and gathers the papers. I look at the door. Should I make a run for it? He clips the papers back together and hands them to me. 'This is a copy of your Nonna's will. She changed it a couple of times in the past month, but this is the latest copy she signed the Friday before last.'

I take the papers, my hands shaking. 'Who was that woman driving your car who dropped you at the hospital the other night?'

He snorts. 'Is that what this is all about?'

'Who is she?'

'Cassandra. My sister.'

I feel my cheeks redden – a flush of shame for doubting him. 'I saw the suitcase. Where are you going?'

'Away for a few days.'

'Where?'

His voice breaks. 'I don't know. All I do know is I can't bear to be in this house without Cara.' He sweeps his hand around the room. 'It's too painful. Everything reminds me of her.' He picks up the cushions from the floor and slumps onto the sofa, hugging them to his chest as he sobs. 'I love her so much.'

Have I got this all wrong? I stand and listen, overcome with emotion for this man who obviously loves Nonna with the passion that she has for him. I sit down by his side, and listen attentively while he maunders on, recalling memories of his time with Nonna. 'Let me get us a drink,' I say, when he apologises for his outburst.

I prepare the cups as I wait for the kettle to boil, thinking about his words. He loves Nonna, doesn't he? His tears are real, aren't they?

We drink our tea as he tells me how he met my nonna. His daughter, Fi, was over from California – a fleeting visit for work. Fi could barely contain her excitement. She had managed to bag a meeting with some big shot in the fashion world, guaranteed to increase the visibility of her fashion blog ten-fold. Given it was around the one hundred thousand mark at the time, Fi said it was well worth the twenty-two-hour return flight. She invited Rik and his sister, Cassandra, to join her and this bigwig – an Italian man named Simone who had long hair and wore a beige trouser suit and floral shirt– for dinner at a fancy restaurant in Mayfair. Rik was bored. Simone was a decent enough chap, but the conversation centred around women's clothes and was hard to follow with the lingo they kept dropping into each sentence.

The warmth in his voice mesmerises me. I've not heard his side of how they met before, only Nonna's. After their first encounter, she said she finally understood what love at first sight meant.

'Cara caught my eye as soon as I sat down. She was sitting on the table next to us, diagonally opposite me, dining with a friend. I couldn't stop looking over at her. It was her grace. The delicate way she used her cutlery to slice her food and feed small pieces into her mouth.' He takes a sip of tea. 'Having lost my fiancé, Silvia, earlier that year, I wasn't looking for a relationship. Silvia's death had left me numb.' He glances sideways at me. 'She died of a heart attack, as you know. We'd been at home alone, and I wasn't able to save her. At work, years ago, I undertook some basic life support training, but when faced with a live scenario, I froze and couldn't remember anything.

'Losing someone while they lay in your arms is not an experience you ever want repeated, neither are two future stepdaughters enraged to discover their mother had cut them out of her will.' He snorts. 'What they failed to understand is, I never wanted their mother's money. I have enough of my own. If the nastiness they had inherited from their father had been less directed my way, I would have signed Silvia's whole estate their way. Instead, the British Heart Foundation found themselves five million pounds better off.'

'You gave your inheritance from Silvia to charity?' I say. 'All of it?'

'Every single penny.'

I can't believe what I am hearing.

He carries on. 'It's funny, because another relationship was the last thing on my mind that night with Fi. But witnessing Cara clutch her chest and drop to the floor, I rushed to help. Everyone was panicking around me, but I remained calm. I knew exactly what to do. After Silvia's death, I took a first aid course with St John Ambulance. I never again wanted to find myself failing to save anyone's life. The guilt is too damn hard to live with. I should've been able to save Silvia.'

I reach over and squeeze his hand. 'You can't blame yourself, Rik.'

He raises his eyebrows at me. 'The same as you can't blame yourself for Matt's death. Cara's told me all about your guilt for not accompanying him here that night he died.'

'I can't help it.'

He continues. 'Cara tracked me down a month or so later. She sent me a hand-written letter.' He smiles fondly at the memory. Nonna loves sending letters. She has beautiful copperplate writing. 'Such a rarity these days, it made me smile as I read her words, thanking me for coming to her rescue. She'd been on my mind every day since the incident. She invited me to dine at a local restaurant. I accepted. The connection between the two of us was all-consuming. Then, as you know, she asked me to move in with her. Cara's a special lady.' His voice is fragile, as if it might break again any minute, like our hearts have. 'I can't bear to think of life without her. Despite what you all think of me, I'd do anything for her, Sienna. Anything. We have so many plans, so many places we want to visit, so many things we want to do. Now all I have is the fear of what we'll probably never have.'

I can't say anything, because I'm trying to control my tears.

'A few weeks ago, she told me she had changed her will and was leaving everything to me. I told her no way. That couldn't happen. I didn't want to be a part of it. I begged her to change it back. From bitter experience, I know how family members can react when it comes to money. You know what Franco and your papa can be like. But for all her alluring qualities, Cara's stubbornness is the least redeeming characteristic.

'I said I was deadly serious. "I don't want your money," I told her. She wouldn't take no for an answer. "I know you'll do the right thing, Rik," she said. She jutted out her chin. You know the way she does when she is being deadly serious. "No more secrets. This family is riddled with them, and there're all going to come out. I'm going to tell them everything, every single detail. No more lies for the De Rosa family. I'm just planning the best time to do it," were her words.'

THIRTY-FIVE

'Did she mean about Papa not being my real father?' I ask.

'You know about that?' Rik says.

'Nonna told me just before she had her stroke. She said it was time to come clean about all the lies in this family.'

He shakes his head. 'It was a secret she didn't want to take to her grave. Over the years, she urged your mother to tell you all the truth. I disagreed with her.'

'Really? You knew all about this? Nonna isn't my real grandma either?'

The sadness in his eyes matches that in my heart. 'You mustn't think that way.' He sighs deeply and thumps the palms of his hand on his forehead. 'It's all so complicated.' He asks me what good can come out of exposing the truth at this stage of our lives. The fallout could be catastrophic. 'Especially with Cara's heart condition,' he says. 'I told her she didn't need the stress. It's all too much for her.'

'But isn't it also about honesty, Rik? Doesn't Papa deserve to know the truth?'

'It all depends on which way you look at it. Perhaps he needs protecting from it?'

'Keeping it from him feels deceitful.' I pause, before asking, 'Why did you lie about Gianni Bellini? You know who he is and his connection to Nonna.'

'That's for Cara to tell you.'

'No, you tell me.'

'It's not my place, Sienna. What I can tell you, though, is I'm not a beneficiary of Cara's will. I was. But under my instruction, she changed it again; put everything into trust and made me the executor.' The sorrow of it all becomes too much. More tears drop down his face.

My heart goes out to him. We're both too upset to be talking about wills and beneficiaries, family ties and family lies. This is a conversation for another time. My sympathy comes out of I don't know where – the depths of my own experiences of grief, perhaps. I remember the excruciating numbness in the early days without Matt. I was beside myself. It was as though I existed on a different plane. There were two of me, my soul on one level, my body on another. I'd be crossing the park, and there I was, walking along, beside myself. I'd be in bed, and there I was lying beside myself.

Knowing how much Nonna loves this man, I can't bear for him to be on his own. It's wrong. Nonna wouldn't want this. She would want all of us to take care of each other. 'Come and stay with me. I can sleep with Lola, and you can have my room.'

'I couldn't do that to you. I'll stay at my sister's or find a hotel somewhere.'

'What are you going to do today?'

'There are a couple of jobs I need to sort out here,' he says in a desultory voice.

'Can I help?'

He shakes his head. 'I'll get up to the hospital as soon as I can. I'll call you later.'

'Promise?'

'Promise.'

I stare at him. Is the change in my feelings justified, or is he a good actor?

The atmosphere is sombre when I arrive at the restaurant.

Like a dark and cloudy winter sky, De Rosa's has lost its star.

Mamma is busy helping another waitress serve the morning customers. Milana is in the office, sitting at her desk, sorting through some paperwork. 'We've got a hell of a lot of work to do here,' she says, lifting a pile of documents into the air and letting them drop onto the desk. She has lost weight. It shows in the jut of her cheekbones.

'Good to have you back. I can't believe this has happened,' I say, sitting on the side of the desk.

'We need to pull together, Sen. Let's be strong for Nonna. She would want us to keep things going. I know she would. This is our busiest week of the year. I've secured extra help with the agency for the coming days.' She picks up a pen and scribbles on a Post-it note. 'I've spoken to Franco. He and Papa are staying at the hospital until this afternoon, then I'm going to pop up there. We're family, and family need to stick together at a time like this.' She drops her head and starts work. I'm dismissed.

Family. Does the fact we don't share the same papa change anything?

'I need to tell you something.' There would have been a better time and a better place to have this conversation, but my mouth seems to have a mind of its own. 'Papa's not my real papa. Nonna's not my real nonna.'

Slowly, she raises her head and looks at me sceptically, her nose scrunched up and her brow knitted. 'What *are* you going on about?'

She doesn't interrupt me. When I finish, she says, 'For fuck's sake. Mamma kept this hidden from us all these years? And Nonna knew as well? Who is your papa, then?' She stares at me aghast. 'And how do I know if I'm Papa's daughter?' She pushes against the desk and jumps out of her chair. 'We need to get Mamma in here. She's got some explaining to do.'

I catch her arm. 'Not now. Let's save it for another time. I asked Mamma that question. She said you're definitely Papa's daughter. She had an affair when you were young. And I'm the result.'

'Does Papa know?'

I shake my head. 'I'm sorry, I shouldn't have brought this up at a time like this. My head's all over the place. There's more. Someone has been charged with Matt's death.'

She stares at me, mouth agape, as I update her with the

news from DS Durant. She gets up and perches on the side of the desk next to me. 'Oh, Sen.'

'It feels strange. It's the news I've wanted to hear for so long.'

She squeezes my arm. 'I hope you can move on now.'

I squint at her. 'What do you mean?'

'It's been five years, and you're still as raw as if Matthew died yesterday.'

I give her a knowing look. She's right, of course. But she doesn't understand. Grief is like a fog. A thick, murky barrier between life before and life after that has become part of every waking moment. Life with Matt and life without him. It has slowly lifted, but the guilt tagging along has prevented it from raising enough to allow me to fully move on with my life.

She grabs my shoulders and turns me towards her. She squeezes them, her lips downturned. 'I know you don't like to talk about it. I can't imagine how painful it is for you. No one can know that. But you have a life to live. And, I know this may sound unkind, but I have to say it. You treat Zach like shit. He's as good a person as Matthew was. You always attract the good ones. Unlike me. I'm so jealous sometimes. I'd do anything to have a Zach in my life.' Her words shock me. It's so rare to see behind the usual façade she wears for the world. 'Hold on to him and get on with your life. It's what Matthew would want.'

'Moving on feels so disloyal.' I swallow hard. 'It feels strange to be having this conversation with you.'

'Because you never open up to me. Never. It's hurtful, you know.'

'Nonna is the only person I can really talk to. I don't know why.'

'Why are you still punishing yourself?'

'Because it was my fault.' A small sob escapes from my mouth. 'I failed him. He'd still be with us if I'd gone to Nonna's that night.'

She shakes her head, squeezing my shoulders again. 'No. No. No. This has to stop. You can't keep beating yourself up for that. Let this be a new beginning.' She tells me it's time to close this door. I'm young enough for many more to open.

If only it were that easy.

'You still don't look well,' I say, unable to talk about Matt anymore. I tell her about Nonna's poisoning accusation, and the police involvement. 'You don't think the same has happened to you, do you?'

She laughs. 'You don't really think that.' She continues laughing. It sounds wrong. 'Seven people at the party I went to the other night came down with the same symptoms. They think it was the prawn skewers. Never trust the prawns at parties, isn't that what they say?'

'I've been worried about you.'

'I think you're letting your imagination run a bit wild here. Everything points to Nonna having had a heart attack.'

I get up and flump into the chair. 'That's all I need to hear from you at the moment.'

She sits in the chair next to me, gracefully. Flumping is not something Milana does. 'Jared has agreed to take over the kitchen until Papa returns.'

'Jared? Really?' I pull a face, questioning his suitability for the role.

'Why? You don't think he's up to it?'

'Nonna said she wanted him to go, and I think he could be the one who poisoned her.'

THIRTY-SIX

Milana slaps my arm and laughs. 'What *are* you on about? You've got it all wrong. Jared handed his notice in. He was headhunted by another restaurant: more money, more responsibility. Nonna and I have persuaded him to stay. We don't want to lose him. He's the best chef we've got. We offered him a job to run the kitchen in Islington when it opens. We matched the current offer on the table, and threw in the flat above the restaurant at a silly rate. You know Nonna, she's not stupid.'

'Has he accepted?'

'What do you think? Nonna is hard to refuse. You know what she's like.' Her brow raises with fondness. 'She told him to take the offer.' She mimics Nonna's accent. '"Islington is the perfect next step for your career, Jared. You won't regret it. I promise you. Give it a year, and it'll be a place where all the staff will want to work." That's probably what Nonna was trying to tell you. She really wants him to *go* there. And he is. He spoke to me about it last week. You've reminded me. That's something else I need to do. I was trying to find his contract of employment, but it's not in the files. We're going to extend his notice period to six months now he's going to be in a managerial position.'

I bite my lower lip and drop my head. 'Nonna made it sound like he needed to be sacked. I was sure of it. His contract of employment is at her house. I saw it in her study.'

'When? I never saw it there when I was looking,' she says.

'You must have missed it. It's definitely there, in the bottom of the filing tray.'

'It doesn't change anything. Not for me anyway,' she says.

'What?'

'The way I feel about you. Sod the half thing. I'll only ever think of us as whole sisters.'

'Same here.' I pause. Might as well get everything out in the open. 'Why are you taking out a loan?'

She scowls. 'How do you know about that?'

'I dumped my bag on your desk, and I messed up your neat pile. I saw the personal loan application.'

'Someone's got to try to bail out this business.'

'Why are you looking at new premises, then?'

'Plan B if we do lose the Stamford Hill lease.'

'Why did you keep it from me?'

'I didn't. I've been so busy. It never came up. You're reading too much into stuff, Sen.' She stands up. 'Come on. We've got a business to run.'

'You'll have to do without me,' I say, smiling with jesting sarcasm. 'I'm too paranoid to be here today.'

Banging at the office door startles us both. Milana answers it to a staggered Jared. 'The police are here. All over the show,' he says, pale with shock.

'That'll be the new team investigating Nonna's accusation,' I say. 'DS Durant said they'd be on their way.'

'What the hell for?' Jared asks.

'Someone is responsible for what's happened to Nonna, and they need to find out who,' I answer.

Milana frantically asks customers to leave as police officers and forensics wearing white oversuits arrive, carrying cameras and wheeling a set of drawers. Most of the customers depart promptly . A few busybodies linger over the last of their drinks. A suited man, who introduces himself as DCI Peter Hobbs, the Senior Investigating Officer, tells them to all leave now. It's so formal. At least the police are finally taking this seriously.

A crowd has formed outside the restaurant. I can see them through the window – pockets of nosy parkers with nothing better to do. Milana is her usual cool self, following DCI Hobb's orders and briefing the staff to stay put. My heart races as the DCI introduces me to another detective who takes me to the office to answer her extensive list of questions. DS Durant must have told them to speak to me first.

I stay for a couple of hours, helping them with enquiries and relaying my concerns. At one point, the line of questioning makes me feel like a suspect. I can relate to how Rik felt that night DS Durant visited him. The DCI hands me a card with his details before I leave to pick up Zach and head to Gianni's place.

I call Gianni before we set off. I want to make sure he is there this time. A hacking cough accompanies his words. It's a quick call which he ends with, 'I'm looking forward to meeting you.' If he didn't sound so ill, I'd think he sounded creepy.

I asked Milana to lend me her car. Oddly, she was more than willing. The barrier that seems to have divided our lives seems to be slowly lifting. Her Mercedes CLS convertible is a far more reliable ride than my Ford Focus that has seen better days and let me down a few times lately. For months, Nonna has been talking about helping me to buy a new car, but I've refused. Matt bought me my Focus.

But perhaps the time has come for an upgrade.

The inclement weather adds to the journey, but it's time well spent. I open up to Zach during the hour or so it takes for us to get there. More than I ever have. His gratified smile, and the constant squeezing of my knee, tells me how pleased this makes him. 'Are you sure about this?' he asks as I slow down at a flashing amber light.

'I refuse to wait five years for the police to find out who has tried to murder Nonna. If they ever do manage to find the culprit, of course. I owe it to her.'

'You don't know that someone has for sure, though?'

I take my hand from the steering wheel and stroke his. 'I do. I'm telling you I do.'

Gianni's housekeeper answers the door and introduces herself as Ksenia. She is wearing the same clothes as when I was last here, her hair scraped back into the same tight bun. We follow her, my stomach turning. I feel odd. I'm walking through a stranger's house, but with a weird sensation that I'm at home. The low heels of her court shoes click-clack along the mosaic-tiled floor to a room at the end of a long hallway lined with impressive artwork of Italian cities: Venice, Rome, Florence, and Milan. Knocking on one of the panelled doors, Ksenia speaks through the crack between them. 'Mr Gianni,' she says, 'Your visitors.'

We enter the imposing room with high ceilings and panelled walls. Gianni is sitting in a wing-backed chair by the fire. A cylinder of oxygen hooked to a nasal cannula, assisting his breathing, rests at his feet along with a disposable bowl. The mop of silver-grey hair and goatee beard are no more. I recall Milana saying she thought the man she saw Cara take off with, from the Islington restaurant, was thinner and older than the image I showed her. His face is gaunt, his skin puckered, but signs of a once handsome man live on in his dark eyes and well-defined bone structure. The collar of his crisp, white shirt suggests he was only recently two or three sizes bigger than he is today. 'Ksenia, be so kind as to get my guests a drink.' He drags up a limp hand, acknowledging us with a quick wave. 'Pull up a chair,' he says. 'Make yourself comfortable.'

A half-empty cup of tea and a sandwich with only one bite taken sit on the elaborate coffee table in front of him.

His hands hold a handkerchief in his lap. When Ksenia leaves the room, he says, 'I'm so pleased you've come today,' and then erupts into a coughing fit.

I reach for the disposable bowl, but Gianni waves me away. While we wait for the episode to end, I gaze towards the large, double-hung window. The impressive crystal chandelier sparkling light around the room is as big as the chair he is sitting in, and the vast display of cultural artefacts suggest a man well-travelled.

He wipes his mouth with a tissue and says, 'Where shall we start?'

'I'll cut to the chase, Gianni. Is it OK to call you Gianni?' I say.

He nods and smiles at me. It's an odd smile. Formal, yet relaxed, as if he thinks we've met before.

'What business dealings do you have with Cara De Rosa?' I ask.

'None at all,' he replies.

'Then how do you know her?'

'She is the mother of my son.'

THIRTY-SEVEN

'You're my granddaughter, Sienna,' Gianni says.

At first, I wonder if he is confused. Thoughts flash through my mind, trying to decipher his words. Is he saying Papa is his son? Or Cara had another son who she has never told us about? But Gianni leaves me with no doubt about the specifics of our family tree.

'I have to meet my son before I die.' With great effort, he raises both arms and opens them wide, casting them out to the grandness of the room. 'Otherwise, who am I going to leave all of this to?' He drops his hands into his lap, the smile on his face heavy with regret.

But he has got it wrong. I'm not his granddaughter because I'm not Papa's real daughter. There are times in your life when you feel as if nothing will ever be able to loosen the knots twisting your insides. Zach shuffles closer, squeaking along the leather sofa until our legs are touching. He puts an arm around me.

'I guess I've some explaining to do,' Gianni says, his

shoulders stooped as if ladened with years of regret. Through laboured breathing, he tells us about when he first met Cara in the summer of sixty-nine. Their fathers were business partners and owned a restaurant in Sorrento, a busy town lined with noble houses along the Amalfi coastline. Trade was good, but not as good as it could have been. Securing good waitresses was a never-ending struggle. They were chefs, their fathers, excellent chefs. People flocked from neighbouring districts to sample their renowned lasagne Napoletana. But their skills lacked considerably in the managerial department. 'It's fair to say, their food pulled in the trade, but the quality of the service pushed it away,' he says, looking from Zach to me.

I sit mesmerised, enthralled by his story. It's such a contrast to what I expected to learn when I came here today.

'One summer, when Cara was still at school, they persuaded her to help them out. The best commercial decision they ever made. She was a natural. Ratings and reviews soared.' He gives a brief laugh. 'They became quite a match for the establishments crowding the Piazzo Tasso in the heart of the town. Everyone loved her. Such a hard-working young woman, it's no surprise she has made such a success of her life.'

I go to speak, but Zach squeezes my shoulder, suggesting I let this man tell his story while he still can. Gianni continues, explaining how, as soon as she left school at sixteen, Cara went to work for their fathers full-time. By the following summer, she was managing the entire restaurant, running a successful team of waiting staff and working behind the scenes addressing all the administration their fathers didn't have the time, or the inclination, to deal with. He worked for a local law firm, amongst other business ventures he had a hand in. One day, he took a high-profile client to the restaurant, and he remembers wondering, who was this beautiful woman taking their order with such grace? He didn't recognise the skinny girl from three summers previously, whom he met before he went away to law school. She had blossomed into this exquisite young woman.

'She was a bright girl. And bold! So bold for a young woman back then. Glamorous, bold and beautiful, such a unique combination. I decided to ask her out on a date, only to learn she had started seeing a local man, Nico De Rosa. He was never for her. Not really. She could've done so much better.'

'That's my nonno you're talking about,' I blurt out, before pausing to think. Nonno Nico wasn't my real nonno, like Cara isn't my real nonna. Because of Mamma's stupid mistake, I'm not a De Rosa at all. Not biologically.

He apologises between his persistent coughing. 'I'll never forget arriving for a business lunch one day to see her walk from the kitchen into the restaurant's tiny office, her expanding belly clearly with child. My heart sank. Disappointed is an understatement. She and Nico had a rushed wedding the following month. The family invited me to attend, but I declined. I couldn't bear to see her with that man. It was all wrong. She wasn't happy. I saw her after the baby, Franco, was born. Her mother looked after him, and Cara returned to work. She'd changed, though.

Postpartum depression, I think they call it these days, but not back then. Doctors didn't prescribe happy pills willy-nilly. Women got on with life.' He tells us how Cara mostly hid in the office after that, only waitressing occasionally when they needed an extra pair of hands. But under Cara's guidance, their fathers expanded the business and bought another set of premises in the neighbouring town. Cara dealt with all the paperwork, communicating with the authorities, sorting out the banks, managing the procurement and finances.

'That's when our affair started,' he says. 'I guess circumstances eventually drove us together. I dealt with the legal matters of the impending deal. Neither of us meant it to happen. It was wrong. A silly mistake. We both knew that. She was married. I was engaged to another woman. But it happened. The affair stopped six months before her son, my son Don, was born. The son I've never met. I knew he was mine. Knew it the night my father came home and said Nico and Cara had announced the news that their second baby was on its way. Cara wrote me a letter – slipped it to me at one of my business lunches – saying she couldn't see me anymore. Reading between the lines, she knew I was the father, but she didn't want to bring shame to her family. She said she had to concentrate on them. The pain was intense. I was heartbroken. Not long afterwards, she and Nico packed up and moved over here, to England.'

'And you never saw her again?'

What he says next floors me.

THIRTY-EIGHT

'I have to confess that, until recently, I've been covertly watching my son and grandchildren. For about a year.' He looks from me to Zach as he tells us about his regular visits to the bookshop diagonally opposite De Rosa's restaurant. 'There's a comfortable armchair in the front bay window, ideal for a quick read, or in my case, perfect for viewing the comings and goings of De Rosa's restaurant over the road.' He points to the floor-to-ceiling bookshelves framing the room. 'I've never left without at least a couple of books to complement my collection. I haven't managed to go there much lately.' He coughs loudly, indicating the reason why.

He looks up at me, a hint of colour tinging his ashen cheeks. 'I've seen you, Sienna, on a number of occasions. I guess it's the time of day I visited, usually mid-afternoon, when you were leaving for the day. One afternoon, I followed you. I didn't plan to. I was leaving the bookshop to catch a taxi home when I saw you walk out of the restaurant. You were going to the school. I crossed the road to the park and sat on a bench, waiting. Not for long, though. Five minutes later, I saw my great-granddaughter, Lola, for the first time.' He smiles with pride. 'Little Lola, what a delight. I followed you through the park. I couldn't help myself. All the way home to your house, Lola skipping and laughing. She's such a happy child, isn't she? It became a bi-weekly habit I couldn't break.'

A shiver shoots through me as fast as I've bolted through the park back and forth to work so many times. It was him! 'Gianni! Do you know how much you scared me? I've sensed someone has been following me for a while. It has played with my head. You can't imagine what you've put me through.' Thoughts flash through my mind. Looking over my shoulder. Running from shadows. Breathless with fear. I turn to Zach. 'See, I was right. Everyone thought I was bonkers, but I knew someone was following me.'

Gianni coughs between profuse apologies, his body jerking with each wheeze and sputter. I'm shaking. Zach tells me to keep calm. Heavy with the punishment of life, my head drops onto his shoulder. He kisses my hair and whispers, 'This'll work itself out.'

Gianni stops coughing. 'Do I wish Cara had left Nico and we'd had a life together, so I could've been a proper father to my only child? We can all live with regrets, wish we'd done things differently, can't we? But if we'd stayed together, I wouldn't have met my late wife, Mary, with whom I spent a happy forty years. Mary knew about Don. She encouraged me to contact Cara and ask for her blessing for me to meet my son, but I couldn't do it to

Mary. Deep down, I knew she'd rather I didn't. But Mary passed away last year, and when I got diagnosed with terminal cancer, I decided the time had come. I had to meet my family in person. So, I contacted Cara. Told her I wanted to meet my son before I died. She was vehemently opposed to the idea; told me it was best for me to stay away. "The past is the past, Gianni," she said when we first met again in the park. She said Don had idolised Nico, and it would break his heart to learn the truth.'

But he couldn't let sleeping dogs lie, he tells us. 'Then there's the money. The wealth I've accumulated with my business empire needs to go somewhere when I die, and I have no other family. I want Don, Milana, and...' He pauses to nod at me. 'You, Sienna, and little Lola, to have it all. And that's what I've told my solicitors.'

I can't believe what I'm hearing. How did all this stay hidden for so long?

'I knew where Cara would be that day I confronted her. I follow De Rosa's Twitter account. Milana had tweeted. In preparation for the upcoming grand opening, Cara and Milana were heading to their new restaurant in Islington. It was unlike me, but you know what? When the pearly gates are on the horizon, you stop caring.'

I wait for Gianni to elaborate, but a violent coughing fit prevents him from continuing. There's a knock at the door and Ksenia enters. She scurries over to Gianni, carrying a tray prepared with medication and a glass of water. 'Give me a minute,' Gianni says, and with a shaking hand, he picks up the glass and swallows the tablets Ksenia drops into his hand. She adjusts the dial on the oxygen tank.

Zach kisses my hair again. 'You're free to go anytime, you know. You don't owe anyone anything.' I lean into the comfort of his muscular broadness, grateful he is here with me, confirming Nonna's words, "He's always there when you need him."

'Gianni, there's something you should know,' I say.

His raised hand tells me to wait. He thanks Ksenia for the tablets, and once she has left the room, he takes a deep inhale of oxygen before he nods at me to continue.

'A week ago, Cara collapsed. All the tests and evidence pointed towards her having had a heart attack, and then…'

'That's not because of me,' he interrupts, coughing again. He takes another sip of water. 'Is it?'

'She went on to have a stroke.'

A trembling, frail hand covers his mouth.

'One of the last things she said to me was, "Gianni, stop Gianni, you must stop Gianni Bellini." What did she mean by that?'

He lowers his chin. Resting his elbow on the arm of the chair, he drops his head into his hand. 'I threatened her.'

I wait for him to carry on, but words are not forthcoming. 'What did you threaten her with?'

He glances up at me. 'I told her, I'd give her until Monday, today, and if she hadn't told Don the truth about me, then I'd be telling him myself.'

'Cara's really not in a good way. She has slipped into a coma.' There is an accusatory tone to my voice. It's unintentional but there all the same.

'This is the most dreadful news.' He is clearly shaken.

The coughing continues in shorts bursts. 'You don't think I caused the heart attack?' he asks.

I don't want to load him with guilt he doesn't deserve. Where's the sense in that? I've lived the past five years with an albatross of guilt plaguing my life. Constantly reminding me I shouldn't have let Matt take the birthday present to Papa that night. Gianni doesn't deserve to live his dying days saddled with a similar burden. 'No, Gianni,' I say, shaking my head. 'You didn't cause it.'

'Now I've met you, I do hope we can spend some time together in the coming weeks,' Gianni says. 'Time is running out. I want to meet my son.'

THIRTY-NINE

Snow lays thick on the ground and covers the body of the car when we leave Gianni's house. It's loose and powdery, but will turn to ice by the morning. Radio One was right to announce a weather warning earlier. 'You OK to drive?' says Zach. 'We could find a bite to eat, or a drink, before we set off.'

'I want to get home to Lola.'

Zach nods his understanding. I start the car. It's freezing in here. He blasts the heating and switches on the radio. The gritters are out and police forces across the country are urging people to drive carefully, describing the driving conditions as treacherous. I make a quick call to the hospital to learn there's been no change. Nonna is still fighting for her life. 'I felt so sorry for him,' I say. 'I should've told him Papa is not my real papa – I'm not related to him at all – but I couldn't bring myself to.' Zach squeezes my knee. 'I knew someone was following me in the park.'

It takes a while to get out of the street, but when I finally manage to join the main road, the conditions aren't as bad. I shake my head as I stop at a set of red lights. 'This is all such a mess. All because people didn't tell the truth.'

'It sounds as if Cara was ready to confess everything,' Zach says.

'Only because she had no choice. It's all starting to make sense. She knew the truth was going to come out about Gianni. I reckon she was planning to tell us all last Monday when she invited the whole family to dinner. Remember me telling you?'

He nods.

'She has always taught me to tell the truth. Lies will always come back to bite you on the backside at some point. That's what she has always drummed into me, but all this time, she's been the one lying.'

'She must've had her reasons.'

I glance over at him. How does he always manage to keep his glass half-full? 'I'll stop at Maddie's and get Lola,' I say. 'I'll drop you both at home and take the car back to Milana's. Maddie would have fed Lola; will you get her in the bath? Then we can tell her about Nonna when I get back.'

'Sure. How about I rustle up a stir-fry for us?'

'I'm not hungry.'

'You must eat.'

Beeping horns indicate the lights have turned green, startling me. 'It still doesn't answer the question.'

'What question?'

'Who poisoned Nonna?'

'If she was poisoned. As the detective said, she might've been confused.'

'It's becoming apparent she wasn't confused about anything else, though. Think about it. Jared, Papa, the decorators, moving house, and even Gianni. She wanted Rik to stop Gianni telling Don about everything. She wanted him to wait until she was ready to do it herself.' I shake my head, squinting. 'No, Zach. The confusion came in the way she expressed herself, but she knew exactly what she was saying.'

After picking up Lola and dropping her and Zach at home, I drive to Milana's, overcome with tiredness. Drugged by the cocktail of thoughts racing through my mind, I could fall asleep. All I can think of is a hot bath and my PJs. I open the window. The cold air hits me. I take several deep breaths as the traffic comes to a standstill. Playing with the controls on the sat nav, I debate taking a detour down Crater Avenue, where Franco and Jenni live. It could take longer, given the weather. I decide it's worth a try and pull into the road. I'm about halfway down, when I do a double take at a woman, the hood of her coat pulled over her head, heaving a suitcase into the boot of Franco's prized Range Rover. At first, I think it's Nancy. Is Franco taking her somewhere while Jenni is at work? He can't be. Something feels wrong.

I swing into a space, blocking the neighbour's driveway, and switch off the engine, watching her. Slamming the boot shut, she turns, and I realise it's not Nancy, but Jenni.

She should be in work. She told me she had a late appointment every night this week. Where is she off to? As she goes back into the house, I grab my phone. Finding the number of the salon, I press the call button. After a delay, a staff member finally answers. 'Could I speak to Jenni, please,' I say.

'I'm sorry. Jenni isn't here. She had to go home sick this afternoon. She won't be in for the rest of the day. Can I help you?'

'Is she in tomorrow?' I ask.

'We hope so. She had a migraine, nothing contagious. Do you want me to get Franco? He's out the back.'

'Nothing urgent,' I say, and end the call. There's no mistaking what is going on here. Jenni has found out about Franco and Nancy. She is leaving him. Oh, God. On today of all days. I wonder how she found out. I want to go and comfort her, but I don't know what to say. Can I feign ignorance when she tells me about his affair?

The house darkens, and Jenni reappears carrying a bulging tote bag. A security light illuminates the porch. Her face is stiffened with a steadfast look of resolve as she squinches up her eyes against the bright light. She has changed into a pair of killer boots similar to those Nancy was wearing at the party. Why is she wearing killer boots in this weather? She'll end up dead. She doesn't look like someone suffering from a migraine. Locking the door, she leans her forehead against the glass panel for a few seconds before hurrying to the car. Another security light brightens the driveway. She tosses her bag in the passenger seat, walks around to the other side of the car and climbs in.

Smoke pumps out of the exhaust as she starts the engine, fogging the taillights. I shiver in the cold of my car. What are you up to, Jenni? Or am I being paranoid like everyone keeps telling me?

When she edges into the road, I pull out of my parking spot. Our cars face each other, her headlights blazing my way like two shining eyes. She flashes her full beam, impatient, angry almost. I get out of the car and walk towards her, waving. When I get to the driver's door, she recognises me and looks put out; as if she is annoyed to see me. She opens her window. 'Sweetie! What're you doing here?' She is nervous, her face strained, and her usually immaculate appearance plain, but attractive, like a catwalk model without her makeup.

'I've been running some errands. Milana lent me her car. I'm on my way to drop it back. Where're you off to?'

She hesitates. 'I had a client cancel, so I came home for an hour to put my feet up. You know what it's like being pregnant. Can never have enough putting your feet up time, can you?' She half-laughs, nervously. 'I'm going back to the salon. I've one more cut and blow-dry.'

According to the staff member, she should be at home nursing her migraine in the darkness. She's not having a breakdown, is she? 'Are you OK, Jenni? I'm worried about you.'

'Never felt better,' she says. 'Must dash. Client waiting.'

She reverses her car and beckons me into her driveway so she can pass. It's like I don't know her. Is this her pregnancy hormones playing up?

I return to the car and pull into their driveway, allowing

her to continue her journey. When she takes off up the road, a little too fast given the weather, I follow her. Snow has turned to drizzle, misting the windscreen. I turn on the wipers, keeping my distance but not allowing her out of sight.

Passing cars prevent me from following her immediately. Three cars later, a van driver reduces his speed and stops to let me out. I pull onto the main road, flashing my headlights by way of thanks. I search for Jenni. I think I can see her, two cars ahead. Traffic is flowing, but there's no opportunity to overtake. I bide my time, keeping her in sight. At the next set of lights, she swerves into the left-hand filter as the lights change red. I veer in behind her. When they switch to amber, she speeds off. I manage to tail her. Ahead, she hurtles through another flashing amber. I can't risk it. Damn. I'm going to lose her. I tap the steering wheel, willing the lights to change. When I see green, I put my foot down. I stay straight, hoping she hasn't turned off anywhere. I hear Nonna's voice as if she is sitting in the passenger seat beside me, tapping the dashboard. "Slow down, girl. You'll have an accident."

A minute later, I spot Jenni up ahead. She deviates left by a small supermarket. I follow her. After a seventies low-rise building, Edwardian houses line the road. Pulling into a residents-only parking bay, under the brightness of a streetlamp, she turns off the engine. Her car fades into darkness. I pull into a space on the opposite side of the road. I should get out and ask her what she is doing here, but a voice in my head tells me to hold fire.

Stepping out, she walks to the rear of the car. She is

holding her phone to her ear, but she doesn't appear to be talking. Rain is lashing down. Lifting the boot, she wedges the phone between her shoulder and ear and opens the suitcase. She removes something and shoves it into her bag. It looks like an envelope. As she turns to walk up the road, she grimaces and throws her phone in her bag. I get out of the car and hurry after her, watching to see which flat she is going to go in. But she doesn't. She walks to the end of the street, where she turns left onto the main road.

Where has she gone? I peer up the street but can't see her. I up the pace, my feet slipping in the sludge. Looking through shop fronts, I try and spot her. I reach a cream building surrounded by black railings. It looks like an office block. The plaques outside announce that a graphic designer, property management company, accountants, and solicitors, occupy the building. The door opens. I step back. Jenni comes out with an A4-sized envelope. She slips it into her bag.

As I debate what to do, she crosses the road. She heads for the cashpoint, where she withdraws some money. Pocketing the wad, she makes a call, but it doesn't look like the receiver answers. She stares at the ground for about thirty seconds before making another call, as she darts into Costa next door. The road proves too busy to safely navigate. I hurry to the pedestrian crossing, seeing her ordering at the counter. I stab the button and wait for the green light to appear. After crossing the road, I stand by the bank, wondering what to do. The wind whips around me. Rain frizzes my hair. Something is amiss. I know I'm not being paranoid. Something is wrong.

FORTY

Jenni needs my help. I'm sure of it. I rush into Costa. She is sitting at a corner table under a red lampshade, aimlessly reading some papers. Her manicured nails tap on the envelope she picked up from the solicitors. 'What's wrong, Jenni?' I say, alarming her.

Milky liquid sloshes onto her hands, and a roll of expletives slide off her tongue. She grabs a napkin, wiping her fingers, and snatching up the papers. But it's too late. I have already seen the divorce application she returns to her bag. 'What're you doing here?' she asks, looking at me intently. Her elfin face is pale, her eyes small without her standard lashings of mascara.

Shouldn't I be the one asking this question? 'I have an appointment over the road, and I'm a little early,' I say. Two can play this game of deceit. I'm winning at this lying lark lately. Not that I'm enjoying it. 'Can I join you?'

She shilly-shallies. 'Sure.'

'I thought you were off to work,' I say.

She picks up her phone. 'Sorry, I need to send a quick text.'

It takes all my restraint not to snatch her phone to see who she is messaging. 'I'll get a drink,' I say. 'Want another?'

I leave her fixed on her phone and join the short queue, listening to the woman in front of me order a slice of salted caramel yule log and a festive spiced cappuccino. Jenni is speaking into her phone as if she is anxiously leaving someone a message. I order a coke and return to the table. 'I thought you were off to work,' I say again.

She keeps looking towards the door as if she is expecting someone. 'Sorry, did you say something?'

'You told me you had a client, a cut and blow-dry, so what're you doing here?'

She bites her bottom lip, silent.

'Are you leaving Franco?'

She lowers her head, massaging her brow with her knuckles.

'His mamma is on her death bed,' I say.

Her head jolts up, her tone aggressive. 'Don't judge me, Sienna De Rosa.' She picks up her phone and makes another call. 'You know nothing.'

Oh, but I do, Jenni De Rosa.

'There's a side to Franco you know nothing about. He has cheated on me for years.' She leaves a message for whoever she is trying to call, telling them to check their texts. Placing the phone on the table screen-side down, she glances at the door and looks back at me. 'So don't feel sorry for him. I've stayed with that man way longer than any sane woman would've.'

I reach over the table and take her hand. 'I didn't know it had been going on for years.'

'What has been going on for years?'

'His affair with Nancy.'

She gives a sarcastic laugh and yanks her hand away from me. 'Oh, that one.' Her eyes roll in a circle of disgust. 'His latest conquest. She's nothing compared to the pain he's caused me throughout our marriage.' Her head tilts to the left. 'So, you knew he was cheating and never said anything to me.'

'I've only just found out. I promise you, Jenni.'

'How?'

'I've known for less than a week, and with everything else going on, I've been debating whether to say anything. I didn't know if it was my place, especially once I found out you were pregnant.'

'Why would that make a difference?'

'I was scared. Scared you would hate me. Scared it might make you lose the baby, and then you would blame me.' I pause before adding, 'Is there any way to salvage this?' But I know it's a fruitless question.

'Nothing you can say will make me change my mind. I'm leaving him.'

'But Cara is dying. Can you at least wait a few days? And what about the baby? You've both wanted a child for so long.'

She shakes her head, her face pained with hurt. 'I've wanted it for years, Sienna. Me, not him. Because he already had you.'

FORTY-ONE

'Me?' I ask. 'What do you mean?' But she doesn't need to answer. The hurt ingrained in the lines of her face confirms the sickening truth.

Franco, my papa?

I swallow the razor blade of pain cutting into my throat.

Nonna once told me, at times, it's hard to face the truth, because the consequences are blinding. She loved relaying her knowledge of Greek mythology. The story of Tiresias was one of her favourites. The prophet who was gifted with information about the future but cursed by losing his eyesight as a result. The truth blinded him. Has the truth been staring at me all these years, but I've been too blind to see it?

No wonder Nonna and Mamma kept silent about Papa not being my real papa. My head spins with family dynamics. Nonna *is* my real nonna.

I am a De Rosa.

'I found out about his affairs, but I stood by him. I loved him.' She shakes her head. 'Then do you know what I discovered?' Her bottom lip quivers, the disgust in her soul feeding across to mine as I guess what's coming next. 'That's right. I overheard a conversation between Cara and Franco. Cara was trying to persuade him to put his hand up about his affair with Bettina because, according to Cara, "It was all going to come out soon anyway." Who knows what she meant?'

'You understand why I'm leaving him, don't you?' Her tone softens. She squeezes my hand. 'I'm sorry to do this to you, sweetie. You're the innocent one in this madhouse of a family. Yes, Cara knew. All these years, she harboured the sordid truth.' Tears cascade down her face. She brushes them away with the back of her hand. 'I loved Cara. Ever since I first met her, I've treated her as my own mother, but she betrayed me. Franco, your mother, and Cara, they all betrayed me.' With a steely edge to her voice, she says, 'Now it's my turn.'

'I've only just found out about Papa not being my real father. You have to believe me, Jenni. Nonna told me before she had the stroke, last week. I confronted Mamma. She said it was a one-night stand she bitterly regrets. She never mentioned Franco was the other guilty party.'

'Why would she let the truth come out now? All three of them have managed so well to keep it hidden all these years. I don't understand.'

'I think I know why. It gets worse,' I say.

She snorts. 'How can it get worse than this?'

'Do you know about Gianni Bellini?'

She shakes her head. 'Never heard of the name.'

'Wait for this.' I smooth the skin above my brows, trying to iron out the creases that have deepened over the past week. 'He is Papa's real father.'

'What?' Her face contorts with confusion.

'Long story, but I met this guy, Gianni, today. Nonna had an affair with him after Franco was born. Nico was not Don's real father. Gianni is.'

Jenni draws the words out. 'Blooodeey heeell.' She grimaces. 'This'll destroy Don. He loved Nico.'

'Gianni's got cancer, not long left. He wants to meet Don before he dies and was threatening Nonna. That's why Nonna was pressurising Franco to come clean. She was also saying the same to Mamma. In for a penny, in for a pound. Get all the lies out in the open in one go.'

Jenni stares at me, silenced with disbelief.

'History had repeated itself, and Nonna wanted to break the cycle, I guess.'

'So all this stress caused her heart attack?'

I shrug my shoulders. 'She told me someone had poisoned her. That's why I got the police involved. They're all over it. Zach told me about Franco and Nancy, but only last week. You have to believe me. He saw them in town together. I've been worried sick ever since, trying to work out a way to tell you. *If* I should tell you. Telling someone their husband is having an affair is not something you divulge without careful consideration. I had my speech all planned, but then I found out you were pregnant.'

She sips the last of her drink, clinking the cup back on the saucer, and stands up. 'Secrets and lies. Cara was right. However far you run, they'll always catch up with you.' She squeezes my shoulder. 'I love you, sweetie. I hope this doesn't change anything between us two. I'll be in touch when I'm settled. I hope we can all find a way to get through this.' She rushes towards the exit. I stare at her. If she has known for all these years what Franco was like, why didn't she walk away earlier? A question, I guess, only the betrayed can answer.

I sip my coke. Poor Jenni. Pregnant by that cheating rat. Matt was such a great husband. Hand on heart, I know he would never have betrayed me. Can I say the same about Zach? I raise my hand and pat my chest. Yes, I can.

We can't part like this. I push myself away from the table and nip to the ladies to wash my hands. They feel exceptionally dirty. I wash them a second time.

Rushing out of the café, I cross the road to get back to my car. Rain is falling, soaking through the snow, and turning it to slush. At the corner of the street where I parked, I stop. The cold air has irritated my airways, triggering a coughing fit. I brace my arms against the wall as I try to catch my breath.

I don't know what makes me turn my head. It's as if I already knew life hadn't beaten and battered me enough this past week, and it was inevitable more was to come. I squint, wondering if my sight is misleading me. A man is loading a suitcase into the boot of Jenni's car. She leans over and kisses his cheek. It's Franco.

This doesn't make sense.

What is going on?

I run towards them, slipping in the slush, each step confirming the answer to this question. It can't be.

It isn't. It isn't Franco. It's Don. My Papa.

FORTY-TWO

'Papa?' I cry out, a question more than a statement.

He is still my Papa, isn't he?

What defines a parent?

One of the many heated debates that has dominated the drunken evenings Maddie and I have spent together when we guzzle wine and put the world to rights. Is it the person who passes on their genes or the person who raises a child? The one who loves and cares for them, puts plasters on their cuts and scrapes, and reads them their favourite story for the hundredth time, just so they can marvel in their child's delight when they arrive at their favourite line? Matt or Zach, or both?

Hearing my cry, Jenni and Papa simultaneously spin around, startled to see me heading towards them. Jenni slams the boot shut and grabs Papa's shoulder, trying to steer him towards the kerb. I stop at a four-by-four parked a few meters behind them and lean against its headlight. Papa takes Jenni's hand and opens his mouth to say something but stops. I look steadily at Jenni, waiting for an explanation. Only five minutes ago, we were sitting opposite each other in that café, spilling the truth. Why didn't she share this scene of the drama? She returns my stare, slipping her hands from Papa's clasp and covering her belly. As if she is trying to cover her baby's ears. Concealing the truth, yet again. 'I'm so sorry,' she says.

'Me as well, Sienna. I'm sorry for everything you've been through,' Papa says. He steps forward, offering out his hand, but Jenni tugs him back.

'We need to go, Don,' she says.

'Is the baby yours?' I ask, my eyes flitting from Papa to Jenni and back again.

Their heads turn to each other, seeking permission to answer me. Papa nods at her. Jenni whispers, 'Yes.'

I exhale a huge puff of breath. 'How long has this been going on?' I point from one to the other. 'You two an item.' Their heads turn to each other again as if they need each other's approval on what to say. I raise my voice. 'No more lies.'

'A while,' Papa says.

My voice is choked with emotion. 'Do you know?' I say to Papa. 'About Franco and Mamma?'

He nods. 'It makes no difference. I love you the same.'

'You knew, and you never told me. All this time. How could you keep that from me?' I throw my hands in the air with disbelief. 'What is wrong with everyone?'

Why all the lies? Brushing everything under the carpet, praying no one ever musters the energy for a spring clean.

In the end, though, someone will always search for the dustpan and brush.

'You're still my daughter.' He chokes on his words. 'Don't you ever think differently.'

'Come on, Don. We need to go.' Jenni pushes Papa towards the driver's side.

'Where're you going?' I ask, confused.

'Away, until the dust settles, and we can collectively find a way to move on.'

'But Nonna's so ill. She could die any minute. You need to stay and face everyone. As a family, let's get everything all out in the open. That's the only way we'll ever be able to move on. You're not thinking straight, the pair of you. I know you're angry with everyone, but the police are all over the restaurant. They'll want to speak to both of you. You can't leave.'

'Don, get in the car. We need to go.' Jenni pushes him again, her rich voice like a blanket around the frostiness of her words. 'Go home and be with your family, sweetie. They need you.'

Don hesitates. He looks torn. He knows it's wrong to slope off. 'But you're my family,' I say. I watch, stunned, as they both climb into the Range Rover. Then it strikes me.

They couldn't have, could they?

They had the motive.

They had the means.

Outside the kitchen door of the restaurant, only a step away, the supply for the heinous act is bountiful. Papa has been creating dishes for the menu for the new restaurant for months, getting Nonna to sample everything. He knew

Nonna was changing her will. They had it all planned. Surely not? Papa is not that kind of man, and Jenni is not that kind of woman. Is he? Is she?

I don't know anyone anymore.

The engine starts. I hammer on the back windscreen. 'Stop. Stop.' Running around to the driver's side, I bang on the door. Papa turns on the inside light. He lowers the window. 'It was you, wasn't it?' I scream.

'What was me?' Papa says, startled.

I look across to Jenni. 'Both of you. You poisoned Nonna. I'm right, aren't I?'

'That's absurd,' Jenni says, frowning at Papa. 'What *is* she on about?'

'Go home, Sienna. You're delirious,' Papa says, pressing the switch to close the window.

I slap his hand away and lean into the space. 'You've had this all planned, haven't you?'

'Had what planned?' Jenni asks. 'I don't know what you're talking about.' She prods Papa's arm. 'Come on, Don, let's go.'

'You're both so angry at Nonna for concealing the truth about Mamma and Franco. You've wanted to run off together for a while, haven't you? But neither of you have any money of your own. It's all tied up in the restaurant and the salon and your homes, which you don't own outright anyway. It would've been convenient for you for Nonna to drop dead. She spoke to you about changing her will, which you were a beneficiary of, Papa. Fifty-fifty split with Franco. You thought you had it all sussed out, didn't you?' I frantically continue this tirade as they stare on blankly. 'Then she and Rik announced their engagement and imminent marriage, which scuppered your plans. So, you thought you'd finish her off. Feed her the oleander plants from the kitchen garden. Do it slowly, and it would be blamed on her heart. She drops dead. You get half of everything. You two fade into the sunset.'

Papa is shaking his head, incredulous. Jenni is laughing nervously.

She narrows her eyes at me. 'I've never heard anything so preposterous in all my life. You should know us better than that.' She looks genuinely shocked at my outburst. Is she innocent in all this?

She elbows Papa. Her cold words are like a snowball in my face. 'Tell her, Don. She's talking utter rubbish.'

Papa starts winding up the window. 'Do as Jenni said and go home, love. This is an impossible situation. We need to let the dust settle. Call me if there is any change in Nonna.' He pulls out of the parking space, leaving puffs of smoke in their wake. Frozen to the ground, I watch them, wondering how this could have all turned out differently.

The truth.

The truth could have saved this outcome.

Exhaustion overcomes me. Home. I want to get home, to hug Lola and Zach. Yes, I want to feel Zach's arms tightly around me, to smell his musky aftershave, to feel the comfort of his kisses on my head as he tells me everything will come good in the end.

But I can't let them get away with this. I move as quickly as conditions allow towards Milana's car. Wind-driven sleet compels me to fasten my pace. I dash across

259

the road, slipping. Slushy mess smears the road. I jump into the car. Shaking, I fumble for the ignition button then dig out the card DCI Hobbs gave me earlier. I dial his number. It rings as I engage the gear selector into drive mode. He doesn't answer. I leave a message.

'I know who poisoned my grandma.'

FORTY-THREE

I navigate the busy roads as fast as I can. As soon as I spot the Range Rover, I negotiate the other cars until I'm behind them. Don speeds up, heading for a red light.

'Call me as soon as you get this. I'm following them,' I add to my message for DCI Hobbs, and stab the end call button.

Sleet is falling fast, the wipers finding it hard to compete. Papa knows I'm following him, I'm sure of it. The roads are skiddy in patches, the grip of the tyres unpredictable. A torrent of emotions floods me. The culmination of recent events and revelations are proving intolerable. I feel sick to the core.

I gasp as the Range Rover zooms through the red light, at an alarming speed. I slam on the brakes, nearly losing control as I skid on the wet surface, gasping in horror at the scene unfolding on the other side of the traffic lights. Papa swerves a motorcyclist, who momentarily loses control. What are they doing out in this weather? The

Range Rover collides with the metal railings running alongside the pedestrian crossing. There's an almighty blast of smashing metal. A horror show slowly follows. As if I'm watching a film at a funeral pace.

I unbuckle my seat belt and run over to the chaos. Debris is scattered across the road. Passing pedestrians on the pavement are screaming and shouting. It sounds like there could be another casualty. Shopkeepers and customers appear from the surrounding shops, and drivers jump out of their cars to view the events that have stopped the traffic. People are videoing from their phones. Small crowds have formed around the Range Rover. A plume of smoke from its bonnet circles the air as a workman dressed in shorts and Timberlands waves the onlookers away, shouting, 'Stay back. Stay back.'

I hear my voice in my head but can't decipher if words are leaving my mouth. 'My family are in that car.' No one is listening, or no one can hear. I shout the words again, as I try to work my way through the onlookers. The two-tone sirens of approaching emergency services announce help is on its way.

A community police officer appears. She rushes towards the Range Rover, talking urgently into her radio. Her wagging hand warns people away. With accelerated force, she echoes the workman's words. 'Back up, everyone. There's a danger of fire here.'

Most of the crowd comply, but I stay put. 'My family are in that car,' I say to her, but she directs me away with the palm of her hand. 'The woman is pregnant.'

'Did you witness the crash?' she asks, inspecting the crowds and surrounding buildings.

Do I tell her about them running a red light?

No more lies.

'They drove through a red light. That's what caused this.'

'They'll be plenty of witnesses, and there's CCTV over there. It should've caught it. You must stay around, though.'

I hear Papa yelling. The community police officer's head jolts around to him. He has managed to escape the car; unscathed it appears. 'Help. Get her out. She's pregnant. Help me, someone. My baby.'

Events advance in a blur. Police cars, fire engines and ambulances arrive en masse, and the crowd of onlookers backs off. Beeping horns drive me back to my car. It's blocking the traffic, which has restarted, but at a snail's pace due to the atrocious weather and drivers rubbernecking at the catastrophe. I find a parking spot in a side street, a few roads away, and return to the crash, watching from afar as the ambulance and fire crew rescue a shellshocked Jenni from the mass of crushed metal. Papa is nowhere in sight. Perhaps he has been taken to hospital.

The crew swathes Jenni in a metallic blanket and helps her onto a gurney. Instinct has me running over to her, despite less than a quarter of an hour ago feeling like I never wanted to see this woman again. She is ghost-white, staring blankly at her hands crossed in her lap. 'She's pregnant,' I tell the crew.

'We know.'

As one of the paramedics opens the ambulance, there is

no containing my words. I lower my head to Jenni's ear. 'Were you part of what happened to Nonna?'

She turns her head, her eyes swimming with sadness and disbelief. 'How could you ever think that of me?'

I sit, slumped in my car, raw to the bone. I know I should have remained at the scene and made a statement, but with plenty of CCTV and a throng of onlookers, I won't be the only person to have witnessed Papa running the red light. Several missed calls from Mamma await on my phone with three voice messages to say Papa has vanished and for me to call her urgently. Rik has texted, thanking me for the offer to come to mine, but he is going to stay with his sister. He sounds different, a choking heaviness to his voice. Milana has been trying to catch me, as well. I phone her, but it goes to voicemail.

A call comes in. It's DCI Hobbs. 'I picked up your message. Want to elaborate?'

'I was wrong about Jared. And about Rik. My papa poisoned Nonna. Except he's not my papa.' I choke on my words. 'I think Jenni could've been involved somehow as well.'

'You're losing me.'

I explain everything as calmly as I can, but I'm fighting tears. I'm done in. I can't take anymore. I want to see Nonna. When I finish, DCI Hobbs says, 'I'll get onto the team. Leave it to us, Sienna. Go and be with your family.'

'The ironic thing is, Don was about to inherit a fortune from Gianni Bellini.'

'Love is blind. Greed is insatiable. Chinese proverb.'

'Not heard of that one.'

Milana isn't in when I get to her house to drop her car off. Always one to thrash out stress in her life on the treadmill, she's probably down at the gym. I drop her car keys through her letterbox and make for home. Despite the darkness of the day, I feel light as I walk through the park.

No one is following me. I know that now.

I see Milana in the distance and hear her call my name. She stops abruptly when she reaches me, hands on her hips, panting. Her cheeks are bright red, and her forehead shines with sweat. 'Whatever's going on? Have you seen WhatsApp? According to Mamma, Papa has disappeared. And the cops are at her house. I've been to the gym. I'm on the way over there now.'

I steer her to the edge of the path. 'You're not going to like this. At all.'

'Why didn't you tell me about Franco having an affair?' she asks when I've brought her up to speed.

'I was going to, then you got sick, and everything has happened so fast.'

'I'm shocked. Franco. Who would have thought?'

As I let myself into the flat, my stomach rumbles at the aromatic smell of ginger and oyster sauce. Zach rushes to the door. 'You look shattered. I've got dinner ready,' he says. He opens his arms, and I succumb to him, clinging to the comfort of his reassuring hug. 'I need to see Nonna later.'

'That's fine.' He kisses my hair. 'Everything will come good in the end.'

He leads me into the kitchen and Lola comes bouncing in, all smiles and sparkles. 'How's Bisnonna? Can I see her yet?' she says, then swiftly tells me she has got something for me, producing a handmade star from behind her back. She has painted it red and sprinkled it with glitter. 'I made it for you at school today.'

'It's beautiful,' I say, propping it up on the windowsill next to the felt sleigh, stuck to cardboard, she made last week. 'A star, like you.' She tells me about a new friend she made at school today – Courtney, who has moved into a house two streets away.

'So, how's Bisnonna, Mummy?'

My heart aches for the news about to wreck her uncomplicated world. Perhaps I'll leave it until the morning. Give her one more night of innocence, I tell myself.

But no, I can't do that. Not anymore.

'She's not good, darling.'

There will be no more lies, no more withholding the truth in the De Rosa family.

'Is she going to die, Mummy?' Lola asks when I put her to bed. 'I don't want her to be on her own.'

'I'm not sure, darling.' I don't know if this is the right thing to say, but I want to lessen her pain.

I lay with her, stroking her head until her sobs fade to gentle snores.

Dinner is ready when I return from a cigarette. The table is laid, and Zach serves up two bowls of delicious-smelling noodles. I wash my hands. They still feel dirty. I can't get them clean today. At the table, I try a mouthful, but I can't stomach it. 'You ready for this? I've got so much to tell you,' I say, crossing my chopsticks across my bowl. 'There are more skeletons in my family than a bloody graveyard.'

He listens intently as he twirls noodles around his chopsticks. 'Would they go as far as to murder Cara, though?'

I can't reply. I want the answer to be no, but I must face reality.

FORTY-FOUR

Milana calls the following morning from the hospital and updates me. I'm outside on the balcony, smoking. The night has left another sheet of snow covering the garden, and wind whistles around me, trying to defy the shining sun. 'There's no change in Nonna. Rik's here with me. Mamma's in a right state. Papa's been charged with dangerous driving.'

'Where is he?'

'Still at the station being questioned over Nonna. I still can't believe this.'

'What about the baby? Jenni?'

'I tried to see her, but I wasn't allowed. Couldn't get much out of them other than the baby's OK.'

'And Franco? I want to go and see him. He must be pretty cut up about everything.'

'He's only got himself to blame. The salon is shut; he must be at home. What a fucked-up family we've got!'

'That's one way to put it. I'm going to drop in on him, then I'll make my way to the hospital.'

'I'm going to need some help to sort things out at the restaurant.'

I tell her not today. Nonna needs me, and I want to face Franco. He has been trying to get hold of me.

Zach knocks together a fry-up – sausages, bacon, eggs, baked beans: the works. I find myself ravenous, despite the plates sparkling with grease. After we've eaten, he fires up the PlayStation. 'I'm gonna beat you again,' Lola says to him, waving a controller in the air. I switch on the Christmas tree lights. Her blotchy skin and red eyes tear at my heart; if it is possible to tear it anymore. It feels more real now I've told her. Nonna might never come back to us. Never. It's the never that terrifies me. This is how I felt when Matt died. He was gone, and he was never coming back.

I can't face never seeing Nonna again. Never speaking to her again. Never hugging her again.

'You sure you don't want me to come with you?' Zach says.

'I would, but I'd rather you look after Lola. I don't want her to be there. Besides, I need to think of what I'm going to say to him.' I shake my head. 'I need to tread carefully with her. Christ, how do you break it to an eight-year-old child that the man who they always thought was their great-uncle, is actually their grandpa?'

'I'll google it when you're out.'

'Not sure you'll come across such a scenario!'

'Believe me, you will. This won't be the first. If not, I'm sure I'll find a case just as screwed up.'

I leave the two of them absently munching a bag of ready salted, while punching away at their PlayStation controllers, and slip out to see Franco. I've been thinking about this all night. My mind is made up. Little will remain of my family at this rate. I don't want to lose him. He's lost his brother, because I know he and Papa will never speak again. He has lost his wife, and he is going to lose his mamma. Franco loves Nonna. I know he has done wrong. He's a womaniser. He's a cheat. He's a liar. But I know he loves us. I am his daughter. Who knows what tomorrow will bring? But, today, I want to see him.

There's freshness in the air as I crunch through the snow to Franco and Jenni's place. The sun is sending some warmth. After bitter days, it's getting brighter.

But as I turn into Crater Avenue, the sky clouds over. A sharpness in the air cuts through me. Another storm is brewing. I admire the efforts people have made with their Christmas decorations, until I arrive at number thirteen. "Unlucky for some", I remember Nonna saying when Jenni and Franco bought this house. The drive looks bare without the Range Rover, like a bullring without a bull. I knock on the door. It takes a while for Franco to answer, and when he does, his face cries out with the impact of the last twenty-four hours. He is usually so perfectly groomed, but today his unkempt hair and sunken eyes shock me. Poor Franco. Despite everything he has done, I can't help feeling sorry for him. Then a voice in my head reminds me;

he is not an innocent party. He has committed adultery. He slept with his brother's wife.

'Sienna,' he says, opening the door wide. His voice wobbles. 'I'm so sorry for everything.'

I step into his hallway, the heat a stark contrast to the cold outside. Putting any awkwardness aside, we embrace. It doesn't feel the same as with Papa. I can't say that anymore, can I? Don, then. It doesn't feel the same as one of Don's hugs. What's missing? History, that's what. And security – a lifetime of feeling safe. But I guess that's another life, and I need to familiarise myself with this new one ahead of me.

'Why didn't you tell me?' I say.

'Life! La mia bella nipote.' He pauses. 'I suppose I should start calling you la mia bellissima figlia.'

My beautiful daughter. I wince. It doesn't sound right coming from him. I draw away from his embrace and lean against the radiator.

He continues. 'I did wrong. I know I did, but life is complex. By the time I found out you were my daughter – when Bettina did the paternity test – we decided it was too late. It was a joint decision. Everyone was getting on with their lives. You were a happy child. What was the point?'

'I found the dustpan and brush, Franco.'

'What?'

'That was the point. You both thought you could sweep your sordid secret under the carpet, hoping no one decided to ever clean under there. But I have, and what a damn awful mess I've found.'

'I'm so sorry. I'll spend the rest of my life making this up to you. I promise you that, la mia bellissima figlia.' He reaches for my hand and guides me into the lounge. Papers cover the coffee table, along with several half-empty cups. 'The police went over the place,' he says. 'Took stuff.' A Christmas tree dominates one corner, beautifully wrapped gifts waiting beneath. Seeing them chokes me up. What a waste. Anger knots my stomach. It's so unfair. They had each other – a life together – but he screwed it up. How come then, I was the one who lost Matt?

He leaves me on the sofa to fetch us coffee. It's an old house but fitted out in black and white, unlike their marriage. But I guess all relationships have their grey areas. The sound of beans grinding in the kitchen flows through to the lounge. I lean forward and glance at the papers on the table. The prominent document is the lease for their new hair salon he and Jenni have been working towards. Half the pages have been flipped over, and his glasses and a red pen sit on top. Several areas of text have been under-lined. How has he found the brain power to concentrate?

He returns, holding out a cup of his flat white. His hands are shaking. 'Just how you like it.'

'I guess you won't be going ahead with the new salon.'

Police sirens whir in the background from outside. He flinches and turns on his sound system. Mellow music fills the room. 'Absolutely, I will. We must move on, Sienna. Mamma would want us to be strong. Jenni isn't coming back here. I know. But you and me.' He points to me and then himself. 'We aren't going anywhere.'

As easy as that? I stare at the flat white in the black coffee cup.

A knock at the door startles us. Looking at me, he springs up and rushes to the window. He lifts one of the slats of the Venetian blind, swearing in Italian.

'Who is it?' I ask, feeling uneasy.

He draws his forefinger to his lips. His face has turned a murky-grey colour. Another knock fills the silence. He tiptoes into the hallway. The knocking turns to banging. 'Franco, are you there?'

I recognise that voice. Who is it?

I hear Franco open the front door. There's a heaviness in my stomach, a pit of pain warning me to brace myself. I walk over to the lounge door and grab the door frame, peering into the hall. Only one thing shocks me more than seeing DS Durant standing at the door flashing his badge, and that is his authoritative words reverberating through the cold air.

'Franco De Rosa. I'm arresting you for the attempted murder of Cara De Rosa and on suspicion of perverting the course of justice in connection with the death of Matthew Mortimer. You do not have to say anything...'

FORTY-FIVE

My fingers dig into the wood of the doorframe. Am I dreaming?

'No, no, no. You've got it all wrong,' Franco says. Running his fingers through his hair, he joins his hands together, supporting the back of his head. He turns to me, his face white, his eyes black. Always black and white. He turns back to DS Durant. 'This isn't true.' He walks backwards, laughing nervously. 'You've got it all wrong.'

I step out of the lounge and glare at DS Durant for answers. At first, he is shocked to see me, then the sadness in his face tells me there's no way this is a mistake. I cower in the corner, my back shuddering down the wall as I drop to the floor. Two officers march in and lead a protesting Franco away. Other officers burst in. DS Durant shouts orders at them and runs over to me. 'I'm so sorry,' he says. 'You shouldn't have heard that. I didn't know you were here.'

'What's happened?' I can feel the desperation in my

eyes, pleading with him to tell me it's all lies. I can just hear Maddie when I tell her. *"What? Your father killed your husband? Your father tried to kill your grandma?"* I'm shaking uncontrollably. I can't feel myself. I'm beside myself. Once again.

DS Durant takes my hand. 'We need to get you out of here. I'll take you home.'

All I can think of is Lola. I don't want her to hear this. She can't find this out, but I can't lie to her. I have become increasingly embroiled in the deceit and lies that have infested my family. No more.

DS Durant gently pulls me up. Everything is out of focus. The hallway is spinning. I can't take this. He leads me outside, instructing another officer to take the lead. The wind whistles around me, a song of utter gloom. That feeling has consumed me again. I'm beside myself. My body is following DS Durant's orders, but I, Sienna De Rosa, am beside my body, stumbling along with DS Durant propping it up. When we're in the car, I follow his suggestion and call Zach, asking him to take Lola out for a couple of hours; the cinema will do. The tone of my voice tells him not to ask any further questions.

When we arrive at mine, I stand at the kitchen sink, scrubbing my hands. I can't get them clean. My joints are aching, my muscles tense. Like I've run a marathon without drinking any water. 'Talk to me,' I say to DS Durant. He is making tea. 'How can Franco be involved in Matt's death?'

He won't say anything until I'm seated. 'You're aware we've charged Jackie Blackstone with Matthew's death.' He pauses and rubs his brow. 'There's no easy way for me to tell you this. Franco was in the car with her when the accident happened.'

'Sorry?'

'They were having an affair. According to Jackie, they were arguing, and she lost control. Franco recognised it was Matthew who was in the other car that crashed and told Jackie to drive off. She freaked out and stopped the car a few streets away. He took over the wheel, dropped her near her home, and evidently, arranged for the car to be disposed of. We need to question him, of course.'

His words are difficult to digest. They've left a rancid taste in my mouth. 'How come this has all come to light now?' I ask. 'And how do you know it was Franco who poisoned Nonna?'

'I told you we got a tip-off which led to Jackie Blackstone.'

He props his elbows on the table and kneads his cheeks with his fingers.

'Carry on.' Why is he holding back?

He sighs heavily. 'I'm telling you more than I should at this stage, Sienna. But it'll come out soon, and I think you need to know. Jackie is Helen Myer's daughter.'

That name. I know it, but I can't place it. I look at him, frowning.

'Cara's friend.'

It takes me a few seconds, then it clicks. 'Helen, who

owns the clothing store near the canal? She is the mother of the woman who caused Matt's death?'

He nods. 'Last month, Jackie was down here visiting her and broke down, confessing to Helen about what happened in that car five years ago. Helen begged Jackie to give herself up, but she wouldn't. Helen had put two and two together, realising the De Rosa family was involved. She told Cara everything, warning her she was going to the police.'

'And Nonna kept this to herself?'

'Apparently not. They jointly decided to give their children each an ultimatum. Helen told Jackie she would give her a week to hand herself in, or she would go to the police, and Cara told Franco the same.'

'And Franco has tried to murder Nonna for this reason? How can you be sure?'

'After what you told DCI Hobbs about Don and Jenni, officers went to your parents' house and Franco and Jenni's place and seized items. What they thought was Jenni's laptop, turned out to be Franco's. The search history revealed several sites relating to the oleander plant. When we questioned Jenni, she expounded on matters. Do you know about the vol-au-vents she makes this time of year for their salon clients?'

Blankly, I nod. 'Jenni's spicy Christmas prawn vol-au-vents. Nonna loves them.' I'm shivering with each word, the bitter coldness of the crimes here, freezing me to the core.

DS Durant continues. 'Jenni believes Franco has been

lacing a few for Cara when she has been at the salon getting her hair done. On the day before Cara collapsed with her second heart attack, Jenni found Franco in the kitchen, preparing some for Cara. He must've put extra chilli in that day because Jenni remembers Cara commenting on how spicy that batch was. They made her cough, and she asked for a glass of water. That's how he hid the taste. Jenni said she thinks he had the oleander wrapped in a piece of foil. She saw him put it in his pocket. We'll carry out a thorough search of the house and salon. Hopefully, we'll find it in the bins, or clothing.'

'Nonna had been trying to persuade Franco to come clean about being my father. I wouldn't mind betting he also wanted her out of the way before she and Rik got married, and she changed her will.'

'There are these factors to consider.'

'This is all so sick.' I plonk my elbows on the table and knock my knuckles against my forehead. 'That's why Nonna didn't feel well the few weeks before she collapsed. All this stress.'

He reaches across the table and takes my hand. 'I'm so sorry, Sienna. You don't deserve any of this.'

'Choose a poison to make it look like it was Nonna's heart.' I shake my head. 'He thought he was so clever.'

'Not clever enough for you, though, Sienna De Rosa.'

'I had to search no further than my own family. Those I know the most.'

'It's often the case.'

An overwhelming need to see my papa comes to me.

Papa.

Not the man who made me, but the man who raised me.

FORTY-SIX

The church is packed, and crowds gather on the outside forecourt where rays of sunshine are peeping through the clouds. Scented wreaths skirt the aisles, hooked over the end of each pew. I inhale the delicate fragrance of lilies and the sweet smell of roses as I step up to the sanctuary. Taking deep breaths, I stand tall and straighten my piece of paper. The occasional stifled cough breaks the deathly silence.

I've prepped myself for this moment. Like I did for the reading at Matt's funeral. Not that I ended up delivering that one. Milana had to take over. Not today, though. I'm going to see this through. I've practiced this speech countless times, rehearsed it alone and in front of Zach. Poor Zach. He's heard it so many times, he could take over if need be and reel it off without a script.

When Rik first suggested I say a few words, I declined. Taking the stage and speaking in front of so many people fills me with utter dread, but I'm glad he persuaded me to do this today. When Nonna was in hospital, Rik told me she loved me with all her being, so I don't want to let her down.

I pause nervously, glancing around the faces in front of me. Many of whom I know, more whom I don't. But they all have one thing in common; I can't see a dry eye. Zach catches my attention and offers a nod of encouragement. My stomach is spinning. I need to get through this. I focus on the stained glass window of the western wall. Taking a steadying breath, I clear my throat.

My reading resonates throughout the church. I can see my words etched in the faces of the congregation, devouring their meaning, as I talk about love and pledges, cherishing and adoring one another, and until death do we part.

FORTY-SEVEN

We hold the reception at the restaurant. When it came to it, Nonna laughed at her original idea of a quiet family gathering. 'Don't you think you'll be over doing it, love?' Rik said when she expressed her meticulous plans to scrap the town hall and find a church in which to exchange their vows.

'Don't talk nonsense,' she replied, dismissing his remark as poppycock. 'I'm alive. It's time to celebrate. We're going to close De Rosa's for the day and hold a lavish party for all to remember.'

Nonna demanded no expense was to be spared. Although, she has never expressly stated as much, I know today's lavish affair is not only about her marriage to Rik, but as a celebration of her remarkable survival. Once oleander poisoning had been identified as a possible cause of her heart attack, and she was treated accordingly, her recovery was quite extraordinary. But then, that's Nonna for you.

Milana and I ended up organising most of today's celebration. Through loving smiles and, at times while biting our tongues, we have diligently obeyed Nonna's wishes to deliver precisely what she wants. It's mostly been fun, planning it together, although exhausting as we've also opened three new restaurants this year. 'I understand now what you mean by tough as old boots, Mummy,' Lola said, after the final fitting for her bridesmaid's dress.

Nonna insisted on outside catering, with strict instructions our staff are only here to join the party. Milana sourced a wedding company who have organised the food and bar. Chianti and Soave are free-flowing, and the music is loud. Papa, Jenni, and baby Olivia keep to one side, Mamma to the other. There will never be any middle ground with them. Papa is running the Stamford Hill restaurant now. With the inheritance from Gianni, Papa and Jenni bought a house nearby. Papa signed over his and Mamma's marital home to her. I smile fondly at Nonna mingling. She walks with a conspicuous limp, hobbling from guest to guest, and she talks with a slight slur, but she refuses to slow down and rest more. 'What's the point?' she says with a wicked smile. 'I'll rest when I'm dead.'

'Well done, darling,' Zach says when the party is over, and we're back at home, unwinding on the sofa. After our hectic day, Lola is in bed, completely sparko. 'Your reading was perfect, and that was certainly a bash to remember. Cara and Rik are so proud of you.'

'Our reading, not mine. I couldn't have done it without your support.'

'I'm sure you could've.'

I stare at the framed photograph on the mantlepiece as I rub cream into my sore-free hands. It's of Lola, Zach and me, with Jared and his family at Disneyland Paris back in the spring. A surprise present Zach and Jared organised last Christmas for us all. Our families have become close friends.

I take a deep breath. 'I think I'll make up a fire,' I say, staring at Zach.

He sits up straight and jolts backwards, a look of surprise widening his eyes. 'A fire. That's not like you.' He glances over to the fireplace, empty since the day Matt died. 'I didn't think you liked the fire lit.' He shrugs. 'You know, too many memories.'

I smile. It's a few more degrees in the right direction.

ALSO BY AJ CAMPBELL

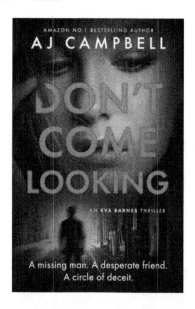

I hope you enjoyed reading my third published book *Search No Further* as much as I adored writing it. If you haven't read my other novels *Leave Well Alone* and *Don't Come Looking*, check them out at Amazon.

THE AJ CAMPBELL READERS CLUB

For me, building a relationship with my readers is one of the joys of writing. I formed the AJ Campbell Readers Club so that I could keep in contact with you all. As a member of my community, you will receive reading inspiration via my monthly newsletter, plus details of giveaways to win book-related gifts, including a Kindle for Christmas. You will always be the first to know about my upcoming book launch promotions and ongoing special discounts. Plus, I'll ensure that you are the first to receive sneak previews of my book covers and exclusive free downloads of my work.

To join, visit my website www.ajcampbellauthor.com. I look forward to welcoming you personally.

PLEASE LEAVE A REVIEW

As for all authors, reviews are the key to raising awareness of my work. If you have enjoyed this book, please consider leaving a review on Amazon and Goodreads to help others find it too.

All my books undergo a rigorous editing process, but sometimes mistakes do happen. If you have spotted an error, please contact me, so I can promptly get it corrected.

Thank you. AJx

BOOKCLUB QUESTIONS

SEARCH NO FURTHER

1. What did you think of Nonna? What are your views about the decisions she made throughout her life?
2. OCD manifests itself in many forms. What was the root of Sienna's OCD, and how did it affect her life?
3. What parallels can you draw between Nonna and Milana's characters?
4. Did you think the person following Sienna through the park was a figment of her imagination or born out of her fragile state of mind?
5. "One lie is enough to question all truths" is one of Nonna's sayings. Do you agree with this?
6. Was Bettina right to keep the truth about Sienna from Don?
7. Do you consider the way DS Durant treats Sienna as unprofessional? Did he get too close?

8. Sienna asked herself, what defines a parent? Matt or Zach, or both? How would you answer this?

9. Jenni suffered Franco's womanising for many years. Why didn't she walk away sooner?

10. If you discovered your friend's husband was having an affair, would you tell them?

11. 'Love is blind. Greed is insatiable.' What does this Chinese proverb mean to you?

12. If you were Helen Myer, would you have gone to the police sooner?

ACKNOWLEDGMENTS

Getting a book into the hands of readers is not the work of one person. I owe my thanks to so many people who have helped me achieve publishing a third novel.

Thank you to my skilful editor, Louise Walters, for helping me develop this story, and to Tim Barber – I love this cover as much as the others you have designed for me!

To my insightful beta readers, Mr C, Christine Henderson, Maddie Standen, John Black, Claire Cook and Melanie Vout, thank you for helping me shape *Search No Further* ready for its final edit. To my ARC team, I can't thank you enough for your support in getting this story over its final hurdle. And thank you to all the book bloggers and media folk who help to spread the word about my work.

A special thank you to Christine and Mel for their continued support with my writing career and for making me laugh every day.

To you, my readers, thank you for reading my books. Without you, I wouldn't be able to carry on writing and publishing my work. For that, I will be forever grateful.

To my three amazing sons, thanks for bringing so much joy into my life. And not forgetting my bestie, Max, who lies faithfully under my desk all day, every day, keeping me company while I write my stories. Finally, to Andy. I love you, Mr C.

ABOUT THE AUTHOR

AJ Campbell is the debut author of the Amazon bestselling novel *Leave Well Alone*. An alumna of the Faber Academy, she writes in the psychological suspense and mystery genres. AJ draws inspiration for her writing from many facets of everyday life. The human mind and how different people react to each other and interact in society fascinates her. She loves settling down with a good book and enjoys thought-provoking stories that beg the question – what would I have done in that situation? AJ lives on the Essex / Hertfordshire border with her husband, sons and cocker spaniel, Max. She enjoys walking Max in the local fields to boost her creativity and cooking oriental food while sipping a good glass of white wine. Connect with AJ online: www.ajcampbellauthor.com.

Printed in Great Britain
by Amazon

86474169R00174